Bronc Man

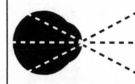 This Large Print Book carries the
Seal of Approval of N.A.V.H.

BRONC MAN

PAUL BAGDON

THORNDIKE PRESS
A part of Gale, Cengage Learning

GALE
CENGAGE Learning

Detroit • New York • San Francisco • New Haven, Conn • Waterville, Maine • London

LIBRARY OF CONGRESS CATALOGING-IN-PUBLICATION DATA

Bagdon, Paul.
  Bronc man / by Paul Bagdon.
    p. cm. — (Thorndike Press large print western)
  ISBN-13: 978-1-4104-1136-5 (hardcover : alk. paper)
  ISBN-10: 1-4104-1136-2 (hardcover : alk. paper)
  1. Abduction—Fiction. 2. Bronc riding—Fiction. 3. Cattle
stealing—Fiction. 4. Large type books. I. Title.
PS3602.A39B76 2007
813'.6—dc22
                                                  2008035369

Published in 2008 by arrangement with Leisure Books, a division of
Dorchester Publishing Co., Inc.

This one is for Doreen Lewis, without whom this book wouldn't exist. She's a wonder and an editor and as sweet as new honey.

Chapter One

The horse smelled awful — like a slaughter-house when the wind was wrong. There was manure pasted to his flanks and a long cut down his muzzle that looked like he'd either ripped his face on a fence nail, or someone had gone after him with a knife. Greenish pus oozed the length of the wound and the scent of it made me gag. When the announcer called out my name through his megaphone — Cal Vesper — the animal snorted, as if in derision.

There was a sporadic tremble that carried through his body; the tautness of a bow string at full stretch, the smallest bit of time before the arrow would be released at its target.

Then he pissed — long and hard — and the stench of ammonia rose like a foul cloud around the horse, me, and the guy who was hanging on to the bandanna over the mustang's eyes. It was the reek of hatred rather than of fear. I know the difference.

I've been riding these hellhounds for money for longer than I care to remember.

The horse sure didn't look like much: short coupled, ribby, mouse-brown coat, pasterns short, stubby, without a degree of slant, a head like a bucket, the chest of a chipmunk. But all that didn't matter. He could buck and twist and spin and drop his ugly head so far down between his front legs, that it looked like he'd been decapitated. Not many of these screws scared me, but this one did. I had to ride him to a standstill or a fall-down, or I was in pretty big trouble.

The timed rodeo events didn't mean much to the cowhands and watchers in Busted Thumb, Texas. This was their Fourth of July Celebration for 1869 — it'd started on the second and was ending today, the Fourth. These folks knew a short ride on a bronc didn't accomplish a thing except make the horse more ornery and confident — and dangerous. If he wasn't ridden to a standstill, dripping sweat, wheezing, unsteady on his feet, the ride wasn't over. If the horse collapsed, that was even better.

I'd done right well since July second. I drew a couple of good horses, bet my own money against prize money with the shysters and gamblers, and I was ahead almost six hundred dollars. I knew I could wear down the horse I was sitting on right now. I knew it — there was no doubt. The problem I might have is that I bet my entire roll — $600 — with two separate gambling men. If I lost I could only pay off one of them, which would purely irritate hell out of the other. Busted Thumb gamblers are tough boys, quick with their .45s. I can handle my Peacemaker with the best of them, but a fast draw doesn't have much effect when a man catches a slug in the back of his head. So, it'd be much better if I rode this horse down.

"Hey, lookit, Cal — you gonna set up there gawkin' 'round all afternoon? This boy is gettin' antsy — he wants to bust you up more'n a little."

The groundman was right. I shrugged my shoulders a bit, settled into my bronc saddle, gripped a bit tighter on the halter rope in my left hand, and nodded. "Let him loose," I said.

The groundman snatched the bandanna from around the horse's eyes and then scrambled for the fence, wanting to get away from the whole affair.

The mustang went straight to the sky, which I pretty much expected. He came down like his legs were solid steel — no give to them at all. I felt the jolt all the way up my spine and my chin smashed against my chest as hard as a good punch from a strong man. He went up again, and came down just as hard. Old busted ribs I hadn't felt much in years suddenly caught on fire and pain seared through my chest.

The horse told me what he was going to do next with the slightest canting of his head to the left. I was sitting good and rode out the spin pretty easily — until he surprised me. One bit of time we were churning to the left. Then, going faster, harder — to the right. My body snapped like a horsewhip and I felt space between my butt and the saddle. I was getting behind his moves and I couldn't let that happen or I'd be eating dirt. It took all I had but I managed to haul myself back into the saddle and centered my body as well as I could.

He was snorting now, a sharp, raspy sound that I knew wasn't running down or fatigue; the snort was a snarl, a very clear "I'm gonna kill you and stomp your head like a rotten pumpkin." He went directly from the spin into the sky, which takes an agile bronc — most would get their legs tangled from the momentum and never get off the ground. He came down on his forelegs, rear end still high, with the force of a runaway locomotive slamming into a brick wall. I felt rather than heard a muffled pop and suddenly blood was gushing from both my nostrils, hot on my face and salty and metallic in my mouth.

The shroud of dirt and grit we'd raised around us made it hard to breathe, like inhaling in a damn sandstorm. I could vaguely hear the cowhands and farmers and storekeepers yelling and cheering, but they seemed far away. The long gun contest must have been going on at the same time my ride was. Every so often the percussive thunder of a Sharps buffalo rifle cut through the horse's snorting, the cheers from the crowd, and my own gasping for breath.

I was getting tired. My muscles — back, arms, shoulders, legs — were beginning to knot up on me, I was pouring sweat, my nose still flooded blood, and I was seeing little black, soft-edged shards of darkness kind of floating in front of my eyes, which is a bad sign. The mustang was wearying, too, though. He tried some high bucking but his power was draining and he didn't grab much sky. He tried a spin to the right and it was a stumbling, awkward use of his body that my grandmother could have sat through without trouble. He shook his head violently and long, ropy strings of saliva struck my face like a cut from a quirt. After the spin he stopped stock-still, head lowered, sides heaving, breath rasping in and out far too rapidly. In spite of my aching butt and almost numb legs, I felt a slow tremble the length of the horse's spine. Then, he collapsed as quickly and as soundlessly as if he'd simply died as he stood there. I managed to shove off so he didn't trap me under him, and I stood there and wobbled, fighting to find my balance. I didn't dare allow myself to fall — some bettors would call the ride a tie if I went down, too. It was a long, drunken, stumbling walk to the fence, but I made it and hung on to the top rail as if it was salvation from the fire and brimstone the red-faced preachers — and my pa — rattled on about.

When I could stand without falling over, I found the first shyster I'd bet against. There wasn't a crowd around him, so not many of the cowhands thought I'd make the ride. That horse had quite a reputation.

The second shyster was sucking beer in a tent set up by the town of Busted Thumb by the merchant's committee. He'd taken my bet on my word that I could cover it — and on the value of my horse, saddle, Sharps rifle, gunbelt and holster, and a sweet Colt .45 that fit that holster the way a child's hand fits into her mama's. I'd filed the front sight away so there was no drag when I drew, and one time when I was rich and a little drunk, I'd had an old Lakota Sioux fit polished bone grips to the pistol. The gambler grumbled a bit as he counted out my money.

"That truck of yours — 'cept maybe the Sharps — ain't worth half of what I'm payin' out here. Them fancy Colts is a dime a dozen, an' I don't know a thing about that crowbait you're ridin'."

I counted my money again, even though I'd watched him count it onto the table in front of me. "That horse," I said, "is a whole lot better bred than you or your pa, mister. You took the bet 'cause you were real sure I couldn't make the ride. You bet wrong. It's as simple as that. You got no call to start runnin' your mouth about my animal or my things." His eyes flicked to mine and we held a stare for what seemed like a long time. Just as tiny beads of sweat began to pop out of his forehead, he looked away.

"I didn't mean nothin'," he said, with a kind of whine in his voice. "I was only . . ." I walked away so I didn't hear the rest of what he was saying.

My horse, Jake, and most of my other

things were at the blacksmith shop/livery down Main Street, and I figured another day of rest wouldn't do my horse any harm. I strode right on past the saloon, which wasn't real easy to do, considering the thirst I had, to the barbershop. He was closed up for the town celebration, but he lived right above his shop and I figured he might be home. I pounded on his door and sure enough, after a bit he opened a window and glared down at me. "That sign sayin' I'm closed ain't no bigger'n a barn door, cowboy. Maybe it's too small? Or maybe you're plain too stupid to read it?"

I flipped a ten-dollar gold piece up to him. He snatched it out of the air, smiled broadly, and said, "Be right down."

The old codger opened the shop door from the inside. He didn't need to light lanterns; the sun pouring in through his big front window provided all the light we needed. He tied on an apron. "You want some coffee?" he asked. "My ol' woman's got a pot brewin'."

"Sure. And I want two baths — fresh water for the second. I want 'em hot — real hot. Also I need a pint of red-eye and a bucket of beer — and maybe a cigar. Yeah — get me a cigar, too."

"Seems like you want a lot, Mister."

I held out another ten dollars.

"I can fix you up with the whiskey, but I'll have to send out for the beer and ceegar. Might take a minute. I tell you what — you set back with coffee an' whiskey an' relax a bit while I bring my fire high for your bathwater, and I'll send a kid over't the saloon."

"Good," I said. "I'm needing a haircut and shave, too."

That barber's wife made a fine, fine cup of coffee. Even mixed about half and half with whiskey, it had that rich, dark taste that makes a man grin and say "Ahhhhhhh," after the first swig. I had a second cup while the barber clipped off enough of my hair to braid a good throwin' rope out of, and shaved me as smooth an' pink as a baby's bottom. I was a little surprised to see some gray in the brownish pile of hair around the barber's chair.

The first bath was steamy hot and I used the long-handled brush to scrub off the dirt and grime and sweat of the last couple of months. When I finished up, the water was murky, brackish, like stagnant water in a horse trough, except not green. The second bath was for soaking, smoking my cigar, finishing off my pint of whiskey, and feeling the hot water suck the pain out of my shoulders and legs and back. I gave the barber another ten dollars to go over to the mercantile and get me a nice flannel shirt and a pair of those denim pants. He'd seen me standing in his shop bare as a newborn rat, so he knew my size. I needed under-drawers, too, and a bandanna. My boots were good ones — they'd cost me a good part of cowboy's pay for a month of trail work, and I'd had them custom-made in a shop in Tijuana. The bootmaker told me not to insult the boots he made by wearing socks with them which, he said, were an eastern invention because nobody in the states could put together a decent boot. I guess he was right; I never raised a blister nor a scrape from the day I hauled those boots on, even when I was carrying a knife with a twelve-inch blade in the right one. Also these were a left and right, instead of both the same like boots made in the States.

I left that barbershop in a cloud of lilac water and talcum powder and fresh clothes and scrubbed-clean skin, and I felt real good about myself, considering I was a man approaching forty-two years of age and I'd just ridden the rankest bronc the promoters could find to a fall-down, and won a bucket-ful of money doing it. Now, I had a drink and another sort of ride on my mind.

I stood just inside the batwings to let my

eyes sort through the smoke and the murky light inside the saloon. Although the sun was a huge white disk that seemed close enough to the earth to touch, the only light entered through the front of the joint. There were no windows and a couple of lanterns sputtered in the rear, where the card games were played and whores spent time between jobs upstairs. I bought a bottle of whiskey and a schooner of beer at the bar and took my drinks to the back of the saloon. A couple of the men who'd bet on me nodded and grinned, and one offered to buy me a drink. I held up my bottle to decline his offer.

The beer tasted wonderful. It was almost as cold as it should be, and the yeasty flavor was the slightest bit bitter, but greatly refreshing. I sat at a rickety table and looked over the batch of women available. They were a scruffy lot, and the reek of their cheap perfume hung over the room like a foul cloud. Some of the women looked to be at least half Mexican; the balance of them were more or less American, I guess. All were fat; rolls of lard were revealed at their waists, straining against the fabric of their dresses.

The owner of the saloon — and in a sense, of the women — sat alone at a table across

17

the room from me, a bottle and a shot glass in front of him. He was a gaunt, greasy looking man with very black eyes, like those of a snake. Like virtually every other man in the room, he had a pistol strapped at his side. His eyes met mine for a second and then flicked away and a quick grimace of disgust appeared on his face. I smiled — he was one of the many who'd bet that mustang would dump me.

I'd seen the sheriff around the festival and now I saw him again. He was a droopy looking ol' codger whose gut hung over his gunbelt by a good bit. He was white-haired and had the loose, lined face of an old, old woman. He was drunk each time I saw him. The day before I'd watched, laughing, as he used the butt of his Army Colt to whack in a tack holding up a poster. The sheriff was sleeping peacefully, head resting on his arms on the table he sat at, an empty whiskey bottle standing guard over him and his dreams, whatever the hell they might be.

One of the heifers approached me, a phony smile on her face, revealing that she was missing some teeth. I waved her off and she muttered something under her breath as she turned away. I slugged down about a third of my beer, then brought the liquid level to the top of the schooner by pouring

18

from my whiskey bottle into it. Another gal walked to my table with that ludicrous whore wiggle, and stood with her hands on her hips, staring down at me from under her thickly pomaded hair. "I'll give you a better ride than that busted-down ol' horse ever did," she said, her voice raw from cheap whiskey and even cheaper tobacco cuttings. I looked her up and down. I guess she saw my lack of interest.

"You think I'm too fat, doncha? I'll you what: takes a real man to mount an' ride a fine lady my size."

I took a pull of my drink and said, "No doubt."

"Well, damn," she said. "If you're after one of those skinny things, we got jus' the woman for you — an injun, or part injun, anyway. You don't mind a injun, do you? Might change your luck or somethin'." She winked grotesquely. Some makeup that looked like reddish plaster flaked away from her forehead and drifted to the floor.

"My luck's fine the way it is. Anyway, that luck thing only works with black women."

"Cain't hurt you to take a look. I'll send her on over."

"How much?" I asked.

"Six dollars, which is a good price."

"It's a damn stupid price, is what it is.

19

Leave me be."

"Four?"

I took another drink and topped off the schooner. The mixture was about eighty percent whiskey now. "Goin' rate's two dollars, right?"

She winked again. "Might be, for the right man, anyhow."

I shrugged my shoulders noncommittally and took another drink. The whore went back to the other side of the room.

I hadn't noticed the woman who was now walking toward me from the bevy of others. She may have been standing or sitting in the dark of the corner. She was no half-breed; she was a full-blooded Indian, at least going by her inky-black straight hair and the deep red tint of her skin. I watched her approach. She was tall and lean and the gaudy dress she wore looked foolish on her. She wasn't carrying much weight and it was easy enough to see the mounds on her chest were balls of cloth rather than her own breasts. I figured her husband — or maybe her father — had sold her to the owner of the saloon. There was a lot of that going on; in most tribes, women were of lesser value than a good horse. She stopped at my table and looked down at me. Her eyes were that obsidian black that I've seen on no other races, and her face, although a bit gaunt, was actually quite pretty, with the prominent features, high cheekbones, large nose, of her race. She was maybe 5'4" or so — about six or seven inches shorter than I am — and looked to weigh about half as much as a fat chicken.

"Rosie said that maybe you wanted me," she said. Her voice was quiet, but she sounded like an original speaker of English, which struck me as odd.

I took a coin from my pocket and handed it to her. "Maybe. Maybe not. You go on over to the bar and get me a beer." As she took the coin from me I touched her palm. It was hard, callused — she couldn't have been involved in the trade too long. A whore's hands grew pasty and soft right quick. She turned away obediently and headed toward the bar. She wasn't a whole lot to look at, but I felt a quickening below my belt.

I pushed back from my table, stood, and walked over to where the owner sat. "How much for a few hours?" I asked.

"How many is a few?"

"Maybe four — maybe more, I don't know."

"That's a long time, cowboy, and she's one of my most popular gals — real prime

21

stock that'll do anything you'll tell . . ."

"Cut the crap," I said. "She's an Indian and you made a mistake in buying her. The cowhands and drifters in this dump want lard-butted sows when they get their ashes hauled. I'll give you ten dollars for as long as I want her."

The owner shook his head. "Ten dollars?" he asked incredulously. "You're way low. I'd need at least . . ." I turned away and took a step.

"Wait, now," he called after me. "We can work something out."

I paid thirteen dollars for pretty much as long as I wanted her and a room upstairs for that period of time. I had her make three or four more beer trips for me, and I sweetened the beer considerably until my whiskey bottle was all but empty. She sat at the table with me, her back straight and erect in her chair. She didn't talk much. I asked her what her name was and she said, " 'Little Dog' in my tribe. Now it's Anna. The good Sisters named me that. My father dropped me at the mission school when I was very young and came back to get me years later. Then he sold me for fifty-five dollars and some whiskey — I don't know how much whiskey."

"Anna isn't a bad name," I said.

"No, it isn't," she answered. I noticed how she had a way of sinking back into her eyes, how any emotion would be barricaded, where no one else's eyes could penetrate.

"Do you like this . . . I dunno . . . work?"

"It's OK. Most men don't want me 'cause I'm an Indian and too scrawny for them." The first bit of emotion I'd seen from her — disdain, disgust — showed on her face. "They like the *gordos,* the pigs." After a moment she added, "I'm glad you chose me. Some of the men here, they smell like a pasture full of manure. They have bugs."

I pushed off the table and stood. I was unsteady — I'd drunk a barrelful of booze and beer over the past couple of hours. I had maybe an inch of whiskey left in the bottle; I handed it to Anna and said, "Let's go." I had to lean a bit on her going up the stairs. Her body felt softer than I thought it would. The room was about the size of a small stall, with a bed and a single rickety chair. I flopped down on the bed and used the two pillows — both hard as boards — behind me. "Shall I take off my dress?" she asked.

"Take off everything," I said.

Her body had a nice symmetry to it: her breasts were small, but her legs were nicely muscled. She turned all the way around slowly, and then came to the bed and dragged off my boots without being asked. She worked the buttons on my new pants and slid those down and off and draped them neatly over the chair. Her dress, I noticed, looked like a small pile of ratty cloth when she tossed it to the floor. She unbuttoned my shirt and helped me out of it.

She felt good under my hands. After not too many moments I exploded like a Fourth of July rocket had gone off inside me. Anna was quiet, but there was a tiny grin of satisfaction on her face. A fat bead of sweat dripped from her neck down to her breast and then onto my chest. I noticed both her nipples were still stiff and that they looked like small, pinkish pearls.

"Damn, Anna," I said. "Damn."

We ended up staying in that room for almost four days, except to use the privy and to get more whiskey and even some food occasionally, downstairs. I learned a lot about Anna. It wasn't that she was a talker, but rather that we had to do something when we weren't goin' at it. She was Shoshone and her mother died birthing her. She vaguely remembered being sold the first time.

"The warrior who was considering buying

me," she said, "had me shuck down to my skin and he looked me over like I was a horse he was considering. He asked if I was a virgin."

"Were you?"

"Yes." Her voice was cold as she said the word.

She didn't say much about how the saloon owner here had come to buy her, which was fine. I didn't want to know. For some reason or other, even thinking about it made my hands curl into fists or worse, my right hand to relax, going almost limp, as it did just before it tightened when I was about to draw my Colt in a bad situation.

I was leaning back against the headboard with the pillow behind me and a shot of whiskey balanced on my stomach. I hadn't heard Anna get up; I figured she was visiting the outhouse or buying another bottle of booze. I heard some crashing around downstairs, which wasn't a rare thing — I figured a few drunken cowhands had gotten into a scuffle they'd all fail to remember the next morning. I was hefting the shot to my mouth when one of the women downstairs screamed, and it wasn't the usual, forced, "it's OK to grab me" laugh that was almost constant in the saloon. There was real fear behind it. Several gunshots got me out of the bed, into my pants, and out the door, strapping on my pistol, still a bit foggy from the booze.

The one almost at the head of the narrow stairway was a grossly fat Mexican with a cut-down twelve gauge. I dove to my left as the two gaping maws of the shotgun swung toward me and I brought my Colt up and fired. A brilliant red splash of blood erupted from the Mex's throat and the impact of the .45 slug hurled him backward into the desperado directly behind him — that man was armed with a lever-action .30-.30. I got lucky again; my round caught him in the chest. The rifle clattered on the landing. That mess gave me a moment to haul up my pants. They'd been at my knees when I drew and fired and it seemed like an awfully long time before my palm slapped the familiar bone grips. Another guy, his red-rimmed eyes the most prominent feature of his face, fired at me. The shot was close, but not close enough; it hissed past my ear and slammed into the wall behind me. I took him down with a single round that must have been a head shot. It left a faint red mist in the air where he was standing. I was firing from instinct, of course. In a fight like this one, the man who takes the tiny bit of time to aim goes down first and goes down hard.

Another of the lunatics was trying to climb over his dead pals to get a clear shot at me. There was a hell of a racket on the stairs — men cursing and yelling in both English and Spanish — but there was much more ruckus from the saloon. It was like the third day of the battle at Gettysburg. Gunfire was steady, as was the terrified screaming of women, bursts of manic, drunken laughter, and the moans of wounded men and women. Chairs and tables clattered and splintered; the reek of cheap whiskey already had reached me from what must have been lots of smashed bottles. The climber stepped on the fallen Mex's back, lost his balance, and began to topple backward. My shot took him in the belly and helped him down the stairs.

I had only two shots left before I had to reload, and I sure didn't fancy standing there like a damn target while I fed bullets into my Colt. My eyes flicked to the rifle the outlaw had pushed away in his death throes. If he was like most desperados, the .30-.30 would be fully loaded. Of course, I had no idea how much lead he'd spread around downstairs, but I figured I had to roll the dice. I placed my last three shots into the knot of men piling up at the bottom of the stairs and grabbed the rifle from where it'd landed. I cranked the lever and fired again into the writhing heap of outlaws. The action of the rifle was smooth and well lubricated. The dead man had taken good care of his weapon.

The best thing I could do to stay alive and to drag Anna out of the mess in the saloon was to haul ass to our room, get my boots, and go out the window. I shot a few more times down the stairs and then raced to the room. I wasn't about to leave those boots for the outlaws. I pulled them on, found my shirt, and hurled the rickety chair through the window. I climbed out just as buckshot tore through the flimsy door and peppered the wall. I lowered myself down in a hurry, hung on to the sill for a second, and then let go. It was a short two-story building — the drop was easy enough.

Except for the horses dancing and shying at the hitching rail in front of the saloon, the street was totally empty. I noticed that a lady's hat store at the end of the strip of buildings was pouring dark smoke out of its windows. So was the mercantile closer to the saloon. The stable at the other end of the street wasn't smoking; I figured my horse, saddle, and Sharps were all right for the time being.

I fumbled a full load into my Colt and cursed myself for having left the .30-.30 upstairs when I went out the window.

The inside of the saloon was chaos. I peeked in from over the batwings and saw Anna cowering behind a table. The card players and the men who'd been at the bar were mostly dead or dying. Still, the outlaws — there must have been thirty or more of them, plus the ones upstairs — kept up a constant barrage of pistol, rifle, and shotgun fire. It didn't seem like they were hitting much of anything except dead men and the bottles along the back of the bar. It was as if they were drunk on the killing and the racket and wouldn't let the moment go. The sheriff was still at his table, but he was now missing a good part of his face and head.

A stray round must have hit one of the lanterns and the wall beneath it was aflame. The fire was spreading slowly, its flames dancing in the fog of gunsmoke — at least until the fire reached the back-bar area. Most of the whiskey served in frontier gin mills was little more than raw alcohol with some molasses for coloring. That combination, which dripped and drained along the full dozen feet of the bar, exploded with a *whomp,* and hungry blue fingers of flame raced to the ceiling.

29

A raider with a pistol in one hand was dragging Anna out from under her table by her hair with the other, his startlingly white teeth far more distinct than the rest of his face or figure in the smoke. At least those teeth gave me a good target. I pushed through the batwings and took him down with a single shot. Inside the saloon all was chaos — a foggy version of hell, screams, and gunfire.

It was as if all the desperados at the same moment suddenly realized that the building was on fire. They started toward the batwings — the only way out of the inferno — like a clutch of demons, wild-eyed, slamming into one another, trampling dead men, women, and their fallen pals in a mad scramble to beat the flames. Several of them had women slung over their shoulders as if they were carrying sacks of grain. I stepped off to the side, going against the tide of raiders, my Colt up and extended at chest level. The panic was such that most of them either didn't see me or didn't give a damn that I was there. The air — the little of it there seemed to be — was as heavy and as heated as that around a good branding fire, and was almost impossible to breathe or to see through. I knew roughly where Anna had been when I did the dental work on the man hauling her up by her hair. I figured she was still there. If she wasn't, I had no idea what I'd do. My mind was screaming at me to get the hell out of there, but I couldn't do that just yet. I figured having to live with myself after turning tail on Anna would be harder than choking or burning to death.

One of the main timbers supporting the roof gave up the fight to the fire and crashed to the floor like a burning juggernaut, a horrific splash of burning embers and flames erupting around it maybe six or seven feet ahead of me. The collapse of the beam brought down a big section of the ticky-tacky roof, leaving a roughly rectangular opening to the intense blue sky above. For the briefest particle of time it seemed like the noise and smoke and killing had been drawn up into that gaping hole and was replaced with a dead calm that was somehow just as frightening as what came before it. I could see to the back wall. The table was there and so was the raider with the big red slash where his mouth should have been, but Anna wasn't.

I guess the opening in the roof gave the fire what it wanted, fed it, turned it into something far worse and far more deadly than it had been. And I'll tell you what: it

31

sure wasn't a damned church picnic before. A pair of outlaws, one dragging a woman by her foot, were in the rear corner of the saloon and they both saw me at the same time. The guy dragging the whore was using both hands to pull her along — I figured he could wait a moment. The other brought up a shotgun as I swung my Colt toward him. I saw both the hammers fall on the shotgun, and it seemed like I could hear the metallic click, too. There isn't much that's more useless than an empty weapon in a gunfight. If that outlaw had lived, I doubt that he'd ever have forgotten that fact. He didn't live, though. His partner was quick on his draw. Maybe he wasn't as drunk as the others. The thing is, I saw a muzzle flash at the end of his right hand, and I heard the woman shriek, and I saw the man's face quite clearly, and that was the end of the day for me.

My pa was way deep into whiskey again. I could hear him roaring at my ma inside the cabin even way out in the barn. Pa's drunks were predictable. He's start off with an easy, happy, almost silly drunk, then he'd get to crying over how he'd wasted his life and taken the youth of a fine woman, and then he'd get as mean as mean could be, slapping and punching both me and Ma around. If we weren't handy, he'd take a whip or his fists to our milk cow or a horse in the corral. Once I saw him kick a pretty good dog to death.

He was at his worst when he'd take Ma's Bible from the shelf where she kept it and start preaching about how he was going to hell to burn forever, and so was everyone else unless they repented and accepted the pain he put on them. That's when he swung his belt or a stick or whatever he could find the hardest. When he got like that his eyes seemed to get smaller and brighter, so that they had a fever-shine to them.

I knew my pa was dead. In fact, I'd killed him out in front of our cabin when I was fifteen years old. I'd stolen a used revolver from the mercantile a few weeks before and I spent lots of time practicing with it. The pistol was a piece of junk, but it fired most times when I pulled the trigger. It wasn't what you'd call accurate, but I got fairly handy with it.

Pa was on a toot, Bible in hand, shotgun in the other. Ma was on the ground, blood running from her nose, one of her eyes already swollen shut. I didn't say a word to the crazy old bastard. When he made to bring the shotgun pointing to me I emptied my revolver into him. I hit him with four out of the six shots — and one was a misfire. It wasn't bad shoot-

ing for a kid.

Like I said, I knew Pa was dead. Yet, there he was with his shotgun and his Bible all over again, and this time I didn't have a weapon. Ma was there, too, and from looking at her, I knew she was dead. Pa's eyes were tiny and hot. My feet were stuck in muck or mud so that I couldn't run — I couldn't even turn away, no matter how hard I tried. The dog Pa had kicked to death was at his side, fangs bared, hackles standing stiffly, and had the small, hot eyes my pa had — and the dog hated me — hated everything and everyone — as much as my drunken father did. How a long-dead man and a dog he'd killed could . . .

It took a moment for the face peering down at me come into focus. At first it gave only a distinct sensation of bigness — bigger'n a good-sized pumpkin, for instance. I blinked away the pumpkin but the image didn't change a whole lot. The man's head was huge and he had a herd of reddish-orange freckles and unwashed hair of the same strange color that hung down around his face like curtain. I tried to sit up and a shot of pain hit me so hard I thought the bigheaded guy had punched me. Instead, he placed a gentle hand against my chest to kind of ease me back to a prone position.

"A slug dug a furrow in your melon is

about all, pard," he said. "That, an' maybe a bit of damage to your left foot. Looks like you took a bullet there, too. Ankle's a long way from the heart. She'll heal, maybe."

I tried to speak but my throat was parched and stuck together somehow and I could taste the coppery flavor of blood. I could barely move my lips. "You'll be wantin' some water," the big fellow said. When he stood up from his crouch next to me I got my first look at the largest man I'd ever seen in my life. I blinked more times, thinking at first my sight was screwed up. It wasn't. I watched his back as he strode away from me, trying to estimate his size. I'd say he went maybe seven feet and probably weighed in at 325 pounds on the hoof. When he came back with a metal scooper of water I could feel him approaching me because of the tiny tremors of the ground his boots and massive weight caused. He crouched back down and put the edge of the scooper to my mouth, lifting my head a couple of inches with his other hand. The water was January cold and sweet and tasted a little of the stones and slate in the stream it came from. After I'd barely got a couple swallows down, the giant said, "Cain't have no more jus' now. You'll puke her right up, an' that wouldn't do your head no good."

He looked a little closer at me. "Can you talk?"

After a bit of gasping and a half-cough that almost tore my head off my shoulders, I said "Yeah."

"You got a name?" he asked.

"Cal Vesper," I whispered. I wasn't trying to whisper, but that was all the sound I could make.

A broad smile cut across his huge face. "Sure — I figured I knowed you from somewhere. You're the boy who put the fine ride on that 'stang. You made me five dollars richer, Cal Vesper."

That didn't seem to require a response, and my throat was on fire once again. I croaked, "Water."

"In a minute. Lemme get my politenesses all over. I'm Ton Harding. My birth name was Thomas but I came to be Ton early on 'cause I was a big fella. Still am. I'm a blacksmith here — or I was 'til them sumbitches burned my place down. I usedta be married, too. I ain't no more. My wife, she either died in the fire or was shot, I dunno which. I hope she was shot. Be a better way of goin' out. Right?"

I nodded my chin the least bit. Ton had blue eyes that, if they belonged to a cow and were brown, they'd look perfectly natural. The blue was like that of the sky on a real good day, and even as he talked about the killing of his wife, I saw no hatred in them. What I did see was that they were beginning to glisten with tears and I looked away. After a moment I asked where we were. "Out in back of what was my stable, Cal. I got your horse and a bunch of others out — got your saddle and Sharps, too. I shackled your horse and I shackled mine, too, and then threw them and tied them off to keep them from a-runnin' back into the fire. I didn't save much else. I s'pose my anvil's in there and some of my hand tools, but I ain't about to scratch around after 'em. I can't see that I need 'em now."

"What are you . . ." I began, but my throat closed up on me. I had to ask the rest of the question with my eyes.

"Do? What am I gonna do? Why hell, Cal, I'm goin' after them raiders and kill ever last one of them 'til they're all as dead as my Priscilla is." His voice had no more emotion in it than it would have if he were giving me his price to reset the shoes on my horse. I noticed his eyes again, and again they showed no fire, no passion, but there was all the determination in the world in that piercing cobalt blue.

I wanted to ask about Anna, see if Ton

37

remembered her at all. I wanted to know if the gang took her or killed her. I wanted to know which way the raiders went. I wanted to know a slew of things but I passed out again before I could say the words. *I didn't have any dreams about my pa this time; instead I was with Anna at a pond I found not far from Busted Thumb. The tracks and scratchings of animals in the dirt around the pond showed that the water was clear and safe to drink. There was no stink of alkaline or sulfur around, either. We were naked and holding hands and walking into that cold water with the sun pounding down on us and not a sound anywhere. I said something — I don't recall what it was — but it made Anna laugh. I pulled her closer to me and . . .*

. . . and I came awake to the absolute worst pain I'd ever experienced in my life. I couldn't move; I was trussed up like a pig for market, my feet tight together and my arms at my sides. Something had a hold of my head. I saw the six or eight inches of half-inch steel horseshoe stock even before I felt the heat it generated. The stock was white hot and had that liquidy texture to it that means the metal is about as hot as it can get without melting away.

There was a sickening stench about me, worse than a dead animal in the sun, worse than any outhouse. When I saw the steel moving toward my head I screamed. I screamed again, louder this time, I guess, as Ton pressed the length of it into the crease on the side of my head. My hair flared up and Ton sprinkled some water on it and patted it with his free hand but didn't move the steel away. Right about then I fell into a deep, dark pit, my scream choking me, the pain unendurable. If my death had come just then I'd have welcomed it.

I don't know how much later it was when I came to consciousness again, but it was dark all around us and Ton had a little campfire going. He was hunkered down next to me, sipping from a cup.

"Had you a bad infection, Cal. Ain't but one way to take care of somethin' like that and I went ahead an' done her. Musta hurt a good bit, no?"

I didn't bother to answer that. "How long have I been out? How long we been here?"

Ton scratched his head for a moment. "Lessee. It'd be six, comin' seven days. You wasn't awake at all for almost four of 'em, but I could see you were breathin' fairly regular. Then you woke an' passed out again. My treatin' your infection sent you back over the hill for a day an' a half or thereabouts." He sipped again from his cup

39

and then nodded at it. "Fancy some coffee, Cal? An' maybe some grub?"

Quite suddenly I wanted coffee more than I wanted air to breathe, and I could have eaten a gopher's ass if someone handed one to me. Ton fetched me a cup of coffee and stirred some stew he'd made earlier. The coffee was bitter and hot enough to scald the inside of my mouth, but I didn't care. The stew was thick with meat and gravy and some sort of vegetables all mixed together. I ate two big bowls of it an' drank three more cups of coffee and nothing offered to come back up, which I thought was a real good sign.

"I'm wonderin' why your foot isn't hurtin' you much," Ton said. "Seems like it would be." He rolled a cigarette that was as tight and pretty as a store-bought, put it in my mouth, and lit it with a twig from the fire. "I wrapped your foot with clay-mud and cloth and tied her up tight an' let the whole thing dry out real good in the sun."

"Hurts some," I said. "But I've busted up that same poor ankle maybe a half-dozen times. Maybe all the pain kind of ran out of it."

"Could be," Ton agreed. He was silent for a long moment. "How long 'fore you can ride?" he asked.

"Give me two days and I'll be as ready as I'll ever be. I wasn't planning on running any footraces, anyway."

"OK. That'll be good." He was silent again for a longer moment. "You know what I'm plannin' on doin', right? About them raiders?"

"Yeah. I know. You told me about Priscilla. 'Course I'll ride with you, Ton. Hell, you saved my life."

"That don't mean nothing, Cal. You got no call to put your life on the line against those outlaws 'less you lost something like I did. See, there's a big jagged hole right through the middle of me that don't let me think of anything else an' won't let me have a second's peace 'til every one of them snakes is crushed an' dead."

"Maybe I did lose something like you did," I said. "I guess I don't know for sure. But if they got her I'll get her back and I'll crush all the snakes I need to get it done."

I told Ton all about Anna and my feelings and all. He didn't say much. When I was finished talking he held out his hand to me to shake. I did so. He didn't have to exert his strength in a power-grip the way some big men do. Instead, his grasp was light, almost gentle, but his palm and fingers were as hard as stone with callus.

41

CHAPTER TWO

The two days turned into three, which frustrated hell out of me, but didn't seem to upset Ton much. I noticed, in fact, that next to nothing upset the big man except any mention of his wife. That brought tears to his eyes. He'd buried what was left of his Priscilla not far from his destroyed barn, on a small rise to the east of the little camp he'd set up.

Ton told me that he'd been picking up supplies at the railroad depot in Porter Flats, the nearest town, which was a couple day's ride from Busted Thumb. He'd seen the smoke from the raid the second day after it'd taken place as he drove his farm wagon home, loaded down with his kegs of nails, bar stock to turn horse and mule shoes from, and a Sunday go-to-meeting hat he'd bought for his wife. He'd unhitched his draft horse and rode him bareback the rest of the way to Busted Thumb. I don't remember any of this, but Ton said I was crawling about in the street with my head seeping blood, calling, "Anna? Anna?" He didn't waste time with me right then — he saw that his barn — which had been packed with good, baled hay — and the little house adjacent to it were smoldering ruins and he hurried there to look for Priscilla. He found her on what was left of the porch. She'd been a blackened, distorted corpse distinguishable only by the gold wedding band on her finger. Under her body was the ten-gauge shotgun she must have used to try to defend herself. The stock of the shotgun was all but burned away.

Ton came back to the saloon and fetched me. There were some town people kind of wandering around in shock, talking to themselves, he told me, and he heard women wailing, too. He said he wasn't sure if I was a raider or just a cowhand, but the barber, who'd had his business burned out, too, told him I was a bronc man. Ton had seen me ride the day before I drew the crazy mustang.

It's a strange thing how a little burg like Busted Thumb can die just as quickly as it was born — like the shantytowns of the Gold Rush in California: there one day with folks doing business, drinking, or looking for work and the next day they're gone, the quickly and shoddily erected buildings waiting for the elements to level them or a fire to turn them into ashes and soot. Ton said that's the way it was with Busted Thumb. The town had never been big — maybe a couple hundred people. Its existence was based on the cattle drives coming through, headed for the depot at Porter Flats. He said the buildings were false-fronted and burned like dry straw. Maybe a quarter or more of the townspeople were killed by the raiders. The folks who were left packed up wagons or saddled their horses, or walked, pulling or carrying what they could, and headed out to Porter Flats or somewhere else — anywhere else.

During all of that I had jagged-edged clouds in my mind, and was seeing things that made no sense at all, but which purely scared the bejesus out of me.

I don't think my foot was as busted up as Ton had thought when he cast it with the clay-mud. It didn't hurt too much. My head ached some. The problem was that if I was standing for more than a minute or so, black specks began floating around in front of me. The specks grew larger and were joined by some red ones, along with a shrill buzzing sound. Then, I'd fall on my ass. I sure couldn't sit a horse like that. Ol' Ton would be picking me off the ground ever few minutes, which would grow real old in a hurry for both of us.

It seemed like I couldn't get enough food into me those three days, no matter how much I packed away. Ton made a rabbit stew that was big enough to feed a whole family and I made quick work of it, eating so fast and so hungrily that Ton had to sit back and gawk. I was drinking water like I was dying of thirst, too.

I hobbled out to the rope enclosure gimping along on a forked branch Ton had whittled down for me to use as a crutch. Once I padded the Y with a folded-up grain sack, it worked pretty well. I was awkward as a two-legged calf, but I could get around. I found, too, that if I stopped and leaned on my crutch as soon as the spots and specks and buzzing noise started up, I could wait it out without falling down, at least some of the times.

I call my horse Jake. He's a five-year-old blood bay stud with a snip of white on his muzzle. He's a pretty boy and he knows it, and he's as arrogant and wild as any stallion I've ever come across. Jake is tall, about sixteen hands at his withers, and he's built real nice, with plenty of chest, good, straight legs, and a broad, powerful rear end. I bought him as a two-year-old and paid a bucketful of money for him, but it was probably the best money I've ever spent. I considered gelding him, but decided against doing so. Hell, I figured, if I was able to get along in my life with a full set of eggs, so could he. Some folks are leery of a stud horse, but I figured the ones that were dangerous would be dangerous with or without their nuts. I stood just inside the rope corral and called out to Jake. He looked at me for a few seconds and then went back to grazing. I knew if I stood there long enough his curiosity would get the best of him and he'd come over to see what I was up to. Sure enough, he kept eyeing me, turning his body so he could keep me in his line of vision. Finally, he picked his head up, snorted a couple of times, and sauntered over to where I stood. I ran my hand down the side of his neck and he grunted. He was rock hard and the few days off hadn't hurt him at all. He had some scorch marks on his muzzle and a couple on his back, but they hadn't gotten right to the skin and didn't bother him when I touched them. I stroked and scratched Jake until he grew bored with the attention and wandered off to where the grass was thicker. As he walked away from me I noticed — for maybe the thousandth time — how a rear hoof would fall precisely into the track made by the front hoof on the same side. That's the way to tell a horse can travel with what's called economy, with no wasted motion in his gait.

Matthew, Ton's horse, was as big as any horse I'd come across. He was a coal black stud, and he stood a good four inches taller than Jake. He was a bit drafty, which is impossible to avoid in a horse of that size, but there was a sleekness to him that was right pleasing to a horseman's eye. Matt had hooves on him the size of dinner plates and was as tight and well-muscled as his owner. Ton said Matthew had a rocking-chair lope that he could keep up for a long, long time without tiring, and I had no reason to disbelieve him. I noticed that Jake gave Matt plenty of room. I supposed they'd had a discussion about things when Ton first put them together and Jake made a wise decision not to screw around with a boy Matthew's size.

I only fell once on my way back and that was because the tip of my makeshift crutch stuck a rock and as I put my weight on it, the rock splintered. I'd need to get handier with my crutch, but I didn't see that as too difficult.

One night as we sat by our small campfire, waiting for coffee to brew, we got to talking about how we were going to handle what we were going to set out to do.

"Handle?" Ton asked. "What's to handle about it, Cal? We're goin' to kill those sumbitches, is what we're goin' to do."

"Right. But, we don't know where they are, Ton. They may have holed up with those women they carried off, they may have gone into Mexico, they may have gone anywhere. Maybe they joined up with border gangs like Quantrill and his boys. Maybe they're going to continue raiding on their own. We just don't know."

"So, how do we find out? You can take it to the bank that they sure didn't decide to give up their evil ways after burning down Busted Thumb. Even little flyspecks on maps like Busted Thumb get some space in newspapers when they're attacked." He was silent for a bit before asking, "How're you on reading?"

"Fair."

"Good. I ain't, though I can sign my name and do some sums, too. I know that Porter Flats has a newspaper that comes out a couple times a week. That might could be a place to start."

"Maybe," I allowed. "But I think our best information is what we'll get out of saloons and girly houses. Those places draw the types of scum who just might know where the raiders are going next." I sighed. "We don't know a hell of a lot about the outlaws, though. I saw that some were Mexicans, some white, and a few Indians. We don't even know what they call themselves."

"Yeah, we do," Ton said. "They're called the Night Hunters. Their leader is an ex-Reb named Danny something-or-other. S'posed to be a gunhand with a rep. I found all that out from a farmer whose oxen I used to shoe."

"Night Hunters? I never heard of them. How long they been together?"

"I dunno. Toward the end of the war, I guess. But my friend said they shot up an' burned a bunch of Mex towns before crossing the river."

We sat silent for a time, staring into the dying embers of our fire, sipping at coffee that'd long since gone cold. Ton tossed the dregs from his cup onto the embers. "How good're you with that buffalo gun?"

"Real good. I can shoot the hairs off a flea's nuts at a half mile, Ton. Don't you worry about me and that Sharps."

Ton nodded, as if he'd just heard something he'd expected to hear.

"I figure I can ride tomorrow," I said. "I been walking around some and I did good — no spots nor dizziness."

"Seems to me I seen you sprawled out by where I've got the horses staked, late this morning."

"I was resting, is all. And that was hours ago, anyway. I got better since."

Ton spit into the fire. "We'll see how it goes tomorrow, then. You figure we should go on over to Porter Flats?"

"It's as good a place as any to start," I said.

Ton had nothing further to say. He stood. I still hadn't gotten used to the tremendous size of the man. It was a clear light with a lot of moon, but as he stood there with his arms at his sides he blocked the moon and looked more like a huge saguaro cactus than he did a man. He moved around to the other side of the dwindling fire and stretched out, using his saddle as a headrest. "Night," he said.

"Night, Ton."

Ton had given me a sheath of rolling papers and a sack of tobacco he salvaged from the mercantile. I rolled myself a smoke. I was pleased to see that my hands weren't trembling nearly as much as they had been the day before. I'd tried to build a cigarette the afternoon before and all I did was scatter good tobacco all over the goddamn prairie. I lit my cigarette and settled back on my elbows, watching the sky and the land around me. The air was still tainted with the smell of burned, painted wood and a heavier, slightly sweetish smell that made me queasy and that I didn't care to dwell upon.

I'd be more than likely setting off in the morning on that good horse of mine, partnered up with a giant I barely knew, with our sole plan amounting to killing a bunch of crazy men who'd do their level best to kill us. I shook my head, almost in disgust.

But Anna — she was worth what I was about to do. Whatever it was that happened between us in the days we spent together was something that'd never happened to me before. I'd been with whores before — a whole herd of them, really, if the truth be known — but Anna was different. Some of those whores I got to like a bit, but I can't say I really cared about any of them. I never mistreated them like some men will, and I always paid what I owed and a touch more, if I could afford it. I took a final deep drag off my smoke and flipped the nub into the fire.

'Course, Anna could be dead or traded or

sold off already. But I don't know that it'd make a damned bit of difference. Those Night Hunters were going to go down whether or not they still had Anna. Tell the truth, I don't know what would have been better for her — being killed right off in the saloon in Busted Thumb or being alive with the Hunters. Either way, a passel of Hunters were going to die. Some things have to be done and never mind the risk. This was one of them.

It was still dark when Ton woke me up by rebuilding the fire and setting the coffeepot at its edge. I looked off to the east and saw a thin line of orange-red along its length; morning was on its way.

The air tasted good. It was still cool from the hours of darkness and there was no breeze, so the reek of the town hadn't yet reached our camp for the day. Ton's coffee smelled great. I got myself to my feet without much trouble and stood leaning on my crutch. Nothing appeared in front of me and there was no buzzing in my ears.

"How you feelin'?" Ton asked.

"I'm ready to ride," I said, "after some coffee."

"I got some hardtack, too. Might just as well eat it up as carry it. We'll have deer jerky for on the trail, a good big sack of it. I had me a little smokehouse where I hung

52

hams an' such when I had them. It burned
but fire don't do much harm to jerky."

"The jerky sounds good. That hardtack —
sheet-iron crackers I've heard it called —
isn't long on flavor but it fills a man's gut."

"If it's good enough for the boys in blue,
I'm thinkin' it's good enough for us," Ton
pointed out. His voice was a little tight as
he spoke.

"Feisty today, are you? I didn't mean
anything about your hardtack."

"It ain't that, Cal. The thing is, time is
runnin' right on by us 'cause we're sittin'
here jawin' about food."

"Fine," I said. "Let's get to it, then."

We got to it.

Ton saddled the horses and brought them
to me to hold. "Look," he said, "I know I
was talkin' about wastin' time, but I'd kinda
like . . ." He let his voice trail off.

"Sure. You go an visit Priscilla. I'll be
here."

Ton walked off in that ground-covering
stride of his, his arms swinging as regular as
metronomes at his sides, toward the small
rise where he'd buried his wife. I built a
cigarette and was just crushing out the nub
when he came back. He took Matthew's
reins from me. It was almost full light and I
could see that Ton's cheeks were wet and

glistening. He mounted without saying anything. I was a bit clumsy swinging onto Jake from his right side, but he didn't seem to mind it. 'Course, I'd trained him to allow me to mount from both sides. That mounting from the left was military dumbness — the officers had to do it or their swords would get tangled with their legs and stirrup leathers. It didn't mean a damned thing to a cowhand or anybody else.

Jake and Matt didn't pester one another, although if Jake got a tad too close, Matt would swing that huge head of his toward Jake and Jake would move back to where he belonged. It felt very good to be in my saddle with the butt of my Sharps a couple inches beyond my right knee, smelling the good morning air and the light sweat of my horse. The day would get hot. That was easy to see from the size of the sun that was rising — like an intensely bright yellow wagon wheel. Morning was the best part of the day in Texas during a summer.

We loped along steadily, following a barely visible road that led to Porter Flats. There were some wagon ruts where people had gotten bogged down in mud, but other than that the road was more of a wide path than anything else. We'd slowed to a walk to let the horses breathe before Ton or I spoke.

"There's a saloon and whorehouse in the Flats," Ton said. "Might be better if you go in alone."

"Why so?"

"Well . . ." Ton began, sounding like a kid admitting he was the one who put the snake in the teacher's desk, "see, I was in the saloon havin' a beer. Priscilla didn't hold with the use of spirits, even beer, so I never had none at home, an' I like a beer as much as the next man. No harm in that, is there?"

"None that I can see."

"So, there I was drinkin' my beer and listenin' to the piano man, when don't three or four boys come in lookin' like they was already drunk, an' belly up to the bar next to me. I had the box holding Priscilla's hat in front of me on the bar, 'cause I didn't want to leave it out on my wagon. The cowhands began talkin' real loud 'bout how they smelled a damn buffalo in the saloon an' carryin' on like that. I didn't want no trouble at all, but they kept raggin' on me. I admit to gettin' a little peevish about it all, though."

"Peevish?" I asked.

"It's a word Priscilla used to use now an' again."

I nodded, pretty sure I knew what was coming next.

"Well, one of them boys reached out to grab up the hatbox and I latched onto his wrist and busted it like a stick. I could hear the snap of it even over the piano music. The other boys piled on to me an' I defended myself, is all. Even the lawman said so. Still, I had to pay for the window."

"Window?"

"Yeah. I hefted one fella out through it." He paused, thinking. "No — I guess maybe it was two of them went through the window. The others I banged 'round some. But my point is, a man my size is hard to miss an' there won't be nobody willin' to talk with the two of us. See what I mean?"

We rode until dark, stopping only once at a small watering hole to rest the horses and ourselves and to fill our canteens. I didn't have much trouble staying in the saddle. I became a little dizzy a few times, but a couple of mouthfuls of water from my canteen straightened me out. My head was healing nicely. I could even feel some fuzz sprouting where the slug or Ton's bar stock had ripped or burned the hair away. My ankle throbbed some, but not a lot.

We got the jump on a pair of fat jackrabbits just before we drew rein for the day and I got them both with my Colt. We skewered them on sticks over a small fire we set up and they made us a real fine meal. After we finished our meal, we smoked and drank coffee.

"I'll ride with you maybe half the day tomorrow, Cal. Then I'll make a camp and you go on in to Porter Flats," Ton said.

"I don't get it. It's a good idea not to go into the saloon, but why can't you just wait at the mercantile or some such place 'til I come and fetch you?"

"I just don't want no trouble," Ton said, his voice sounding strange to me, as if he was embarrassed or something. "See, that sheriff said he'd put a bullet or two in me if I ever showed up in his town again, Cal. I know when a man is serious and when he ain't. He was serious."

We were up with the very first light of the false dawn — the little splash that comes just before real dawn. I felt good and my head hardly ached anymore. My ankle was sore, but not terribly so. I'd gotten pretty handy using my crutch. I carried it atop my bedroll behind my saddle, which kept it out of the way and didn't distract Jake. Ton and I drank a pot of coffee and then saddled up and lit out.

We walked our horses for a mile or so to loosen them up before settling into a lope. I brought up something that'd been bothering me. "Ton," I said, "how about I pick up a new pistol for you at the mercantile? That ol' Army Colt you carry doesn't look like you could do any damage with it unless you threw it at someone."

Ton drew his pistol and looked it over like he'd never seen it before. There was a patina of light rust around the cylinder, one grip was missing, and the barrel had a patch of deep rust on it. "I guess you're right," he admitted. "I haven't fired this thing in maybe a year and even then it didn't work worth a damn. I was trying to pick off a big rattler that'd slid his way into my barn. I pulled the trigger a bunch of times and when she did fire, I missed the snake by a yard or better." He eyed his weapon again and then tossed it aside into the scrub next to the road.

"How're you with a rifle?" I asked.

"Fair to middlin', I guess. I like a shotgun, though. Pricilla and me, we liked rabbit and I'd go on out with three shells and come back with three rabbits. You might pick up a twelve-gauge while you're in town, along with a pistol."

"I'll do that," I said. "I'll stock up on what we can carry, too — tobacco, coffee, ammo, maybe some canned peaches."

"I don't know a single soul who don't like

58

them canned peaches," Ton said. After a moment, he asked, "You got money?"

I still had a fair part of my winnings from the celebration in Busted Thumb, and I told Ton that.

"Good," he said. "I got some, but not a lot."

We rode on into the heat that had become strong enough to sap the life out of any living thing. Great shimmering sheets of heat rose ahead of us and our horses had frothed up and were sucking air hard. We walked them a good ways before going into another lope. Neither of us mentioned how damned hot it was. It didn't make any sense to do so, and it'd just make a man hotter to jaw about it. We rode with our own thoughts.

I've only known her for a few days, yet I'm here to end some lives and maybe take a bullet or two myself to get her away from the Night Hunters. What the hell? Truth is, she's a soiled dove and an Indian to boot. I don't much care about her being an Indian, but the whoring part kind of bothers me. Of course, she didn't choose to sell herself out like a livery horse; she had no say in it. Maybe that's what makes the difference. Anyway, I have this feeling for her I never had for a woman before. I learned early on that when something nags and prods at me and I can't get it out of my mind, I need to do something about it. That's the way it is with Anna.

About midday we reined in near a shallow water hole that'd soon be finished for the summer. It only held a couple of inches of water, which was warm and kind of brackish tasting. We drank it anyway, and so did our horses. The thought of a schooner of beer flitted about in my mind. "I'll see if I can't bring us back a bucket of beer, Ton," I said. That brought a quick smile to his face — one of the very few I'd seen since I met him what seemed like a long time ago, but was really a matter of a few days. Ton stayed at the water hole and I went on to Porter Flats.

The town was interchangeable with all the other cattle-depot towns in Texas I'd ever seen: false-fronted buildings, two or three saloons, a sheriff's office, a decent-sized mercantile, a livery, and some other small businesses. I left Jake at the livery for some grain and good hay, and crutched my way down Main Street, which was almost deserted, given that it was early afternoon and the stockyards were standing empty.

There were a half dozen horses tied in front of the Apex Saloon & Hotel and a couple of buggies parked in front of the mercantile. I headed there first. It was an impressive place. The precisely lettered sign read, SCOTT'S MERCANTILE EMPORIUM, and the long front window was sparkling clean and sent back sun rays like tiny daggers that made me squint against them. Inside, the store was orderly, with neat rows of merchandise and glass-fronted cases, hanging shirts, pants, jackets, and even a couple of men's suits, and a sizable display of patent medicines. I stopped to take a look at those, because they always gave me a chuckle. The various potions promised to cure any ailment ever known to man and some that weren't, such as "restless liver," "atrophied lung tissue," and "thrombosis of the female reproductive parts."

I'd always enjoyed the smells inside a good store like Scott's. The clean, oiled-leather scent of the saddles and horse gear, the new-clothes smell, the freshness of the oak ax handles, and the pungent yet pleasant aroma of cigars, barrels of pickles, and the big wheels of store cheese just naturally slow down my stride as I wander through the store.

The weapons selection was good. I picked up a Colt .45 and a plain looking but rugged double-barreled twelve-gauge for Ton, and bought sacks of ammunition for my Sharps, the two Colts, and the twelve-gauge.

I picked out a quart of whiskey and several pouches of tobacco and rolling papers. Then, I bought two large cans of peaches in heavy syrup. Mr. Scott himself waited on me. I know that because I heard a stock boy call to him by his name. Mr. Scott packaged up the goods and sent the boy to the livery where Jake was being cared for. When I went to hand the kid a nickel for his efforts, Mr. Scott stopped me. "Thomas is well compensated for his duties, sir. I don't allow my employees to solicit or accept gratuities for their services," he told me. He sounded like a damned schoolteacher.

I left the store, waited until the kid was trotting back to the mercantile from the stable, and handed him a ten-cent piece. He seemed right pleased to get it. "That mean ol' woodchuck," he said, "pays us next to nothing an' works us like mine mules. One day I'm gonna twist the bastard's nose 'til he screams, darned if I ain't."

I like a boy who has a little grit and pluck to him.

The Apex saloon and whorehouse, although they called it a hotel, was mid-block down from the mercantile. The water in the trough looked fresh and clean, which impressed me. Most joints'd put pig piss out there for the horses if they could get away with it. I gimped my way through the batwings and to the bar. Most of the heads in the place turned toward me as I crutched to the bar and took hold of it to steady myself. The bartender was an old guy who had mean, sharp eyes and the quick movements of a bird. I ordered a taste of red-eye and a schooner of beer. "Cold will cost you an extra nickel," he said to me. "Make it cold," I said.

In most of the gin mills cold means tepid but not quite hot. At the Apex cold meant just that: cold. The beer tasted sharp and yeasty and I downed the schooner in one long, throat-sweetening, dust-cutting attack. I put the schooner down and asked for a refill. The red-eye tasted like turpentine.

The cowhand next to me at the bar eyed my wrapped-up foot. "Have an accident?" he asked. *Me? Hell no! I done this on purpose for laughs.*

"I don't know I'd rightly call it an accident," I said. "I got caught up in the raid on Busted Thumb and caught a slug with my ankle." I said the part about Busted Thumb a little louder than I needed to. Some who'd been looking at me earlier and then looked away were interested again. The man next to me said, "Lemme buy you a beer. Anybody who lived through that deserves a free drink."

"You heard about it, then?"

"Hell, yeah, I heard about it. So'd everybody else in town. Our paper done a story on it, even before the folks who left Busted Thumb started pullin' in. Here — I'll show you, if you can read."

"I can read."

"Jacob," the cowhand called to the 'tender, "how about bringing that *Eagle* over for this poor fella to look on? He was there, he says." Jacob reached under the bar and found a six-page newspaper called the *Porter Flats Eagle* and put it on the bar in front of me. "Them cost me three cents apiece," he said. I pushed a nickel across the bar to him. He didn't offer to make my change. I took the paper and the beer the cowhand had bought me to a table. I spilled some beer, but not a great deal of it. I spread the *Porter Flats Eagle* out in front of me. The headline, page-one story was about Busted Thumb and the Night Hunters' raid. It read:

NIGHT HUNTER RAID KILLS HUNDRED!
TOWN OF BUSTED THUMB BURNED!
Bloodthirsty fiends who refer to themselves as Night Hunters attacked and destroyed the quiet and Christian town of Busted Thumb.

The notorious gang of cutthroats and brigands arrived en masse, shooting, looting, burning, and killing. Danny Montclaire, a deserter from the Confederate Army at the battle of Antietam, has gathered scoundrels, cowards, and misfits around him and began his predatory actions in Mexico before bringing his vile troops across the Rio Grande.
BODIES LITTER STREETS!
Intrepid *Porter Flats Eagle* reporter Oliver Twerpwell wrote that . . .

It was obvious that the reporter hadn't been anywhere near the town when the raiders rode in. For one thing, there was a line drawing of a five-story building engulfed in flame. Nothing in Busted Thumb stood more than two and a half stories. And, Twerpwell referred to what happened as ". . . a treacherous and cowardly midnight attack . . ." I pushed the paper off the table and onto the sawdust sprinkled floor in disgust — and then noticed that several men were standing around me and apparently had been watching me read the piece of drivel and nonsense the reporter cobbled together to see my reaction. Actually, this is pretty much what I wanted to happen. "This here is horseshit, boys. Look —

someone fetch a bottle and we'll talk about Busted Thumb, OK?"

I told my story without lying too much. I made myself into a cattle buyer's representative, didn't mention Anna, and didn't point out that I'd killed a handful of the outlaws. When I'd finished my story, I asked the men what they knew about the Night Hunters.

"Well," one gent said, "they's all crazy as shithouse rats, for one thing. They don't do any real robbin', like banks or stores. They like to kill folks and burn buildings, and that's about it in a nutshell. I hear they fetched up some whores in Busted Thumb. Them ladies will most likely end up in Mexican cathouses or dead. Some they use up an' some they sell."

"How long have they been together?" I asked. "Do they have any gunhands worth a damn? Is this Danny Montclaire any kind of a leader?"

"Maybe two years. I dunno about gunhands," another fellow said. "Montclaire, he was a colonel in the Reb Army, is what I heard. Used to have his boys flogged for fallin' asleep on guard duty."

That was all good information, but it didn't tell me anything about how Ton and I could find them. I paid for another bottle

66

of rotgut and when it'd gotten some use, I asked, "Do these Night Hunters operate only in Texas? Where do you think they headed after Busted Thumb?"

"Hard to figure," a grizzled older man who looked like he'd been baked under the Texas sun for lots of years, said. "They're crazy, you see. There's no rhyme nor reason to what they'll do or where they'll go. They hit a ranch 'bout sixty or seventy miles east of here, shot it up, burned the house an' barn."

"Where'd you hear that?" I asked. "There's always rumors going around about . . ."

He cut me off quick. "I don't truck with no rumors, mister. I talked right face-to-face with a hand worked at the ranch. He buried the family — and when a man has planted a whole damned family, what he's sayin' ain't no rumor."

I nodded at the old fellow. "I wasn't questioning your word, sir. Not at all."

He took a long swallow directly from the bottle of rotgut I'd bought, wiped his mouth, and set the bottle back on the table. There was only an inch or so of booze left in it and no one figured I'd buy another and they began wandering back to the bar or their card games. The old fellow stayed with me, sitting across the table.

"You goin' after the Night Hunters?" he asked. "If you ain't, you're one nosy son of a gun."

"I might be," I said.

"You'll most likely get your ass shot off, then. Unless that Danny can take you alive. If he does, it'll take you a real long time to die."

"What about him? He's nothin' but a chicken-shit deserter, right?"

"He's pure cruel, is what he is. I dunno what turned him that way — maybe too much war. I heard tell his folks an' family are good people — rich people — from around Atlanta. They treated their darkies good, let them have a taste of whiskey on Saturday nights, let 'em breed amongst themselves. 'Course, they got burned out in the march to the sea by the Union, an' all their slaves was set free, an' the bluebellies looted everthing they could carry off. I heard they raped Danny's sisters and his ma, but I ain't certain that's true."

"How'd the Hunters come to be together?"

"Well, hell. You know as well as I do that more than a few boys was flat-out crazy after Appomattox, ridin' alone or in ones an' twos, doin' what they'd been doin' for the past one, two years — killin'. Maybe it's like that opium the Chinks smoke, is what I figure. Once you get into it you can't get out of it."

"Lots of good men saw and fought in the same battles and didn't turn into lunatics," I said. "Boys on both sides."

"True 'nuff. Like you said, lots of boys did come home an' try to take up where they left off, but some didn't, too. Them that didn't joined on with men like Danny Montclaire."

I pushed the bottle closer to the old gent. "Thanks for the information," I said, hefting myself out of my chair.

"Here's a bit of advice whether you want it or not: Leave the Night Hunters be. It ain't smart to die 'cause of a shot foot, but it's your funeral, I guess."

"Maybe so."

The old fellow held my eyes with his own for a long moment and then picked up the bottle and drank from it. "Look," he said, "If you're tryin' to find them, they burned a rancher's house and barn about two days' ride from here an' left the crowbait they were ridin' an' took blooded horses that rancher had. If I was to speculate, I'd say they was headin' back across the river to raise some hell in Mexico. Nobody can burn a damn town and not get the cavalry dog-gin' them."

"There's more than a foot involved," I said. "Any idea where in Mexico?"

"I heard they hole up in a pissant town or village or whatever the hell it is, called Santa Lucia — Saint Lucy, if you don't speak Mex."

"Do you know where this Santa Lucia is?" I asked.

"More or less — mostly less. I can probably put you close to it. See, there's a good, shallow crossing spot called Chowder Bend. You cross there . . ."

The directions weren't perfect, but I figured Ton and I could find the place once we got the Rio Grande behind us. I gave the ol' boy a five-dollar gold piece.

Carryin' a bucket of beer would be difficult, so I had the 'tender fill three dead whiskey bottles with his cold beer an' cork them up tight. I figured they'd make the ride back to Ton just fine if I stuck them into my bedroll, so they didn't touch one another.

I got back before dark and found Ton skinning out three cock prairie chickens he'd taken down while I was gone. "Wait jus' a moment here," I said. "You tossed that busted-up Colt. What'd you take these birds with?"

He grinned. "I got a good eye and a strong arm, Cal. I picked these boys off with rocks I pitched at them. I didn't have no heart to take hens, but these'll cook up nice." He helped me unload the packages I'd laced onto my cantle and into my saddlebags. "I guess you forgot about that beer we talked about," he said.

"Then you'd guess wrong. Lookit here." I slid the bottles out of my bedroll. They were in fine shape — a bit warmer than when I'd set out from Porter Flats, but still plenty good to cut a man's thirst.

"Double-damn," Ton said just before he pulled a cork with his teeth, put the bottle's neck an inch or so into his maw, and drained it in a matter of maybe a minute and a half. He picked up the second bottle and did the same with it. Before I finished the third one, Ton finished his second. I handed over my bottle that still had three inches of beer left in it. While he was dumping beer into his gullet, I took his shotgun from my bedroll and his Colt from my saddlebag. There's never been a Colt that I've ever seen that was tight on a target when it first came into the hands of the buyer.

Don't get me wrong — Colt is the best

gunmaker in the country, except for Sharps, of course. And the Sharps brothers didn't build guns for the average sodbuster or shopkeeper or cowhand who'd pull the pistol when he was drunk to shoot the sky. Sharps made killing weapons — and a round from a Sharps, even after carrying hundreds of yards, would kill anything it was aimed at, from a bull buffalo weighing a thousand pounds more than a good horse, to a man who needed to die.

"Ton," I said, "let's put some rounds through that pistol, see if we can't get her to shoot where you want her to."

"Hell, Cal, we got us three dead soldiers" — he grinned down at the empty whiskey bottles at his feet — "let's set 'em up."

We picked up the empties and walked out twenty paces and set the bottles into the ground, scuffing little holes that'd keep them upright. I went on back to stand next to Ton, and suggested he have at the bottles. He had a full load of six cartridges in the cylinder and he purely shot the shit outta the damned ground, and the sky, and made a whole lot of noise, as well.

"Dammit, Ton," I said, "I doubt you've ever handled a decent pistol before. This ain't goin' to work. If you can't drop these bottles with a nice new Colt, you might just as well throw tumbleweeds at them. And remember, the bottles aren't firing back at you, but you can bet those outlaws will be."

Ton's face flushed. "This here gun is one of them defects that they made up for the war. It ain't my fault the sumbitch don't work right."

I extended my hand and Ton gave me the Colt. I looked it over carefully, listening to the quiet *whirr* when I spun the cylinder, feeling its weight in my hand, swinging its barrel in long sweeps from side to side.

"Go on, Cal," Ton said, "you're the shootist here. Make that pistol do what it's supposed to."

I put six rounds into the cylinder, snapped the weapon shut, felt the weight and promise of it, handed my own pistol to Ton, and let his slide into my holster. I gotta admit that the pistol kissed my palm and that the first finger of my right hand fell into that sweet leading edge of the trigger.

I draw real well when I need to, and I can put a bullet wherever I need it to go.

My first round dug in a foot in front of the bottles. My second hit a rock and screamed off.

Jesus.

The third and forth didn't even dig up sand nor rock — the goddamn bullets went

73

off at the moon, or some place. Numbers five and six made me cringe. Five was about a yard to the left and six the same distance to the right.

"Well," I said. "Damned if you're not right, Ton." He handed my own Colt to me and I pitched the new one off into the scrub. "This pistol's useless as teats on a boar hog. We'll pick up another somewhere. That piece of junk cost me six dollars, but that ain't worth goin' back to town to switch with the storekeeper. Let's see if the shotgun works." The bottles were still standing there, untouched by our twelve rounds. That bothered me. Ton turned to walk back to get the twelve-gauge. I drew and with three very quick shots took the necks off of each of the bottles. That made me feel better. Ton turned back and grinned. "I guess your pistol ain't a defective one," he said.

"You betcha," I said.

The shotgun did its job just fine. From about twenty feet away from the now-headless bottles, Ton pulled both triggers. The shot pattern had enough time to open and he purely blew hell out of his targets. "Nice gun," he commented.

We talked about what I'd heard during the day as we roasted the prairie chickens. The meat was a little dry and stringy, but it beat gnawin' on jerky. We also had the peaches and the bottle of whiskey I'd bought in Porter Flats. We cut the tops off the cans with Ton's sheath knife and let that thick, sweet syrup slop down our chins and enjoyed the hell right out of that treat.

When we were tipping the whiskey bottle a tad, Ton said, "There hasn't been any rain, at least anywhere around Busted Thumb or the Flats," Ton said. "Twenty-five or thirty men on horseback make a whole lot of tracks. Maybe we can pick up something at the ranch the Hunters burned."

"Yeah. There's a good chance of that. I don't doubt we could find them on our own, but havin' tracks to follow would make things easier."

Ton tore a piece of chicken from a bone with his teeth, chewed it a couple times, and swallowed. "You got a plan about how we'll go about this, Cal?"

"I figure'd it'd be a bit like buffalo hunting. Set us up on a rise out of their rifle range and pick them off like they was a standing herd."

"No," Ton said. There was power in his voice and in the single word he'd uttered. After a couple of seconds, he added, "I want to look at least some of them in the eye as I take them down. Otherwise, it won't mean

75

nothing. I want to see fear in their eyes like the fear that must have been in my wife's eyes. I gotta do that for Priscilla or she won't rest easy."

I'd told Ton about Anna early on, and he brought her up now. "If you start shooting down Night Hunters, they ain't gonna stick around. They'll run for cover or attack if they've got enough men, and they won't be taking the women with them, that's for sure. They won't leave them alive, either."

"I thought about that, an' you're right. But there's nothing stopping me from dropping one now an' again from behind good cover, is there?"

"Not a thing, pard. Not a damned thing."

It's funny. I never really traveled with a partner. I rode with some boys for a month or two, but always went off on my own way. This thing with Ton felt right, and it felt good.

He sure does snore like a dull saw tryin' to hack through a nail, though.

We set out with the first of the light the next morning. Jake was fractious and wanted to run. I wrestled with him for a few minutes and then said, "What the hell," and gave him all the rein he'd been tugging at and fighting for. Jake was the fastest horse I've ever owned. He'd stretch out like a greyhound, reaching out with his front hooves to pull long sweeps of ground behind him. When we topped a slope I reined him in. Down below a few hundred yards away, smoke was rising into the dawn sky. It could have been drifters or saddle bums or even a minister ridin' his circuit. Ton saw the smoke when he caught up with me and Jake. As I looked, I could just barely make out a couple of moving figures standing there looking back at us.

"Probably nothin'," I said.

"If they got a fire, odds are they got coffee brewin', Cal."

"Wouldn't hurt us to stop an' maybe share in it, now would it?"

One of the men waved as we rode up, me a bit ahead of Ton. We held our horses at a walk so's not to rile anyone up. I saw one fellow's leg just above his knee was wrapped in what must have been a shirt. It was hard to determine what color it was; it'd bled through and looked to be still bleeding.

They had their horses staked and hobbled a little ways away from their fire, but even at that distance I could see they were fine stock — darn good horses. "You boys got some coffee goin'?" I asked, although I could see the pot already resting at the edge of the fire. The one with the injured leg snarled, "You don't carry supplies, ya gotta do without."

His friend nodded his head. "My friend here got bucked offa his horse and a rock cut into his leg. We heard there's a sawbones up in Porter Flats, an' that's where we're goin' before he bleeds out. I can't stop the damned blood."

"You might want to get rid of that cloth and use a fresh one and wrap her good an' tight," I said.

"We don't carry — wait a minute! Might be you're right." He scuffled about in his saddlebag and pulled out a crumpled mess of calico cloth. "This'll do . . ."

"Make sure you sock it down good and tight," I said. "Your pard is losing too much blood."

The explosions behind me were so quick and so loud I was stunned by them, frozen right there in place where I sat my horse.

CHAPTER THREE

The man with the fabric in his hands was thrown backward a good six feet and he landed like a child's rag doll, all twisted up, arms splayed out an' head back. There wasn't much left of his chest. The bleeder was reaching for his sixgun when Ton's second shot wiped off a good part of his face.

"That was Priscilla's dress," Ton said. "Leastwise, part of it. I'd know it anywhere. She had to mail-order for the cloth."

I took the piece of fabric from the dead man's hand. It was oil-stained. I noticed that there was a .30-.30 across the back of the cantle of one of the horses. I sniffed the cloth. "Gun oil," I told Ton. "He must have been using it to clean his rifle."

"He won't be needing a rifle in hell," Ton said.

"No. I suppose not. But look, Ton, you were a little quick here, don't you think? We could have gotten some information out of them — then we could kill them. Now, we got nothin' but a pair of corpses."

"That's not all we got, Cal. Both of these snakes are carrying pistols and there's that .30-.30 on the horse, plus what's in their saddlebags. I'd say we done good here."

I couldn't argue with him about that.

We gathered up what we wanted, unsaddled and unbridled the outlaws' horses, and sent them on their way, figuring they'd join up with a herd of mustangs or wander to a town. "Nice-lookin' horse," Ton said, as I was just about to slap the bay on the rump. "Yeah," I said, "but look at the spurmarks on his flanks. The other one has them, too."

"No reason to gouge up a horse like that," Ton said. "Hell, that alone was a shootin' offense."

Again, I couldn't argue the point with Ton. He was right. We left the two Night Hunters for the buzzards.

We covered some ground for the balance of the day. I noticed that Ton was more quiet than usual; I was used to hearing him say something every so often, but he wasn't doing that at all. When I looked over at him his face was kind of pasty looking — pale, like frost-bit flesh looks. Once, I asked him what was wrong, and he grunted "ain't nothin' wrong." I let it go at that.

We pulled in shortly before dark. We could have gone a few more miles but we came across a puddle-size water hole and figured we might just as well stay where we were and let the horses drink and get some rest. We weren't pushing them hard, but we were keeping up a good pace and they deserved to be tired.

Ton started up a little campfire while I rubbed the horses down with a piece of grain sack I always carry with me. Jake grunted like a happy sow in warm mud and so did Matthew as I worked on them. I picked their hooves clean with my pocket knife, making sure there were no pebbles nor anything else wedged up into the frog. Something like that'll gimp a horse up real quick. While I was doing that the good, rich aroma of coffee reached me. Ton already had the pot on. I fetched the remainder of the bottle we drank half of the night before and poured a good glug into each of our cups. We ate jerky, which wasn't too bad if we used a stick of it to stir our coffee and booze. It softened that dried meat up almost enough so that a man could chew it. Ton was still saying nothing. I thought I knew what was grinding at him.

"You ever kill a man before?" I asked. If I hadn't been looking directly at him in the glow of the fire, I'd have missed the almost imperceptible shake of his head. "You?" he asked.

"A few, not counting the ones in the war. In a war there's no choice. The other man is trying to kill you and you're trying to kill him and that's that. I never thought about them too much. At second Manassas I sent a few Union boys to their graves, but that wasn't hand-to-hand. I picked them off with my Sharps — officers, mostly."

"What about face-to-face?"

I hesitated a moment. "Some," I finally said.

"When? Where?"

"I faced another man down on the street in Houston. He was the local gunhand, trying to build up his rep. Fancy sonofabitch — a pair of Colts backward in his holsters for a cross-draw, silver conchas on his vest, all that. He'd been goading me all afternoon. Finally, he called me a coward and challenged me. We went outside, maybe thirty paces apart. I watched his eyes more so than his hands. Something in a man's eyes — a little flame — will tell when he's going to make his move. I saw the flame and I pulled my Colt. That cross-draw thing is nothin' but show an' bullshit. I put two slugs in his chest before either of his pistols cleared leather."

Ton nodded. "You didn't know him other than that he was raggin' on you?"

"No."

"Thing is, I've been thinkin' of those two I shot today, Cal. I never took a life before and didn't think I ever would take one. Now, I up an' take two. Feels strange, like those two outlaws are hoverin' around me. I keep on seein' their faces, specially the second one, 'cause he knew what was coming. He seen his friend get hit and he seen the double barrel swinging toward him and his eyes . . . his eyes didn't have no flame like you talked about. They was like the eyes of a snake got a mouse cornered. There wasn't fear nor even hatred, just that oily-shiny blackness. He had snake eyes, Cal."

I poured the rest of our booze into Ton's cup. "He had it coming. If you hadn't dropped him, someone else would have. The way I see it, though, is that you probably saved a slew of lives of good people by stepping on a couple of scorpions."

"Think so?"

"Yeah. I'm sure of it. Each of them we kill we're saving lives. Think of it that way."

We both stared into the fire without talking. Eventually, Ton asked, "Why do you think them two was riding alone?"

"I'd say the wounded one caught a bullet at the ranch the Hunters burned. I can't see Danny Monclaire nursing cripples."

"What about the other one?"

"Well, he wanted to keep the gimp alive for one reason or another. Maybe the guy knew something the other wanted to know — hidden money somewhere, or something like that."

"Could be they was just partners, too," Ton said.

I had to consider that for a couple, three minutes. "Men like that — the ones that love the taste of blood, of gunnin' down women and children — don't have partners. Not real ones, anyway. I'd bet my boots that there isn't a man in the Hunters who wouldn't shoot another Hunter in the back for a ten-dollar gold piece."

There was another long silence. I decided to brew up some more coffee and had started doing just that when Ton asked, "What'd you do before you started ridin' for money?"

I had to laugh at that. "I been ridin' for money since I was maybe fifteen years old. I wasn't doing much of anything before then."

"You talk like you had schoolin', Cal. Priscilla, she had some schoolin', too, and I recognize some of the words she used when you talk. Like, Priscilla wouldn't say, 'it scared hell outta him,' she'd say 'he was frightened.' That's the kind of thing you sometimes say."

"I'll tell you about that," I said. "I was dragged off every Sunday and at least once or twice a week to these goddamn church services my father was involved in. I've seen those crazy bastards handle rattlers. One time I was messin' with the box of snakes out behind the church and I noticed something strange. There were some of those big, fat rattlers in that box — and their fangs had been busted out or pulled out with pliers. I picked up a little guy — no more two feet long — and he opened his mouth to threaten me and his fangs were gone, too. Damn, I thought, if the snakes are phony, it follows that the whole horseshit thing with four-hour meetings and folks bayin' like sick dogs and so forth is just as phony. Then . . ."

"But what about the schoolin'?"

"Like I said the damned services lasted three, four hours. I read hell outta the Bible during that time, Ton. When I came across words I didn't understand, why, I'd look them up in the dictionary in my school."

85

Ton chuckled. "Toothless rattlers. Damn. I always kinda thought there was a way for a reverend to get fat behind them gatherings an' shows in tents. Hell, they get folks all worked up so they spout gibberish and crawl around on the floor and faint right out — an' they always pony up on the collection. An' believe this or not, but I come across Rev. Hollins right out behind the big tent with Monica Turnbull settin' on his lap not wearin' a stitch. That's the truth."

"I don't doubt it for a minute, Ton. How about getting some sleep? We can make that ranch tomorrow if we keep moving good."

Just before I dozed off, I heard Ton say, "I'm glad I killed them two. I'd do her all over again."

Before we set out the next morning we ran some bullets through the two pistols and the rifle. Both Colts worked perfectly, and so did the .30-.30. Ton took the cartridge belt and holster off one of the dead outlaws. He had to dig a new hole in the belt because it wouldn't make it around his girth. As it was, it barely made it.

Ton did fair to middlin' firing the Colt. He shot at a rock about twenty-five feet away, and did a whole lot of missing until he calmed down a bit and got the feel of the pistol. The Hunter had filed the front sight off just as I did with my pistol, but the sight wasn't worth a damn, anyway. I watched for a while and then gave some advice. "Pretend that Colt is an extension of your hand, Ton — like an extra finger. Then, point that finger at what or who you're shooting at."

Ton did as I suggested and before long he was chipping pieces off the rock. I tried the rifle and found it to be accurate, with a smooth, well-oiled lever mechanism that had a short stroke to it. By that I mean a gunsmith had worked on the rifle and made the swing of the lever to feed a new bullet into the chamber about half of what it was when the rifle left the Winchester factory. It was a nice touch: a man could get his finger back on the trigger a part of a second faster, and that snippet of time could make all the difference.

We saddled up after Ton was comfortable with the Colt he'd chosen. The other one we put in his saddlebag. The heat made it difficult to breathe, so we didn't talk much as we rode. The times we loped the horses became shorter; we spent most of the day at a walk, and even then both Jake and Matthew were frothy at the chest, as if they'd just run a long race.

Early in the afternoon Ton reined Matthew to a stop. I moved up next to him. "We ain't seen water in hours, Cal. These boys need it bad."

"I've been thinking the same thing. The horses need the water worse than we do." I swung down, got my canteen from my saddlebag, and teetered a few steps to stand at Jake's head. I took off my Stetson and dumped my canteen into and held it to Jake's snout. He sucked it dry in a few seconds, and I swear my throat moved right along with his, as if I was doing the drinking. Ton gave Matthew water in the same way.

I took a pinch of flesh on Jake's neck, held it for a bit, and then released it. It went back to its original lay too slowly. What I was doing was checking how badly my horse needed water: the slower the skin is to return to its natural state, the more the animal needs water. "How bad?" Ton asked.

"I've seen worse, but this goddamn heat is sapping these two. How about Matthew?"

"I've been pullin' skin every so often. He needs water."

I looked around us at the shimmering waves of heat that rose, taunting us, looking much like waterfalls. "You a gambling man, Ton?" I asked.

Ton looked at me as if I'd asked how many

legs a dog has. "I don't hold with it," he said. "An' why'd you ask?"

"The way I see it, we got two choices, and only two. We can go back to where we camped because we know there's some water there. But, we gotta figure the ranch the Hunters burned has a stream or pond or well, right? Otherwise, the sodbuster wouldn't have picked the place to settle and build his house and barn."

"Well, sure, Cal. But we don't know where the ranch is at."

"That's the gamble. We can roll the dice and hope we come upon the ranch. If we don't, we're pretty much out of luck."

Ton didn't need time to think. "We'll find it. Let's quit wastin' time standin' here jawin'."

We rode at a walk until dusk, when the light was fading. Ton was ten feet or so ahead of me. Jake's head was hanging somewhat and he wasn't sweating any longer, which is a bad sign. He wasn't weaving yet — his gait was still true. Both Jake and me flinched as Ton fired six shots at the ground a few feet ahead of him. "What the . . ." I began.

Ton grinned at me. "You ever eat snake?"

"Hell, no."

"You will tonight, 'less you're so partial to

jerky you can't get enough of it."

I climbed down from Jake, took my crutch, and hobbled over to where the snake was. He was a good, fat diamondback, about five feet long, and he was far from dead. Only one of Ton's rounds had hit the snake, a few inches below its head, and it was pumping some blood there, but it was doing its best to coil, too, so's it could strike.

"Keep the horses back," I said to Ton, "and you stay back, too. This sumbitch is unhappy an' he's got lots of life left in him."

I drew my pistol and fired twice. I missed with one shot but the other hit the snake a couple of inches lower than the Ton had. I must have hit something vital, because the writhing all but stopped. I blew most of its head off with two more rounds. A dead rattler's mouth keeps on opening and closing for a few moments, and it can drop a man if he gets too close to the head.

"I ain't eating that," I said.

"Up to you — but I sure am. I'll skin him out and get myself a good feed."

We made camp right where we were. It was as good a place as any and we'd been seeing some prairie dog holes. Stepping into one of those was a good way to snap a fetlock on a horse. During the day the horse can see them and avoid them on his own,

90

but night's a different story.

Ton skinned out his rattlesnake, and I can't say I enjoyed the sound of the scaled part being ripped off the meat. It was like the sound of tearing cloth, but different enough to make me shudder. Ton cut the meat — it was white — into pieces about six inches long, poked a stick through them, and held them over the fire, a couple at a time. Like I said, it was a fat rattler; the dripping grease made the small fire flare up and lick at the skewered meat. It didn't smell half bad. In fact, the scent reminded me of how a chicken being baked smells. I ate a few sticks of jerky, which is tough to do without something to wash it down. Our horses had gotten the last of our water, so although we had a sack of Arbuckle's coffee, we couldn't brew up a pot. Ton was about halfway through his rattlesnake when I asked him for a piece. He grinned at me. "Sorry, Cal," he said. "This here is snake meat and I know you wouldn't eat no snake."

I told Ton right where he could stuff his damn snake. He handed over a stick with a nice chunk on it. I let it cool a bit and took a small bite. It was good — real good. I'd once eaten buffalo hump, a piece cut just barely below where the fat ends and the

91

meat begins, and that was as sweet as cane sugar, and fine eating. This snake tasted much like the buffalo hump, only milder, maybe. It wasn't that the snake was bland, but it didn't have the texture of buffalo. That could be because the hump meat was cooked rare — bloody rare — and the snake meat was all white and cooked all the way through. Anyways, it was good and I told Ton that.

"Priscilla's pa was a practical man," he said. "A pain in the ass, but a practical man. He learned Pricilla how to snare an' kill a snake an' how to skin him an' cook him up. Even when my business was goin' good, we'd have rattlesnake two, maybe three times a week. There's sure no shortage of 'em around Porter Flats."

I dreamed about water that night. I saw myself pushing my face into a cold, fast-running river with my mouth wide open and letting the current shove that water down my throat. I saw myself dumping buckets of well water over my head, and I saw Jake drinking 'til he turned away from the trough. I saw a grand, big pond that I stood in with the water up to my chest. It was a shame to leave those dreams behind when I woke up the next morning with a throat as dry as a wagonload of sagebrush and with pictures of what I dreamed running in my mind. Ton and I didn't say much as we saddled up. The horses were listless and it was easy enough to see that they hadn't grazed much — they stayed where we staked them, not wandering out to the end of their ropes, looking for good grass, as they generally did.

The sun started flexing its muscles real early. We rode at a walk, stopping fairly often to give the horses a break. Then, into the afternoon, Matthew turned his big snout up into the air and whinnied. A moment later, Jake did the same thing. My throat was too raw and dry to holler out a "Yahooo!" but Ton's wasn't. "They smell water," he bellowed. "I knew we'd get through!"

We gave Jake and Matthew as much rein as they wanted, except to haul them in when they tried to go into a run. They were too dry to let that happen — could be they'd drop before they got us to the water.

I swear I'd never seen anything as precious and beautiful as that scum-covered, shallow, sulfur-smelling tiny pond. It was drying up; it'd be gone in a matter of days if it didn't rain, but it still had water, and that's what counted.

I slid down from Jake and he waded right in, and I doubt that I could've held him back if I'd wanted to — which I didn't. I could hear Matthew and Jake sucking hard, that kind of whistling sound, moving their snouts from one side to the other, clearing the scum, but drinking all the while. I was clumsy without my crutch, but I didn't give a damn. I let myself fall forward, facedown, into the pond. I'd guess I swallowed maybe a pound of those little green pebbles or crystals or whatever the hell they are as I was taking in water. Ton was in a second before me and he put a hell of a splash into the air. When I came up for air, his head was still down under the surface and the scum was beginning to close back over him. I started toward him when he stood up, puked a gallon or so of scum and water, and said, "Damn! I needed that."

We had to drag Jake and Matthew out of the water. A horse will drink too much and the overage can hurt him. It's much like a horse wandering into a grain storage barn and eating until he near kills himself — or does kill himself. We led them back a few times after maybe fifteen or so minutes away from the water, and eventually, they'd had enough and went to grazing on the sparse grass.

We camped right there. We ate jerky and were able to make coffee. It tasted a little rank because the water wasn't pure, but it was still coffee, and we drank it down.

We sat by our fire and rolled cigarettes. "We ought to find the ranch tomorrow," Ton said.

"Yeah. And I saw that off to the east there are some pretty steep foothills. If we need to, we can top one of them and get a good view of the lay of the land. The ranch should be easy enough to see from up there."

Ton lit his smoke with a twig from the fire. "Times like this when I get the most mad, Cal," he said.

It was a pleasant night, a little too warm, but clear, and there was a bright half-moon and a thick scatter of stars. "Mad?"

"Yes. It's a time when I get to thinkin' about Priscilla and how she'd love a night like this — how we used to set outside an' talk an' hold hands together. It was real good."

I was about to respond when Ton added, "That's why I ain't gonna rest 'til the last one of them Hunters is bleedin' out in front of me. I want to watch his eyes while he dies." He paused again, and then said, "We'll get 'em, won't we, Cal?"

"Yeah," I said. "We surely will."

Ton didn't speak again and I brought Anna to mind, although she was never really

95

far from my thoughts. I knew about the anger Ton talked about because I felt the same thing. A man can't let his woman be hurt or killed or carried off without taking down whoever did it. That's as simple a rule as you don't lay up with another man's wife or mess with his children. Those Beadle's dime novels yap about some half-assed code of the West. I don't know that there is such a thing, but there are some rules to how we live out here.

I thought about Anna a lot that night. As tired as I was, I couldn't get to sleep. I kept on seeing her in my mind, and then I'd start to imagine what the Hunters might be doing to her, and my fists would clench real tight. I guess I eventually dozed off, but it was a restless, sweaty sleep and I was as beat in the morning as I was the night before. Plus, my foot was giving me grief. It seemed like the cast had gotten larger and was free to rub against the skin and it hurt like hell.

I told Ton about it as we were saddling up, which was always a pain in the ass to me, hefting my heavy stock saddle onto Jake's back and pulling the cinches standing on one foot. 'Course, I wasn't about to let Ton saddle my horse for me. I wasn't a cripple.

"That's a good sign — the cast ain't gettin' bigger, your foot is losing the swelling. You still got your boot in your saddlebag? Might be just as good if we cut the cast and got the boot on. You'll be gimpy, but it'll get better. You probably won't win any footraces, but what the hell."

"Let's do it," I said.

Ton cut the cast off, using his sheath knife. It struck me that I'd never seen a man as big as Ton who was so gentle. His touch was as light as a mama cat's tongue on a brand-new kitten, and he kept on looking into my eyes to see if I was in any pain. When he got to the layer of dried clay-mud, he emptied both our canteens on it to soften it up and then peeled it off. My foot looked bad, and I said so. It was pale and it looked too small and it hung uselessly at the end of my leg.

"Don't get your bowels in an uproar, Cal," Ton said. "That's what it's supposed to look like. I ain't sure, but I think maybe it wasn't broke like we thought but that the slug had a tough time getting through your boot and whacked you a good one, but didn't shatter no bones or nothin'."

"But Ton — there's a hole in both sides of the boot. The bullet must have . . ."

"Lookit: I ain't a sawbones. I just told you what I think mighta happened, is all. But

97

the more I look at that paw, the less I think it was busted."

Getting my boot on required considerable cussin'. It felt awful good to be able to slide my boot into my stirrup — because of the size of the cast, I'd let the foot kind of hang there as I rode.

We decided that topping a rise to look around might save us some wandering, so that's what we did. There was one long hill with a fairly gentle slope to it, and the footing wasn't bad. Once we made the climb we let the horses breathe and Ton and I each had a drink from our canteens. Jake and Matthew were OK; they drank well before we broke camp.

"There she is," Ton said, pointing.

It was still early and the ranch was lightly enshrouded in ground fog that'd clear as soon as the sun got directly to it. The ranch was a sad place. The house was nothing but charred timber with a still-standing fireplace and chimney standing guard, like a faithful dog over a dead master. The barn — and it was a good, big one — was charred, too, and it looked like a giant fist had slammed down on it, caving in the middle. "Main beams burned out," Ton said, "nothin' to hold it up."

We picked our way down the slope and

rode up to what was left of the house. A dead milk cow had gotten ripe where she lay with a half-dozen bullet holes in her. Not far from the milker was a dead dog, not much more than a puppy. There were lots of holes in the little guy and he was rotting as fast as the cow. We turned away from the animal corpses and walked our horses over to the barn. Ton climbed down and wordlessly handed his reins to me. I stayed in my saddle. I could see where the old cowhand I'd talked to had buried the folks who were killed. Their graves were slightly mounded and there was a wooden cross stuck in the ground at the head of each of them. There were five of them. One had a little girl's rag doll tied to it with twine.

Ton walked around the edge of the burned wreckage that'd been the barn. "Couple dead horses inside, but I didn't see nothin' much else. There's a passel of tracks just over the other side — shod horses, lots of them. The tracks are real clear. A blind man could follow them."

"How old are they?"

Ton's tone of voice and his answer to my question were unexpected. "Dammit, Cal, there's no way to figure how old tracks is by looking at them. Sure, a little dirt will fall into a clean shoe impression within a few hours, but after that . . ."

"Little feisty today?"

"Damn right I am, after seein' all this. Let's ride." Ton took his reins and mounted up and we walked around to the other side of the barn where he'd seen the tracks. "See?" he said.

I saw. There was a wide expanse of horseshoe impressions in the soil, many — or most — of them doubles, steps upon steps. "Looks like they might have switched their saddles to this poor fella's horses before they headed out," Ton said. "Their own wandered off."

We asked our horses to lope, the trail was so clear and obvious. It was hot, but not as hot as the day before. When we stopped to roll smokes and give Jake and Matthew a break, Ton looked over at me. "I didn't mean to bite your ass off earlier, by the barn," he said. "Thing is, I feel like there's something goin' wrong with me, Cal. If I ain't dwelling on Priscilla, I'm thinkin' about gunnin' down Night Hunters. I can't seem to get nothin' but those thoughts in my head." After a few seconds, he added, "Gets old real quick. Makes a man . . . I dunno . . . *different,* I guess."

" 'Course it does. I'm feelin' much the

same way. An' for sure, it was a stupid question."

"Naw, Cal. It was . . ."

I cut him off by extending my right hand to him. We shook solemnly, as if we were concluding a big deal of some kind. That kind of embarrassed us both a little, so we mounted and headed out again.

Not much conversation passed between us for the balance of the afternoon. We hit decent water a couple of times, and I shot three jackrabbits shortly before we pulled in for the night. We unsaddled the horses and staked them to graze and Ton began to skin the rabbits. I took my Sharps from my saddle scabbard and sat down on a rock, my little bundle of gun oil and some pieces of cloth in my lap. That rifle was too good a piece of equipment to leave be; I kept it clean, oiled, and ranged in up to about a couple hundred yards. The 1859 Berdan Sharps .54-caliber isn't what you'd call pretty, I guess, but it's one hell of a weapon. Hundreds of boys on both sides during the War died as the result of a good man with a Sharps. Fact is, they called them Sharpshooters. I worked the action and dry-fired a few times, enjoying the solid, finely lubricated metallic click of the mechanism and the feel of the warm cherrywood stock against my cheek.

We ate our rabbits after full dark and had our coffee and smokes as we stared into the embers. "I got a feelin' we might be gettin' close," Ton said.

"Feeling?"

"Right. I can't put words to it, but something or other is tellin' me."

I considered for a few moments. "Come to think of it, I've been twitchy all day, too. Like something is on my mind that's important but that I can't get a handle on it."

I slept soundly, but as I drifted off I heard Ton moving around. He might have walked out into the dark a bit, 'cause I thought I heard his boot steps, but maybe not, too. It was the smell of coffee that awakened me the next morning. Ton had a fire going and the pot perking. I stood and hobbled away from the camp a little to water the buffalo grass and when I came back, Ton had a cup of coffee ready for me.

" 'Member we talked about those feelin's last night," he said. "Well, just before dawn I walked out beyond the horses and I smelled a fire, and roastin' meat, Cal. I swear I did. An' the breeze was blowin' toward me, not from behind me, so it wasn't our campfire I was sniffin'."

I took a half-cup gulp even though it was

still hotter'n the devil's ass. "What say we take a walk?" I said to Ton.

"Jus' what I was thinkin'."

We didn't have far to go — maybe a few hundred yards, mostly up a gradual rise. My bad foot was troublesome, but not bad. Ton had been right. I picked up the weak but distinctive smell of scorched meat and a mesquite fire. As we came near the top of the rise, we crouched down. Even though it wasn't full light yet, we had a horizon behind us and we'd stand out like a couple of scarecrows if anyone was looking our way. The downside of the hill spread out below us, blanketed with morning fog. The fire we smelled glowed red and white through the fog. Nothing appeared to be moving. I could barely see a group of horses — a big group, almost a damned herd — well beyond the fire. I figured they'd staked their horses or maybe set up a rope corral.

It was a good thing the hill was between the band of horses and Jake and Matthew, or they'd have been snortin' and whinnyin' back and forth all night.

Ton and I, on our stomachs now, stared down at the camp. "Figure it's them?" he whispered into my ear.

"Could be. Dumb bastards don't have a guard posted, so they must feel they're pretty safe. And it isn't a wagon family passin' through, either. They always have a dog or two that'd be barkin' up a storm about now."

"Seems to me it's worth goin' back and fetchin' your buffalo gun and the .30-.30 and a couple sacks of ammo. If it turns out it ain't the Hunters, nothin's been lost. And if it is, they ain't gonna like their wake-up today."

"Could be anybody," I said. "Maybe someone takin' those horses to sell in Porter Flats, stoppin' for the night."

"Could be," Ton agreed. Then, he added, "But it ain't."

Light was coming on fast. Funny — my foot bothered me some going out, but not a touch going in to get our arms or walkin' back out. When I picked up my Sharps and a sack of ammo, I also grabbed my tripod. It's a short, stubby thing, built to accept the stock of my Sharps. I figured if I was shooting downhill it would be handy.

We didn't talk as we climbed the hill. Ton's face was taut and I'd seen his hand tremble as he worked the action on the rifle. I was settling in to the place where I go when I'm in a situation where I need to draw on another man, or at a time like we were facing right then. There's a stillness that comes over me, a coldness, that makes things slow down around me, until I can see an ejected shell flip into the air and have time to study it before it strikes the ground.

We crawled the last two feet. The fog was still fairly thick, but it was burning off well. I planted my tripod good and solid, packing handfuls of dirt around each of its legs. When it was steady, I rested the stock of my rifle in it. I emptied the sack of bullets out next to me and then put them in a nice, even line I could get to without looking away from the sights of my Sharps. Next to me, a yard away, Ton was stretched out, clutching his rifle. I got his attention and waved him away. His face showed confusion for a quick moment and then he saw what I wanted. He moved across the crest of the hill twenty yards and set himself up again. It always makes good sense to get the enemy in a crossfire.

We waited, the sun growing stronger on our backs and lapping up more and more of the fog and the dew. Figures were becoming clearer now. I watched as a man in a sombrero stepped away from the camp and pissed onto the ground. He had a bandolier of cartridges slung across his chest and over his back like a sash.

There were some sizable boulders adjacent

to the fire that made what amounted to a ring. It wasn't a bad place to defend, I noticed. Maybe this Danny Montclaire did know something about fighting — or maybe he just stumbled onto the site. A breeze began moving, spreading the remaining tendrils of ground fog into nothingness. A tall gent prodded a group of five women who were tied together at the ankle and waist out from behind a boulder. I was jerked out of my quiet place for a moment; I was certain that the woman second in line was Anna — her long, black hair made her stand out from the other captives. The tall man had a quirt in his hand. He shouted something I couldn't quite hear and took a long swing at the first woman with his quirt. I eased my sight onto him and hit him mid-chest, and he was dead before he had time to hear the shot. Over to my side, Ton was firing quickly, pumping the lever of the .30-.30 like he was trying to draw water out of a tired well. "Aim, dammit!" I shouted to him.

As I eased my rifle on the tripod to the left, seeking a good target, a geyser of dirt and grit exploded a foot to my side, projecting shards of stone in all directions. A piece hit my forehead and the blood ran into my eye. The pain was quick and sharp and like the cut from a well-honed knife, and it came as a partner to the throaty, percussive roar of a big gun — a Sharps or maybe a Spenser. I ducked down, keeping a good bit of hill between myself and the outlaws. Ton was firing more logically now, squeezing off rounds, picking his targets. From his cursing I figured he wasn't hitting anything or anyone, which didn't surprise me at all. The range was long and Ton wasn't much of a shooter. The same applied to the Night Hunters, at least the range part of it. Most of their rounds were dropping harmlessly out in front of us, thudding into the downside of the grade, putting spurts of grit into the air where they hit.

The big gun in the camp roared again and the slug screamed by over my head as I crawled back up to my rifle and tripod. My Sharps was about the only advantage Ton and I had, and another such rifle in the hands of a good shot would swing the odds way back to the Hunters. If I could kill a man at better'n a half mile away, so could the outlaw. I peeked over the top of the hill and scanned the area where I thought the rounds came from. I was right; an outlaw leaned out from behind a boulder and I saw the distinctive short stock and long barrel of a Spenser. I didn't give a damn about the outlaw shooting the rifle just then — taking out the Spenser was what I needed to do. I waited out the outlaw's shot and drew a solid bead on the boulder. He popped out again and fired at Ton's position, peppering my partner with a hail of stone and dirt.

There was a slight breeze from left to right as we faced the camp, but nothing that'd cause a problem with any of my shots. Firing from down below was steady now. The outlaws had decent cover — the rocks and boulders — and it looked like they could hold us off forever, simply by keeping their heads down. They'd gotten over their initial surge of stupidity when Ton and I first started firing, and now they were defending themselves capably. My big worry was that they could send out men to our flanks and close in on us in a pincer-like attack.

I watched that boulder down there very carefully. My forehead was still seeping blood, which mixed with sweat and ran down into my left eye — my aiming eye. I missed an opportunity when I was wiping away blood, cursed, and tugged the bandanna I had around my neck up my face to just over my eyebrows to act as a sponge. With the headband in place, I didn't think I'd miss out on any more good shots.

It was getting hot. The sun baked Ton and

me mercilessly, a great, huge, malignant fireball directing all its power at us. 'Course the outlaws had the same sun draining them, but they had at least limited shade behind the rocks and boulders. I knew they'd catch on quickly that there was only two of us up here, and then it'd be over. If they amassed a charge, Ton and I could drop a bundle of them, but there's no way in heaven or hell that we'd kill the thirty or more men coming up at us.

"Ton," I called over to him. "We gotta get out of here. No way we can win this battle."

"You go on," he shouted. "I ain't done here yet."

"Yer ass, Ton. Don't be a damn fool — you'll be shot to hell up here an' leave most of them goddamn killers alive. That what you want?"

I'd kept my cheek to the stock of my rifle as I yelled at Ton. Could be that the Spenser man thought he had an opportunity and he showed himself and his weapon, the blued steel barrel pointing at me like an accusing finger. I squeezed my trigger gently, like I was stroking a day-old puppy, and fired. The Spenser exploded like a canister bomb, ripping big pieces out of the rifleman, putting that red mist in the air that means a kill, whether a man is shooting buffalo or outlaws. My slug must have hit one of his bullets, either in the chamber or one waiting to be levered up to the chamber, and the whole thing blew up. The Spenser was dropped out where I could see most of it. That blued barrel was torn like a piece of paper down its entire length, and the wooden stock was ripped and splintered so that the polished wood was gone except for some pieces that somehow hung on, and they were white — wood, not polished. I suppose most of the damage took place a few inches from the desperado's face — that's where his bullets would be. It wasn't a bad shot on my part, but I wondered if I wasn't a hair low. I kinda figured on killing the rifleman and then, with my next shot, blowing up his Spenser. The way it worked was fine, though.

I was more than sure that the Hunters had sent men out to our flanks. I didn't really see any of them, but I damned well knew they were there. I yelled to Ton, "Let's haul ass!" and scrabbled back a few feet, clutching my Sharps and my tripod. Ton was jamming bullets into his .30-.30, dropping more than he chambered.

"Idjit — come on!" I yelled. "They're gonna flank us!"

I worked my way down until I could safely stand up and hustle back to our horses. Ton was my friend and my partner, but sweet Jesus, I didn't need to have my ass shot off to prove any of that. I was already stumpin' back to our camp, but I was looking over my shoulder. Ton fired three or four times more and then crawled back and stood and began running, following me.

Our fire was down to white ashes with no or very little heat, and as I hustled by on my way to the horses, I grabbed up our coffeepot. I made it to where Jake and Matthew were standing, wild-eyed at all the gunfire and shouting, and tugging at their stakes. Ton and me had dropped blankets and saddles on them, but we hadn't cinched them tight. Matthew gave me a little argument but I twisted hell outta his ear until he stood still, and then pulled his cinch, leaving the back one free because I didn't dare reach under him to grab it. He was swinging his huge ass around in fear and if I got unlucky one of his hooves would have crushed my foot like a man stepping on a grasshopper.

Jake stood good for me as I tightened him up, although he was pushing out nervous sweat. I smelled the fear, but didn't have time to calm him. I was stepping my right foot into a stirrup when a slug came along and pierced our pot and tore it outta my hand. Ton was up near Matthew by then and saw that I'd gotten his horse ready, and climbed aboard. He saw the pot get hit and started cranking that nice rifle toward the Hunters who were coming from our right. I saw two shot off their horses, and it looked like Ton wounded a couple more — or at least shot the horses out from under them. Could be he was more skilled in shooting than I gave him credit for.

We rode straight back the way we'd come, asking a lot of our horses in that stultifying heat, but finally cleared the outlaws; we could see the dust they raised swinging back to their camp.

CHAPTER FOUR

We put a few more miles between us and the Night Hunters before we reined in to a little spring-fed water hole that had lush green grass around it. The water was clear and sweet and cold enough to hurt a man's teeth when he drank it. That didn't stop Ton and me, and it certainly didn't stop our horses. We let them drink and then staked them in the grass to graze. We loosened our cinches but didn't unsaddle the horses. We weren't planning to stop for the day, although the water hole was tempting.

Ton checked the shoes on both horses and I sat in the grass near him, gnawing jerky. "We done pretty good earlier," Ton said.

"We did. I was real happy to blow hell out of that Spenser."

"And the guy holding it — he went off like one of them Chinese firecrackers, the tiny ones that explode and send shreds of paper all 'round," Ton said. He grunted as he picked up Matthew's right rear and used his knife to cut off a bit of excess frog. "How many do you think there are?" he asked.

"Twenty-five, thirty, right 'round there. When they figured out what was goin' on and got cover and started shooting, it seemed like a whole damned regiment."

"You think they'll come after us?"

"I dunno. Maybe not this time, but if we keep doggin' them, they'll have to. That won't be good for us. No way on earth we could hold off that many men, no matter what kind of cover we had. Hell, they'd have a circle around us quick as can be, an' then they'd commence to shoot our asses off."

"Maybe so," Ton said. "So what do we do?"

"For one thing, we sleep one at a time with the other man on watch, looking and listening. Could be Montclaire will send a couple or three Hunters out to track us down. That's what I'd do, was I in his position."

Ton set Matthew's hoof back on the ground. "Was one of them women your Anna?"

"Yeah."

"I kinda thought so when I seen the one with all that black hair, jus' like you told me Anna has. So, least we know she's alive."

I didn't know how to answer that. Yes, Anna was alive. But who knows how the Hunters were treating her? If they were going to sell her to a whorehouse in Mexico, they'd at least feed her and give her water. But the Mex vaqueros like a layer of fat on their women, just like most American cowhands. Anna was lithe and hard 'stead of fat and soft.

"Right," I said to Ton. "We know she's alive."

"What do we do now? Them sonsabitches'll be watchin' for us, won't they?"

"Probably they'll stand a couple of guards. That don't mean much, though. I figure it this way, Ton: we can't win an outright war against the Night Hunters, but we can pick them off one, maybe two, at a time if we play our cards right."

"How so?"

"Sneak attacks, some at night, some during the day. If we can get a good position, my Sharps will do our talkin' for us, and we can be far gone by the time any of them could reach where we were." I stood up, still a little clumsy as I put my weight on my left foot. "One thing, Ton — Danny Monclaire is mine. I want to face him and I want to kill him."

"Long as I'm there, I don't care whose bullet it is takes him down."

"Good."

"I been thinkin'," Ton went on. "We dropped a few outlaws this morning an' maybe wounded a few. They'll stay where they're at, 'least for tonight, tendin' to the wounded an' draggin' off the dead ones 'fore they start to stink. So, if we was to slide on back there after dark, maybe . . ." He let the sentence die.

I guess it'd been some time since I smiled, but that's what I did just then.

Riding at night beats hell outta being pounded by the sun all day, but there are problems with it, as well. For one thing, like I mentioned before, there are prairie dog holes. Second, all the ground looks pretty much the same after dark, 'specially now that we were down to only a small slice of moon. A rock, for instance, blends right in, and if a horse bangs a pastern against it, he's liable to lame up for a while. Rattlers do their food shopping at night, too, an' unless they're startled and get their warning rattles goin', a horse, or a man steppin' down from his mount to take a leak, can get bit real easy. So, with all that in mind, we kept Jake and Matthew at a fairly quick walk.

The air was much cooler, of course, and it felt good to ride in it. The thing is, though, that sound carries farther and louder at night than during the day. A hoof clipping a pebble sounds as loud as a church bell, and even the creaking of a saddle reaches out like a gunshot.

Ton was right about the Night Hunters staying put; we could see the orange blaze of their fire from a distance off. "Big fire," Ton said.

"Makes for better targets."

We staked our horses a good piece from the grade we'd used that morning and walked on in. I carried my Sharps and tripod and Ton his .30-.30. What little moonlight there was made the empty shell casings we'd left behind sparkle like morning dew on grass. "Good thing we bought plenty of ammunition," Ton whispered to me. "We sure touched off a slew of it this mornin'." I could hear the grin in his voice.

We didn't have to crouch down as we reached the crest of the hill; the night was too dark to show us against a horizon, or even a horizon itself, for that matter. Below us, the outlaws seemed to be having a hell of a good time. Many had whiskey bottles in their hands, and staggered about as if they were on the deck of a ship pitching in the ocean. Their fire was huge and it was feeding on a prairie wagon that hadn't been there at the last go-around. There was lettering on the side of the rig turned toward us, but it was mostly aflame. Still, I could make out the words, "Spirits and . . ."

"They got a whiskey drummer," I said to Ton. "Poor fella was probably going along minding his own business, and then all of a sudden he ran out of luck. Shit."

I set my tripod up and packed a bit of extra dirt around each of the legs, just so it was real secure. The Hunters had no doubt killed the drummer and whoever else might have been with him. That didn't set right with me at all. Killing a man in a battle is the way the world runs — you get him before he gets you. But to attack one man when you've got thirty or so on your side is just plain wrong. I was laying out bullets next to me when down below, a pair of women were pushed out from behind a big rock. They were naked. The Hunters yelled at the two, who stood paralyzed with fright, their hands tied behind them. Over the cackling and drunken laughing and shouting Ton and I heard the words that were, in a second, picked up by all of them: "Dance!

Godammit, dance!"

Both women were heavy, and when they began to shuffle their feet in a mimic of a dance, their breasts flopped about grotesquely. One of the Hunters drew his pistol and began putting rounds close to the women's feet, forcing them to step higher and faster.

"Cal . . ." Ton began.

"I see it. He's going down first."

At times that rifle of mine purely has a mind of its own. The long barrel swung smoothly on the tripod and eased to a stop with the front and rear sights lined up perfectly on the pistol man's chest. It was like I didn't even have to squeeze the trigger — the Sharps all but did that for itself. The shooter's pistol flew from his hand and arced off and into the fire. He stood there for a little piece of time with a hole big enough to pass a wagon wheel through in his chest, and then dropped over backward.

The effect of all the whiskey they'd stolen was obvious. The Hunters scrambled about, running into one another, falling, crawling, stumbling for cover behind the boulders. It was then I got my first view of Danny Montclaire, ramrod of the Night Hunters. I'd heard him described, but those giving the descriptions were afraid of him, so their words were suspect. Still, there was no way the man I was looking at was anything but a leader. There was an air about him, a sort of power, that drew one's attention to him, as if he were a shining lantern on a dark night.

Montclaire was tall — maybe 5'11" — and his dark hair flowed to his shoulders. His skin was dark, but no darker than mine; his color was from the sun, not from his ma or pa. He was thin but not gaunt, and he moved quickly, liquidly, with no wasted motion, much as a snake slithers across sand. He wore a pair of pistols — one on each hip — on a broad gunbelt. The butts of the guns faced out. I'd heard that his cross draw was faster'n a mean dog can bite, and that he doesn't often miss what he's shooting at. He was out in the open, grabbing up the lead rope that bound the women together, and I sighted on him as he dragged the whores to cover. I could have taken him easily. I didn't. I wanted to face him one on one. That's the only way I can even begin to pay the bill he owes Anna. Also, I figured if I killed him, the rest of the Hunters would just naturally kill the women, after using them a good bit. I suspected Montclaire was the only reason Anna and the others were still alive. The entire gang outside Montclaire probably didn't have the brains of a damned potato, and they wouldn't put off what they could have now for a profit later.

I had a few targets, but the booming of my Sharps and the constant fire from Ton sobered the outlaws up and they got to cover and began to return fire. Ton, I noticed, had figured out to shoot high to allow the slug to drop in its flight, and he was chipping hell out of the boulders the desperados were hunkered down behind.

I held my fire until I had a target, and I shouted to Ton to save his ammo. I wanted to see what the Hunters would do, how long it would take them to figure out that there were only two of us at our vantage point, and all they needed to step on us would be a charge. They'd lose some — maybe many — men, but I doubted that would stop them.

The return fire from the outlaw camp was sporadic; they didn't have targets and now that they'd put the boulders between them and us, neither did we. I motioned Ton back from the crest and he nodded, but then called, "Their coffeepot, Cal — it's there by the edge of the fire! See 'er?"

Well, hell. After what they'd done to ours, it was only fair that we'd blow the shit out of theirs. I drew a good bead and squeezed the trigger. I'll tell you this right now: a .54 caliber slug does a real fine job on a coffeepot. It flipped straight up maybe eight or ten feet, dark liquid gushing from the small hole the slug made going in and the great, large one it made going out. I had a round left in the chamber and I tracked the pot in the air and fired again. That hit blew the pot into two pieces of raggedy-assed metal that didn't at all look like a coffeepot. That little show made Ton happy. He whooped at my second shot.

We hustled back to our horses, and again the best speed we dared was a fast walk. "Ya know," Ton said, "if them Hunters have half the brain of a cow pie, some or most of them are goin' to be doggin' us. Hell, we hit them twice today, Cal. They won't like that."

"Yeah. I suppose they figured out that there isn't a whole bunch of us by now. That's the kinda odds they like. I been thinkin', though. It doesn't seem like the Hunters carry or haul supplies with them. So, they gotta go to towns once in awhile, right?"

" 'Course. They went to Busted Thumb, didn't they?"

"But I don't think they stocked up on anything 'cept booze. What do they do for coffee an' tobacco and so forth? Hell, Ton, they gotta get provisions every so often — ammunition, at least, and some grub."

"Well, yeah, I guess so. But what's that do for us?"

"Here's the thing — there ain't much 'til you get fairly deep into Mexico. No towns I know of, anyway. There's a couple of ranches, but I don't know exactly where they are." I chewed and swallowed a small knob of jerky and then went on. "I'm thinking that the Hunters'll need to supply up before they cross the river. It makes sense."

"Could be, I guess."

"How well do you know the area, Ton? Is there a town they'd likely hit before goin' into Mexico?"

"I know it a bit," Ton said. " 'Fore I married Priscilla, I traveled with my tools an' forge, workin' on ranches an' in towns an' such." He thought for a moment. "I don't recollect any little Busted Thumb–size towns anywhere near here. There's just Stanton, but it's too big for the Hunters to try to raid. They got good law there, too. The Sheriff, he don't put up with no shit 'tall in his town. Hell of a man with a pistol, too. Like I said, the Hunters ain't about to burn Stanton."

"Is it big enough to have a couple mercantiles? See, I don't think Montclaire would raid a place like this Stanton, either. But he's gotta get supplies. So, he'd send two, three men in with a wagon. If we can get hold of even one of them, we can find out exactly where the Hunters are headed." I grinned over at Ton, even though it was too dark for him to see my face clearly. " 'Less, of course, you shoot them down before we get a chance to grill 'em."

"Seems to me . . ." Ton began, but stopped mid-thought.

"What?"

"I ain't sure of this, Cal. But I recollect that Dawson's Crossing has a Founder's Day celebration right about now every year. It kinda gives the cowhands from the ranches and the city folks a break in the summer."

"The Fourth of July wasn't long ago. How many breaks do these folks need?"

"They don't do much for the Fourth — maybe a band concert an' some speeches, is all. They save up their piss 'n vinegar for Founder's Day."

"Do they have contests an' such? Any bronc riding?"

"Oh, sure. All the usual stuff for the hands to show off at: ropin', bronc ridin', bulldoggin', shootin' contests, all that."

124

"Good. We've gone through a good amount of ammunition and need more. My poke is getting a little light, too. Some of it either went to the Hunters or got burned in the fire when the saloon was touched off. I put a good bit out for Anna when she went downstairs to get food or whiskey."

"Tell you what," Ton said. "Let's ride 'til daylight or so, get some sleep, an' light out for Dawson's Crossing an' see what there is to see."

That's what we did.

Dawson's Crossing was clean — that's the first impression I had. The buildings were whitewashed or painted a white that was bright enough to cause pain to a man's eyes. There was a wooden sidewalk the length of one side of Main Street, and it looked like they were starting a sidewalk on the other side, too. I don't recall any other Texas towns with sidewalks on either side. The street itself was a dust storm, but I don't guess that could be helped, since there hadn't been enough rain to drown a flea in a good bit of time. The ruts made during the spring had been filled in and the street was fairly level, which was another surprise. The big cities like Dodge and Laramie had big plow-like blades they'd drag the street with, hauled by a stout team of horses, but I'd never seen a smaller town that did it. We rode past a mercantile and I glanced into the trough and hitching rail. The trough was filled with clean water with no crud or scum or horse slobber in it. I figured the mercantile owner had somebody scoop it out every so often. The hitching rail was mounted well and the rail itself looked secure.

I was even more surprised when we rode past the first saloon we came to and saw that the trough there was clean enough for a man to drink from. Most gin mill owners didn't give a damn about their customers' horses.

Dawson's Crossing itself was probably four times the size of Busted Thumb. There was lots of horse and wagon traffic, and more people walking than I'd seen or cared to see in a long time.

There was a banner stretched above Main Street between the tops of two three-story buildings, that read FOUNDER'S DAYS. The whole affair was being held way down at the end of the street. I could hear the snap of pistol shots and the band music and the laughter of people. There was a good cloud of dust over the celebration, but that didn't seem to bother anyone. I noticed that even though the town looked real civilized, almost all the men I saw had pistols on their hips. The sign for the Sheriff's office was in mid-block of the side of the street with the sidewalk.

"I think we ought to stop by an' have a word with the law," I said.

"Why don't you go on an' take care of that, Cal? I'm gonna stop over there," Ton said, pointing at the front of yet another saloon. "Maybe they got cold beer."

Ton swung Matthew into the rail in front of the batwings. I grinned when the three horses already there moved as far away from Ton's horse as they could, giving him all the room he wanted. I'd gotten used to the sizes of both Ton and Matthew, but every once in a while, something would happen that showed me how others saw them, just like the reactions of those horses did.

I tied Jake to the rail in front of the sheriff's office and walked to the door. I didn't know if I should knock or just walk on in, then decided that there was no reason to knock. I turned the handle and looked inside. The Sheriff was at his desk with a bunch of papers in front of him. His head was down as he read one of the papers. "Shit," he said, without looking up, "one day these addlepates who make the laws will figure out what real life is about. Jesus." He

127

looked up at me.

He was maybe thirty or so. His hair was brown and showed no gray, and his sleeves were pushed up, revealing whipcord-like muscles. His face seemed to be planes and angles — high cheekbones, straight nose, strong jaw. His eyes, a chestnut shade, fixed on me. "Help you?" he said.

"Maybe so, Sheriff," I said. "I'm here to talk with you about a gang called the Night Hunters. Maybe you've heard of them?"

"Heard of them? You're goddamn right I've heard about them. They put the torch to a little place called Busted Thumb, shot lots of good people, and dragged off a passel of whores."

"I know about that, Sheriff . . . uhh . . ."

"Warner. Sheriff Luke Warner."

"Yessir. I'm Cal Vesper."

He stood up behind his desk. He was a bit taller than I am, but built about the same way. His eyes narrowed some as he looked me over. "How'd you get away without being shot?"

"I didn't. I caught a round in my foot and one ripped a furrow along the side of my head. I musta got knocked silly. Next thing I remember I was crawling 'round on the street in front of the saloon where I was laid up with my woman. I guess the Hunters

128

figured I was dead, or maybe didn't notice me before they rode off. I got out of the saloon somehow, but my clothes and hair was all singed by the fire an' my foot and head was bleedin' hard."

"A head wound'll make a man bleed like a stuck pig. But, you're lucky. You could have gotten a lot worse than a shot foot and a headache."

"I did get something worse, Sheriff. They took my woman."

The office went quiet enough so that we could faintly hear the sounds of the festival. "I'm sorry that happened," the Sheriff said. He was quiet for a few moments longer. "What brings you here, Cal Vesper?"

"A couple things. First, me an' my partner can take you an' a posse to the Night Hunters. We've battled with them a couple times and they aren't real far from here."

Warner picked a printed page from his desk. "That's Army business. I got no jurisdiction unless the sonsabitches attack my town, and they're not going to do that. This here letter," he shook the page he held, "spells that out real clear."

"Then where the hell is the Army?"

"Killin' Indians. The boys left at the end of the war who could still sit a horse and pull a trigger are off killin' Indians."

"But . . ."

"No buts about it. That's the way it is. I got a good town here. I can't leave it to go off runnin' after outlaws, even if I wanted to. Like I said, it isn't my jurisdiction."

I sighed. "So I guess that's that. I need to let you know that I'm going to kill Danny Montclaire and as many of his men as I can take down. I don't have jurisdiction problems, Sheriff. I'm going after the Hunters and I'm going to get my woman back."

"Might be you don't want her after those outlaws had her. That's up to you. You just keep things quiet in Stanton."

I turned and started toward the door when the Sheriff called, "Hey! Now I've got it — you're the bronc man who rode in Busted Thumb, right? I knew I'd seen you somewheres before, but I couldn't put my finger on just where it was."

"No law against ridin' broncs, is there?"

"Don't go getting smart with me. I'll clap you in a cell faster than you can spit."

I put my hand on the knob to open the door. "We got some good riders an' hard stock at our Founder's Day hooha." Before I could speak, he went on. "Now, I don't allow gambling in my town, but I've heard a rumor that a man can make some money if he can ride."

130

"Can't trust a rumor, can you, Sheriff?"

"Nossir. Sure can't."

Ton was at the bar in the saloon, one foot on the rail, a schooner of beer in his hand. When he saw me come through the batwings he nodded to the bartender and pointed at me. The barkeep drew me a schoonerful of beer and set it in front of me. I was reaching into my pants to pay up, but Ton pushed a twenty-five-cent piece out in front of him. "I got it," he said.

I stood next to Ton and tried the beer. It was cold, which is the most important quality of beer. It had a strong taste — like the joint might have poured some wood alcohol into the barrel — but it went down fine.

The saloon looked pretty much like any gin mill in the sparsely populated parts of Texas: a long bar, a half-dozen or so tables with chairs, a sawdusted floor, and flickering light from the hanging lanterns toward the rear. There was difference, though. There was no card-playing going on and there wasn't the usual bevy of whores trying to drum up business.

"We won't get any help from the law," I told Ton. "The Sheriff has his hands tied up in laws and shit like that — can't even raise a posse."

"I didn't expect no different, to tell the

truth. I knew Warner's a hardhead but I figured you'd want to find that out for your ownself."

I finished off my beer and wiped foam away from my mouth with my sleeve. "You hear anything?" I asked.

Ton motioned to the 'tender and then pointed to me and then himself. "Could be. The rummy who cleans up here told me a pair of Mexicans rode in yesterday, carrying everything but a damned cannon — a pair of pistols each, a rifle slung over their shoulders, bowie knives on their gunbelts, and probably hideout single-shots in their boots."

"How'd the swamper see the hold-outs?"

"He didn't see 'em, but he told me he was cleaning out one of the spittoons an' he looked over at these two boys standin' at the bar, and each had a lump on the outside of their right boots. You can bet that lump wasn't no letter home to mama."

"They still in town?"

"The rummy said they were. He tol' me their supply wagon is at the livery, loaded up with provisions, and the men was at the celebration."

I drained my second beer and Ton emptied his schooner down his gullet. "Ready?" I asked.

"Directly I will be. I'm goin' over an' take a look around the mercantile. Whyn't you have another beer? Time you finish it, I'll be back."

I met him out in front of the saloon. He was walking down the street from the livery. Together, we headed to the celebration. It was easy to see how much larger Dawson's Crossing was than Busted Thumb by the size of the crowd. There were kids rammin' about all over the place and women with baskets of lunch and men in nice clean pants they sure didn't wear to work in. There was a steer on a spit over a white-hot bed of embers, and the roasting-meat smell made my mouth water.

There was four music makers on a little wooden stage — two guitars, a fiddle, a Jew's harp, and a washboard. They were playin' up a storm, and lots of folks were standin' an' watching and listening, some of them clappin' in time with the music.

Maybe a hundred feet or so from the stage was the long-gun contest. A hay bale with an empty whiskey bottle on it was set out a good two hundred yards. We watched some men shoot. Hell, seemed like the safest place to be in Dawson's Crossing was sittin' next to the empty red-eye bottle. The shooters were either too long or too short. A kid maybe fifteen or sixteen was using an old Springfield, which is a fine weapon, and he showed some promise. He needed a couple more years an' some more experience. He was aiming and firing too fast, an' was more interested in the girls standing in a cluster who were watching him than he was setting his sights for the distance an' taking a solid aim on the bottle.

There was a crowd of men standing around a decent-sized corral that must have banged together been real recently, since much of the wood was still green. That's where the bronc riding was going on. The riding stock was in another, much smaller corral. I looked over the horses. Most were ribby with bad, grown-out hooves. That doesn't mean that a horse that isn't perfect won't give a man a hell of a ride for his money. Them mustangs can live on eatin' sand and taking a sip of water every few months and still have all the heart in the world.

Ton and I watched a rider and, at the same time, tried to pick out whoever was takin' bets. That wasn't hard to do. Gamblers mostly look alike. They never button the fancy jackets they wear because doing so would cost them some time in getting to their holstered pistol. Most of them smoked cigars, although it wasn't rare to see one chewing on the end of a stogie rather than lighting it up an' smoking it.

I counted out what I had left. It came out to be two hundred and fourteen dollars and a couple of ten-cent pieces. I put the fourteen dollars and the change back in my pocket and eased through the crowd to get to the gamblin' man. I learned from a cowhand who'd lost some money to him that the gambler's name was Stoddard. He was in the crowd like I said, but there was considerable space around him, like he was diseased or smelled like a cow flop or something. A man will bet with a gambler, but he doesn't care to be near him after the bet is down.

I approached Stoddard and said, "Your choice of the horse an' I'll make the ride. What odds you payin'?"

"Best I can do is even odds."

"Yer ass. I'll find another slickster to take my money."

"Look," the gambler said, "I'll go two to one, but that's my top — and I pick the horse, right?"

"At two to one, you can pick your goddamn nose 'stead of pickin' a horse for me, Stoddard. Gimme five to one."

Well, we went on like that for longer'n I

135

cared to, but got to three to one, which isn't half bad. Ton, who'd been standing kind of behind me, pushed past, holding out some paper money to the gambler. "Here's sixteen dollars," he said, "I'll go with the rider." That made feel good. Now, all I had to do was make the ride.

Stoddard and Ton and me walked on over to the corral the horses were kept in. They were standing in a bunch, like horses will, swattin' flies for one another, except for one big stud that was at the edge of the rope corral, cropping the dry grass. He was what's called a splashed white, which means he had a white belly an' legs an' white on his back end. Most of his face and muzzle were white, too. The rest of his coat, like over his withers and along his sides, were a sorta washed-out chestnut. His white was none too white: he was grass stained and muddy and there were places on his flank where another horse had gotten its teeth into him and ripped away a palm-sized patch of hide and hair. Splashed whites always make me a bit nervous. For one thing, they have pale blue eyes, and for another, I've never come across a single one of them in life that wasn't pure crazy or mean.

"That one," Stoddard said, pointing to

136

the horse grazing alone. "That's the one."

"Fine. Can you dig up a bronc rig? Mine's under the burned-out carcass of my partner's barn."

"I won one just yesterday," the gambler said. "It's over there, in the back of my wagon. Go an' fetch it. I'll talk to the announcer. What name are you usin'?"

"My own. You afraid I'm on the run from the law?" Stoddard didn't say anything. "Cal Vesper," I said.

The rig was a sorry-looking piece of equipment that smelled moldy. I let the stirrups out an' tested the tree — the part right in front of me when I sat down into the saddle — and it seemed like it'd hold together for a ride. The leather was dry, which is just plain stupid, if you ask me. Takin' care of leather is simple, yet lots of men don't bother with oilin' and saddle-soapin'.

While I was looking the rig over the announcer called through his megaphone, tellin' the crowd, "We got a new man here, name of Carl Whisper. Carl, he thinks he can ride that blue-eyed screw out there. Mr. Stoddard here thinks Carl's gonna get dumped, and he'll be glad to talk to anyone who favors the rider. One of you boys get a rope on that splashed white an' bring him

137

on out an' we'll see who's right and who's wrong."

I put the rig on an' cinched it up myself. It ain't that I don't trust people, but I wouldn't allow my sainted ma herself to strap on a rig for me. If somethin' is wrong I want it to be my fault, not someone else's. I handed my gunbelt an' Colt over to Ton.

The big stud was a tad fractious on the way to the ridin' corral, but he stood pretty good after the groundman got the bandanna over his eyes. I climbed on from the right side, which brought some conversation from the pile of men watching. There was a stout piece of rope looped over the horse's muzzle, with a single length about four feet long dangling, which the groundman handed to me. I worked the rope in and outta the fingers of my right hand, and that got the watchers buzzin'. It's what's called a Dead Man's Hold, because it's damn near impossible to let go of in a hurry. Thing is, I didn't plan on letting go 'til I wanted to.

I looked around the crowd as I was settling into the saddle and my eyes stopped on a pair of men armed to their teeth and wearing sombreros. They looked wolfish an' cruel just standing there. I didn't doubt for a second that they were Night Hunters. As I watched, one of them spit a stream of tobacco juice onto a fellow's boot. The farmer turned, red-faced, about to tear into the Mex — and then he stopped dead, hesitated for a couple of seconds, and turned away, digging his way deeper into the crowd. The two gunsels laughed louder than they needed to.

My eyes found Ton easily enough. He was the tallest man there, and he was standing right tight to the gambler. Ton expected me to make the ride and he didn't want Stoddard slidin' off without payin' what he owed.

The horse had tightened up as soon as he felt my weight in the stirrup. Now, when I was sitting on his back, all thousand or so pounds of him was quivering like a strummed string on a guitar. I nodded to the groundman and he pulled the bandanna and ran for the fence. The splashed white went straight up on his first jump, bending himself into a inverted U shape, shaking his head crazily. We landed hard and he swung his head back, yellowed teeth bared, to try to rip into my left leg. I booted him in the nose and he went up again, sunfishing, twisting, slamming down on all four hooves so the impact probably hurt him as much as it did me — and it hurt me a lot. It was like getting hit in the ass with a thick stick of wood by a man with Ton's strength.

I figured he was going to try a spin and he did. The damn fool cranked so hard to his left that he almost tied his legs up. He stumbled slightly, snorting his anger, taking in air in short gasps. He reached for some sky right out of another spin, but I could see that coming by the flex of the muscles in his shoulders, and stuck to the saddle.

It seemed like I'd been riding that fool of a horse for most of the day, but it couldn't have been more than maybe a pair of minutes. There was the usual shroud of dust and grit around us. I felt and heard the familiar "pop" and my nostrils gushed blood. That was getting old; the same thing happened at Busted Thumb and at Powder Chase, the town I'd ridden in before Busted Thumb. It was embarrassing to sit up there with blood all over my face an' the front of my shirt, an' still more flowing out of my nose. Hell, I recall thinking maybe I was too long in the tooth for this shit anymore.

My right hand was getting awfully sore from all the jolting pressure on it from the rope. My arm felt like it was about to come apart where it was connected to my shoulder. My legs were doing all right, and my left wasn't giving me any particular grief.

The thing was, the goddamn horse didn't seem to be tiring, but I sure was.

We went sky-high again, but there was a little surprise for me in that leap: we went on through the corral fence, the horse smashing the top rail with his chest and kicking hell outta the bottom one as we went through. The lookers-on hauled ass in all directions, ramming into one another, shouting curses, taking swings at anyone blocking their way.

The horse spun again, taking down three fellas who were busy pummeling on one another in a frenzy to get away. A front hoof came down on the arm of one of them who was stretched out on the ground, and even over the shouting and cursing, I could hear the sharp crack as the bones snapped.

That devil horse had to wind down eventually, and he did. He'd done his level best. He was dripping sweat and heaving as he sucked air. He stopped, standing on trembling legs, and lowered his head until his gaping mouth was almost touching the ground. I sat there for what seemed like another day or so and then unwound the rope from my fingers. They — my fingers — wouldn't move at all. They stayed in the fist-like position they'd been in for the entire ride. When the blood began to flow back into them, they felt like someone was squeezing each of them with pliers. 'Course

141

my nose was still bleeding and I was as sweated as the splashed white. I looked around for the announcer and held his eyes with mine. He pointed to the ground with an exaggerated sweep of his arm. I could climb off; I'd made my ride.

Stoddard paid up. It didn't bother him to do so, since he had a basketful of bets on the horse. Ton and I walked back to the nearest saloon. My hand was giving me a tough time. It was still claw-shaped, and when I tried to straighten my fingers it hurt like hell. "I seen a man use that death grip once before, Cal. He didn't do so good. Why'd you do it? We still had some money."

"We got more now," I said. That seemed to satisfy him.

The bar had cold beer, so they obviously had ice. I asked the bartender for a couple of pieces. "We ain't runnin' a charity here, mister. Ice is expensive."

"How expensive?" I asked.

"Four dollars a beer bucket."

I was about to tell him where to stick his ice when Ton spoke up from next to me. He held out two dollars. "You'll take two dollars and you'll fill the bucket real full," he said.

The 'tender looked Ton over carefully, took the two dollars, and scurried down the bar for a bucket. Ton an' I sat at a table pouring down cold beer, me with my paw stuck into the bucket of ice. It kind of hurt at first, but then it began to feel good — or numb, at least. Ton made several trips to the bar to refill our schooners. I took my hand out of the ice every so often and tried to flex my fingers. They were working a whole lot better.

I sat facing the batwings. When the two vaqueros pushed through the batwings I nodded to Ton. "They're here," I said. "Take a look an' see if you remember either of them."

It's hard for a man as large as Ton to do anything at all without being noticed, without drawing attention to himself, and when he turned in his chair to gawk at the Mexicans, both of them picked up on the move. "I can't say I recollect them, Cal, but they're Night Hunters sure as you're born."

I took my hand out of the bucket and rested it in my lap, forming and releasing a fist of sorts. Another half-hour in the ice and a few more beers probably would have fixed me up jus' fine. I didn't think I'd have that time, and I knew a fast draw'd be impossible. I leaned back in my chair. The vaqueros were glaring toward us — or Ton, mainly — and they didn't look pleased.

They started over to our table; those huge gut-ripper spurs they wore jangled with each step.

It's funny how that works. Not a word had been exchanged between the two men and Ton and me, but of a sudden the saloon was as quiet as a crypt at midnight, and the air was almost crackling with the "somethin's gonna happen" feeling.

They were both relatively small men, but the pistols, rifles, and knives they carried made them seem larger than their 5'4" or so. A stink of sweat, whiskey, and long-unwashed hair drifted in front of them as they approached us. From a bit of a distance they looked intimidating; up close they looked silly in their ill-fitting clothing and their foolishly large sombreros. One was carrying a good bit of lard around his gut and he had one of them faces that remind a person of a pig. The other man was rail-thin and had a twitch in his left eye.

They stood together at our table, across from me and almost on top of Ton, who'd turned in his chair to face them.

"You stare at us, no?" Twitch said. It wasn't really a question.

"Yeah," Ton said. "I do stare at you. I think you're both Night Hunters, is what I think. That means my pard here an' me

144

gotta kill you."

Both of them snickered. "Night Hunters? What is this Night Hunters?" Pig asked, his sarcasm — or maybe it was disdain — heavy. "Is like a gang or somethin'?"

"We're kinda wondering where you boys are going next, so's we can get there before you do and shoot your greasy asses off when you ride in," I said.

"You talk crazy-stupid, gringo," Twitch said. "You think 'cause you ride a horse for a couple minutes you can talk like this to us?"

Still looking at Twitch, I said to Ton, "It's a damn sure bet we're not going to get anything outta these two pieces of garbage."

Ton didn't turn back to me when he answered. "I never figured we would. I sure did want to meet up with a couple of Hunters right face-to-face, though. Looks like my wish come true."

The vaqueros separated, each taking a step or so to the side. "I got the pig," I said to Ton. "How 'bout you take care of ol' twitch-eye?" Twitch's face reddened, even through his fairly dark skin and his years of exposure to the sun. Pig didn't seem real fond of his new moniker, either. The men at the tables behind and to the side of me an' Ton scrambled to get out of the potential line of fire of the two Mexicans, leaving their beers and their hats behind in their rush.

Pig's eyes were slits and the set of his shoulders and the throbbing of a vein in his neck showed that he was ready to fight. Twitch was balanced, feet apart, one planted several inches behind the other, his body angled toward Ton and me. The best of the gunfighters — those who live a few years — never stand with their full bodies facing an opponent, particularly in a fast-draw situation. I didn't know how fast Twitch might have been, but he was Ton's problem, not mine. Pig was my man and I concentrated on him, knowing that he was teetering on the very edge of making his move.

I don't remember ever hating a man as much as I hated Pig. At that moment I was holding him personally and directly responsible for the treatment of the women, the sacking and burning of Busted Thumb, and the killing of the whiskey drummer.

"Pig," I said. "It's my understanding that when your mama birthed you with the rest of the litter, she puked the first time she saw you, an' that she up an' cut her own throat to make herself into a side of bacon rather than look at you. That true, Pig? 'Course, some say your mama is whorin' out of Juarez an' that the best she can get for a ride is a nickel."

As I was talking I eased back the hammer on my Colt. I'd drawn it and rested it in my lap the moment the Hunters came into the saloon, and I had the barrel angled at Pig's chest. I'd have to shoot through the table, but that flimsy piece of shit wouldn't even slow down a .45 slug.

My little speech pushed Pig over the edge and his hand flashed to his pistol. I hadn't done much shooting with my left hand, but I could pull a trigger, an' that's what I needed to do. Pig's draw wasn't bad, but a strong voice cut into it, demanding, "Goddammit, hold on there!"

CHAPTER FIVE

Pig's pistol had already cleared leather when Sheriff Warner's words crashed into the silence that'd taken over the saloon. I did the only thing I could to save my life: I began squeezing the trigger of my Colt. Even though I was shooting with my left hand, I'd say I did real good. The first round tore a jagged hole in the tabletop and took Pig in the gut. His pistol continued to move upward to where it would be leveled at me, and I kept on firing. Two more slugs hit Pig, one in the throat and the other in his chest, pretty much right over where his heart would be, if the sumbitch had a heart.

Twitch was a bit slower with his draw. It seemed like the throaty roar of Ton's shotgun was what threw Twitch back several feet to the wall, but of course it wasn't — it was the load of double-ought buckshot that tore a hole in his midsection big enough to pass a fist on through. That twelve-gauge is a hell of weapon.

Warner aimed his pistol in the space between me an' Ton. "Drop the weapons," he shouted, "an' get your hands up or I'll drill the pair of you!" Warner's face was an apoplectic red and I didn't doubt for a second that he'd start throwing lead at us if we even hesitated. My Colt hit the floor at the same time Ton's shotgun did.

Warner nudged Pig with the toe of his boot. "I guess it'd be real hard to get any deader than this one," he said. "Looks like the other boy is out of the game, too." He called over his shoulder to the bartender, "Todd — you get these two over to the furniture store so's we can get them boxed up and in the ground before they start to stink."

"You there, bronc man," Warner said, "stand up real slow. And you," he said to Ton, "keep your hands up just like you got 'em now. You make a move and I'll empty my gun into you — my .45 don't give a damn how big you are. Got it?"

I didn't want to take my eyes away from the sheriff's gun hand. If I saw his trigger finger move the least little bit I was going to dive to the floor. His face and eyes told me real clear that he wouldn't mind taking us both out, an' I wasn't about to give him a reason to do so. I heard Ton mumble, "Yes-sir."

"Hiram," Warner called to one of the gawkers standing near the bar, "pick up the shotgun and pistol and run them down to my office. Take the weapons off the two Mexes, too."

Warner took a couple of steps back, his gun still at the ready. "You two are going to walk ahead of me to my office," he said. "You get cute and you die even before the folks of my fine town of Dawson's Crossing get the chance to see you hang. Go on — move on past me, an' out to the street."

It wasn't what you'd call a Sunday stroll as we walked down Main Street to Warner's office. I could feel the sheriff's pistol centered on my back with every step I took. There were people on both sides of the street, watchin' us go by. A kid threw a stone that bounced offa Ton's shoulder. "Cut that shit out," Warner warned, but he didn't sound like he really meant it. Sure enough, a stone caught me on my shoulder. It stung some.

There were two cells in the sheriff's office, connected to the business part of the office by a door. Warner took a ring of keys from his desk and motioned me to the door with the barrel of his gun.

The cell area reeked of vomit. There was a pair of young guys in one cell, passed out. One or both of them had unloaded the booze he drank and what appeared to be whatever he'd eaten in the past six months or so. The second cell was open. Me an' Ton didn't need to be told where we were going. I walked in and Ton followed me. Warner slammed the barred door closed and locked it. He holstered his weapon and stood for a moment looking in at us like we were a pair of buffalo turds on the food table at a church picnic.

"I told you I don't allow trouble in my town," Warner said. "You two ain't been here a full day and you killed two men. I told you I didn't give a damn about where or how you chased down the Night Hunters, as long as you didn't cause me any grief. Well, hell, you boys . . ."

"Sheriff — what you saw was pure self-defense an' you know it. The one I dropped was drawing — hell, had drawn — on me, and the one Ton shot was going for his gun, too. You can't . . ."

"Don't you tell me what I can and can't do!" Warner snarled. "You two caused me a good bit of trouble. I gotta keep you here 'til the circuit-riding judge comes through, which I means I got to feed you at least once a day. That's a pain in the ass. Plus, you're tying up a perfectly good cell."

"Any decent judge will see it was self-defense," I said.

"Could be you're right," Warner said. "But I didn't say a word about a 'decent' judge did I? Hizzoner Malcom Stoneworthy is due here in two, maybe three weeks. He's a cranky old sonofabitch for true. The law of the sixgun doesn't carry any weight with him. He'll string the pair of you up just as sure as I'm standing here."

"But, Sheriff," Ton protested, "them two was Hunters an' needed to die. An' like Cal says, it was self-defense. We wanted to get some information from them, is all."

"I don't care if they were angels come to lead you to the promised land. You gunned down two men in my town and you're going to swing for it." Warner turned and walked back to his office, slamming the door a good deal harder than he needed to.

The cell was a little smaller than the size of a good horse stall, maybe eight feet by ten feet. There was a single, barred window that faced south with no breeze coming in through it, and the reek of the cowhands was overpowering, making me gag, bringing hot bile up to the back of my throat. The bars were three-quarter-inch solid steel, both in the door and the window. The floor was a mix of clay and dirt — hard, flattened by the boots and the bodies of the men before us who had to sleep on the floor, just we would, since there were no cots. There was a slop bucket that from its smell hadn't been emptied recently.

"Well," Ton said. "Damn."

"Yeah. This is bad, Ton. There's no way outta here unless Warner gets real careless, and I can't see that happening."

"I heard of that judge, that Stoneworthy. Everybody calls him 'String 'em up Salsworthless.' He hangs more men than he lets off. Some say he's a drunk, but I don't know 'bout that." Ton stepped over to the window and tested a bar. "Set good," he murmured. "Good steel, too. I dunno, Cal. Seems to me we might be screwed."

"Maybe so," I said. "There ain't much we can do right now but think this whole thing over — try to figure some way to get us outta here."

Ton nodded without enthusiasm. "We can think all we want," he said, "but we're still screwed."

We watched as the cowhands were taken out and sent on their way the very next morning, looking sheepish and queasy. The first couple of days passed very slowly. The cell got hotter'n the deepest part of hell in the afternoons. Warner brought us water to drink but not nearly enough of it. There was a little rectangular opening at the bottom of the cell door where food was slid in, and the sheriff gave us a full canteen once a day. Hell, we sweated out that much every day.

There isn't much to talk about when a man is locked up. It seems like the real world is so far away, so unreachable, that yapping about it is like talking about heaven or some such place.

I spent a lot of time thinking about Anna. If it hadn't been for her, I wouldn't have been in the fix I was. That thought kind of made me cringe as soon as I had it 'cause I knew that her fix was one hell of a lot worse than mine or Ton's.

I recalled one conversation Anna and I had the night before the Hunters rolled in.

"Where will you go from here?" she asked.

"I'm not real sure. Wherever I can do some ridin', I guess. I'm not in no hurry to leave."

"You like Porter Flats?" she asked, grinning.

"Hell no, Anna — but I'm sure findin' you tolerable."

Anna didn't say anything for a long time. In fact I'm not completely sure I didn't dream this, but I think she then said, "I will go with you when you leave."

I can't swear to that, but something sure happened 'tween us up in that crummy little room. Love? I dunno. I never had any before so I didn't know what it was like. Lust? Maybe so, but even freshly sated I still wanted to look at her, watch her move, see her smile, look into her eyes. I been with some whores in my time, an' I never felt anything like that before. After I was done with them I jus' wanted to commence drinkin' and maybe playin' some cards an' I never gave the woman I'd just used a single further thought.

With Anna, everything was different.

The third night, Ton gave the window bars a try. There was a full moon and I could see him fairly well. He looked exactly like the picture in that damned Bible of my pa's, where Samson's pushing down the columns and wrecking the temple.

Ton grunted like a draft horse laying into a load, one hand on one bar and the other on the bar next to it, and he strained until beads of sweat popped out of his face 'stead of flowing like normal sweat does. His back muscles began to quiver, and the veins in his arms stood out from flesh like fat worms, and I could hear his teeth grindin' on each other from the effort he was making. He kept on for what seemed to me to be a long

155

time. I was actually scared his heart would bust if he didn't ease up. He sucked in huge draughts of air as he hauled on those bars, sounding like a locomotive building up power. Finally, he had no choice but to give it up. He fell back like he'd been hit on the head with a stout club and crashed to the floor of the cell. He was soaked in sweat and the muscles in his arms trembled. Seeing Ton laid out there on the floor, I again realized what a massive man he was. Being with him as much as I had kind of took the awe away. But just then I wasn't seeing my partner, I was seeing the most powerful man I'd ever seen in my life. If he couldn't bend those bars, there wasn't a living man who could.

When Ton's breathing came back to normal, he said, "Sorry, Cal. I couldn't do 'er. I gave her all I had but it wasn't near enough. Damn." I didn't know what to say to that, so I said, "I know that," and let the matter drop. We both slept where we were at that moment, Ton spread out on the floor with his arms splayed out like a fallen tree, an' me sittin' with my back to the wall, knees up, head resting on my arms.

Both of us were aware that the more time passed, the chance to strike at the Night Hunters became more an' more remote.

'Course, there was the matter of getting strung up waitin' on us, too.

It was the day after Ton tried the bars, or maybe two days later — time gets all mixed up in a cell — that the storm began. We heard the thunder rolling across the prairie early on an' then began to see the glistening, white-hot bolts of lightning cutting across the sky. It was daylight, but the lightning was brighter than the sun ever could be. The rain began, soft and cooling at first, but then it got some wind behind it and it poured down to be whipped about in whatever direction the wind took. I never saw such a changeable wind: one second it was blowing due east, and in the next south or north or whatever the hell. The heat got washed away right quick, and the cell became as cold as it had once been hot. We'd both taken our shirts off and we put them back on.

We sat against a wall to avoid the rain being huffed in. "You know what I miss more'n anything except Priscilla?" Ton asked between bursts of thunder.

"What?"

"A cuppa coffee and a smoke. Been some time since I had either."

I waited for another break. "I wouldn't mind some decent food. Warner's slop isn't

157

fit for pigs. That coffee sounds awful good though, an' so does the smoke."

We passed the rest of the morning and then the afternoon sitting there next to one another, but completely separate, each of us with his own thoughts. The storm didn't seem to be settling down: the sky all around us flickered with lightning, and when it struck anywhere we could see from the window, the light didn't flicker, but instead hit our eyes and made us see it long after it was gone.

I was about half asleep when Ton asked me, "You ever see a man get hung?" he asked.

"Once in Yuma I did."

"What was it like?"

It was a foul old memory that came to me in nightmares every so often. "Isn't much to it if it's done right, Ton," I said. "You drop on through like a trapdoor an' your neck gets broke, an' that's it."

Ton absorbed that for a good long while. "Did you hear the guy's neck break?" he asked.

"Yeah. It was like the sound of a whip hitting a mule's ass — kind of sharp an' quick an' gone before you know it."

There was another silence from Ton. The rain continued to pelt down. "I ain't gonna

158

do it," he said. "Ain't nobody gonna hang me up like a slaughtered pig."

I didn't think Ton had much choice in the matter, so I didn't say anything.

"What I'll do if it comes down to it, is run. The sheriff or somebody'll pick me off, but I'd rather croak from a bullet or two than dangle at the end of a rope."

I didn't tell Ton that more'n likely his legs would be shackled together, and his hands tied behind his back, an' that he'd have a black hood over his head toward the end. I figured if Ton thought he could beat the hangman outta a job, that was fine with me. Maybe that thinkin' gave him some comfort, an' it wasn't my place to put an end to that.

See, the thing of it is that I lied to Ton. The cattle thief I saw strung up in Yuma did a hell of a dance for several minutes before he quieted down an' strangled to death. His neck wasn't broke by the drop, an' a soldier there told me that happens lots of times, maybe even most times. The rustler wet his pants, too, an' his bowels let loose as he was dangling there, tryin' his best to reach out with his feet for somethin' to stand on to support himself for a few seconds. Ton didn't need to know any of that, and I hoped he did get a chance to run an' catch a bullet 'stead of dyin' at the end of a rope, but I knew it wasn't gonna happen.

We'd both dozed off when we heard a *psssst!* from right outside our window. I stood and looked out. There was a wagon of the type used to deliver big things with two draft horses in the traces. An old fella — or white-haired at least — stood on the back of the wagon. He was not a big man; maybe 5'4" and didn't look to weigh more than a fat hen. He was dripping wet. He saw me looking out and moved closer to the window.

"I'm gonna bust you boys outta there," he said, whispering. By that time, Ton was standing next to me. "These two horses here could pull over a goddamn building. I'm gonna hook this here rope to the wagon an' you boys tie it 'round them bars. Got it?"

I guess I'm a bit suspicious, but I'd heard of breakouts like this set up by vigilantes who wanted their own crack at the condemned man, an' would tar an' feather him before they hanged him from a tree branch. "Why you doin' this?" I asked.

Ton banged his elbow into my side hard enough to come close to knockin' the wind outta me. "What the hell difference does it make why he's doin' it? He's *doin'* it, ain't he?"

The old man passed the end of a thick

160

rope to Ton, the kind steam wheelers use to tie up to the Mississippi piers when the weather's gettin' frisky. Ton pulled in some slack and took two wraps around the bars and then handed the tail of the rope back to the man who was about to save us. "I heard one of you askin' why I'm bustin' you out. Here's your answer: them Night Hunters killed my Aunt Clara an' burned her house an' barn an' I ain't about to let that set. I don't see real good — got some bits of Yankee shrapnel in my eye at Antioch. So, I ain't much with a rifle. But I seen you two take care of the Hunters in the saloon, an' that was enough for me. 'No way in hell are those boys goin' to swing,' I promised myself."

He put his face closer to the window. "Your horses are at the livery, all saddled an' ready to go. Your Sharps an' so forth're there as well. I'd suggest that you get mounted an' get the hell outta Porter Flats in a hurry. I had to wait 'til somethin' like this storm made 'nuff cover noise to get the job done here. Warner'd shoot me down as soon's he would you, if he saw me tryin' to help you escape. Now, get ready to run for the stable, hear?"

He moved to the front of his wagon and climbed up into the driver's seat. He shook the reins over the horses and they started forward. When they hit the end of the rope, their hooves threw clods of mud into the air as they fought to get traction to do their jobs. The rope came tight between the rear of the wagon and the bars in the window until it was taut as a guitar string. The bars didn't move. "Hell's fahr," the old boy cursed. He backed his team until the rear of the wagon was almost touching the wall of the jail under the window. This time he slapped the reins harder and those two big horses took off like they were running a race.

When the team hit the end of the rope the entire back wall of the cell came down just as pretty as you please. Me an' Ton scrambled out. The ol' fellow was cutting the rope an' then was back in the driver's seat without another word. He slapped his team again an' hustled off into the storm. Ton an' me didn't waste any time — we ran to the livery, slippin' an' slidin' in the mud, soaking wet by the time we'd gone ten feet.

The old man was true to his word. Jake and Matthew were saddled and bridled in a pair of stalls. All we needed to do was take up the reins, lead them out the back door, and climb on. You can wager that we did that in a big hurry.

I'm not sure if we rode out of the storm or that the whole thing slowly abated, but by the time dawn came, the rain was gone and the wind had dropped. The sun began its climb above the purplish line of the eastern horizon and the heat began to set in early.

"If it ain't one damned thing it's another," Ton said. "Last night I near to froze my ass off, an' today we're goin' to be fried up like a couple of chickens." He said it with a grin, and I knew he was purely overjoyed with our escape, just like I was.

"You think Warner'll be after the ol' boy who saved us?" Ton asked.

"I've been thinkin' on that," I said. "An' I don't think there's a thing Warner can do. There are a passel of big rigs in Porter Flats like the one the old man brought — beer deliverers, grain carriers, all that. An' each wagon has a pair of draft horses pullin' it. So, I think our friend is safe."

"Good," Ton said. "Good. I can't feature the Sheriff ridin' out after us, either. Doesn't seem like he'd leave his precious town to chase down a couple of fellas didn't do nothin' but lower the rat population in town by two."

We rode on until we were worried about our horses. Truth is, both Ton and me would have ridden for another week straight if our mounts could have taken it. We wanted as many miles between us and Porter Flats as possible.

We came upon a good water hole about midday an' decided to rest up our horses an' maybe catch some shut-eye our ownselves. All that rain had filled up the water holes that were near dry before the storm, which meant we had sweet, clean rainwater to drink.

Ton stripped the horses down and I walked out from the water hole, looking for some rabbit meat on the hoof. We were hungry enough to eat a jackrabbit, fur an' all. I got lucky on the first two an' brought them down with a single round apiece. The third one took a quick turn an' I missed with the shot, but did him in with my next one.

I put up a little fire while Ton skinned out the rabbits. The fire took some coaxing 'cause of everything being so wet, but I finally got it going. We skewered our first real meal in too long, and made short work of it. Ton eyed the third hare we'd put aside. "You still hungry?" he asked.

"Go on," I told him. "I couldn't eat another bite."

We decided to wait out the rest of the day

and night where we were an' get started with first light an' fresh horses in the morning. That raised a question: where the hell were we going? It'd been either five or six days since the saloon, and there was no chance of picking up tracks after the rain and driving wind had wiped them all away.

We talked it over that night. Ton was of a mind to head to the river, find a place we could cross, an' then hunt up that town of Santa Lucia. We weren't positive that's where the Hunters were going, but it seemed like a good bet. "How long you think it'll take us?" I asked Ton.

"I can't say. See, I don't know where we are, but we know the river is due south, don't we? Let's find it first an' then worry about where we're goin' after we cross."

That's exactly what we did.

The Rio Grande is a mean ol' bitch who's quite fond of upsetting wagons, pulling horses and cattle under her surface, and drowning good men who've never done a thing to her. Cowhands moving cattle dread water crossings more than anything else they encounter on the way to the railroad shipping yard. Heat an' rattlesnakes an' lamed-up horses an' too many meals of beans an' hardtack are all part of the business, and they accept that. But it's the rare hand who hasn't had a friend — or at least an acquaintance — drowned in a water crossing.

As we rode toward the river, I asked Ton if Matthew had ever been in water. He shook his head no. "Only up to his pasterns, an' then only to drink. I don't think he cares for water much. For that matter, neither do I. What about Jake?"

"I've swum him a couple of times and he handled it good. Scared the piss outta me, though."

"Why so?"

" 'Cause I never learned how to swim, is how so. Can you swim?"

"Feisty this mornin', ain't you?" he grinned. "I swim like a damn anvil myself. I never learned to do her."

"Well, look," I said, kind of thinking out loud. "All that rain is gonna make the Rio Grande roar, an' she doesn't need any help with doin' that, even durin' a dry spell. I guess the best thing we can do is when we strike the river we head one way or the other alongside it 'til we come on a place we can cross without drownin'."

"Yeah. It'll take at least a couple of days for the runoff to clear and the river to calm down a hair, an' we ain't got a couple of days to waste."

That day we rode on into the night 'til the dark was so thick even the horses were nervous about movin' ahead in it. We'd had no sign of water since mid-afternoon. We didn't make a fire when we stopped 'cause we had nothing to cook. We each had a sip of water from our canteens, then emptied them into our hats for our horses. We were back in the saddle with the first little glimmer of light.

About mid-morning we were all thirsty enough to drink lamp oil. Ton and me gave our horses all the rein they wanted whenever their ears flicked forward or they raised their muzzles to sniff the air, hoping they'd smell water an' take us to it.

The heat was an ongoing pain in the ass. Both me an' Ton had been in the West most of our lives, but there's no way a man can get used to the heat of deep summer in Texas. It simply can't be done — one scorching hot day is as miserable as one a week ago or a year ago, or wheneverthehell.

"I had me an uncle who drowned in a little fishin' pond," Ton said as we rode. "I don't recall much about him. I was a kid then, maybe five, six years old, is all. Even so, I still dream of how he looked when my Pa and some other fellas hauled him outta the water. He was kinda gray, Cal, and his eyes were open an' they were flat, like all that water had washed away most of their color. Some water, it run outta his mouth." Ton cleared his throat and licked his already parched lips. "He owed my Pa four dollars for a shoat he bought offa us. Pa never did see that money."

My throat was so dry and swollen that I didn't bother to croak an answer. I nodded, is all.

"Shoat died anyway, of the scours," Ton said.

A walk was as fast a gait as we dared. We couldn't ask anything more of the horses. Both of them were frothy at the chest and soaked at the flank. Jake was one of those proud horses who always liked to carry his head high, like he was somethin' special. This day his head was low, muzzle not real far from the ground. Matthew was the same. I felt sorry for the critters but feelin' sorry didn't accomplish anything, an' it wouldn't bring us any closer to water, so we kept on going.

It was well into the afternoon when both the horses' heads jerked upright as if they was puppets pulled up by the same string. They flared their nostrils for a moment, drawing in the scent. Then both of them got cantankerous, pulling at the reins, wantin' to step up the pace a good bit. Ton and I exchanged a grin; even a mare in heat wouldn't have affected those two horses at that point. Nothin' would 'cept the smell of water.

We topped a gentle rise and down below us, there she was, the Rio Grande, with cottonwoods and grass along her shore. The water was rushin' along, carryin' limbs an' even trees, an' it was a murky, muddy brown color. None of us gave a damn about that. We charged down the slope and right on into the river. I held a rein in my hand and pushed off my saddle and the feeling of being in that cool water was better'n any heaven my pa's preacher ever rattled on about. I took in great, gritty gulps, almost choked, an' then stood up. The river was about boot-top deep and I could feel the pressure of it as it swept along. Both horses were sucking water hard. Ton was sitting on the bottom, his face buried under the surface. I swear we lowered the level of the Rio Grande a foot an' more that day.

Jake an' Matthew had to be dragged out before they busted a gut. There was some grass along the shoreline, but right then they weren't interested in it — they wanted to drink. We gave them some time onshore and then led them back in an' let them suck again. After three times of doing that, they began to graze, happy as a pair of sows in a muck pile.

The sun was touching the horizon in the west, although there was still good light left. But, me an' Ton an' the horses were drawn thin by the day's ride. "Might just as well set up here," I said to Ton. "We can look for a crossing tomorrow."

"I'm right sick of rabbit meat," Ton said. "I tell you what: I'll get us some fish for supper — see if I don't." He drew the bowie knife he carried in a sheath and walked over to one of the cottonwoods. There he selected a branch maybe an inch or so thick and cut it from the tree. He used a length of latigo — a flat leather string attached to a saddle to tie things down to it — to bind his knife to the end of the branch, making an awkward-looking but serviceable spear. He set out walking down the river going with the current and I gathered up some sticks and twigs and started a fire. Once it was going I shucked off my clothes and set them around the fire to dry them a bit.

Maybe an hour later Ton came struttin' on back with a half-dozen big fish strung through the gills on the same piece of latigo he'd used to tie his knife to the branch. He was as proud as the king of the world. "These here are what're called trout," he said. "I found a little swing in the river where the water was calm an' I speared these boys as easy as can be. I'll clean 'em up an' we'll have us a real fine meal for once."

"For once?"

"Sure. Like I said, I like rabbit as well's the next man, but it gets old. These trouts are somethin' completely different."

I hadn't eaten much fish in the course of my life, and when I did it was generally catfish pulled out of warm, silty water where they hung around, waiting to be speared or caught on a hook an' line. They were the ugliest goddamn things you ever saw, an' their meat was fatty an' tasted of mud. Ton's trout weren't like that at all. The meat was pure white and firm and tasted of the mesquite branches we cooked the fillets over. There was no mud taste at all.

Ton had bought a couple cans of cling peaches in heavy syrup while I was jawin' with Sheriff Warner an' put them in his saddlebag and we each had one after we finished the fish. We boiled coffee in one of the cans and it began to smell awful good as we rolled smokes. Ton had picked up the most important things — coffee, peaches, an' tobacco, but he'd forgotten to buy a coffeepot. He got us one of them canned hams, too, which we decided to save 'til we were desperate. We'd planned on buying ammunition, too, but we felt compelled to get out of Dawson's Crossing without doin' any more shopping.

We smoked an' drank coffee. "I guess if we keep headin' north after we cross, we'll come to somethin', right? Maybe a road or a village or some such."

"Seems like we would. Thing is, from what I've heard, Mexico is a lot like Texas — all the space in the world with nothin' in it but scrub an' buffalo grass an' rattlers."

The night didn't bring much coolness with it, but at least the sun wasn't pounding down on us as it had during the day. The sound of the river a few yards away made everything seem peaceful-like. I guess water kind of does that.

Ton hadn't dried out his clothes at all, an' I asked him about that. "The sun'll dry 'em out soon enough," he said. "Tomorrow afternoon when I'm bein' baked like an apple pie I'll be wishin' my clothes was still wet."

"You think we'll have the river behind us by then?"

"I do. There must be a passel of places we

can cross. We'll come up on one soon enough," he predicted.

The next morning we discussed how we could most quickly find a point where we could cross the Rio Grande without drowning. "How about this," I said. "You ride upstream an' I'll ride downstream and whoever comes on a good spot fires his rifle twice into the air. I'll come runnin' if I hear your shot an' you do the same with mine."

"That makes good sense," Ton said. "I figure we'll be across before midday."

Ton was wrong.

I rode downstream, kind of enjoying the sound of the moving water as I followed the shore. A few miles out that sound became louder, and then louder again, and then, as I rode around a bend I saw the cause of the racket. For whatever goddamned reason the river became narrower and it looked like the water was battling the huge boulders that were scattered there, bashing against them, spewing water ten or more feet into the air, churning so wildly that the water was white rather than the dull brown it'd been earlier. All that noise and movement made Jake antsy and he danced around some, his eyes as big as dinner plates, snorting and carrying on. I got a handle on him, but he was soaked in nervous sweat. I figured the only thing I could do was ride beyond the whitewater, keep goin' in the same direction I had been.

It may have a mile or a touch more before Jake settled down. The river had widened again. In fact the spot where I sat my horse made the river look like a small lake. The current was still moving faster than I liked. I watched a dead cow, battered in the white water but still pretty much hanging together except for a foreleg being torn off and a two-foot-long gouge in its gut, as it swept past me. The cow was moving right along — faster'n a man's quick walk. I wasn't sure how the horses would do swimming against the current an' that bothered me. I didn't want to see Jake or Matthew with a ripped gut from a rock.

After a while the river narrowed back down from lake size, and again the sound of it was peaceful. I'd been thinking about Anna as Jake picked his way along the shoreline. Truth to tell, I'd been thinking about her a whole lot, and what we'd do after I got her free of the Hunters. In the back of my mind I kind of saw a little piece of land I could run some horses and maybe a few head of cattle on. I'm getting too old for getting my ass kicked around by rank horses — that's a young man's game. So, I thought maybe Anna and me could get together and make a go of it on a spread. I knew horses well enough to buy, sell, and train them. Maybe there'd be work for Ton as a blacksmith wherever Anna and me settled down, too. That'd be good.

It's strange, but Ton's and my friendship — our partnership — is based on hate. It was true, though: we both hated Danny Montclaire and the Night Hunters, and we both wanted to see as many of them dead as we possibly could.

Thinking that way — about the Hunters — eroded hell out of the good thoughts about Anna and replaced them with gunfire and blood and revenge. I refused to let my mind wander to what was being done to Anna, how she was being used, because I'd get crazy then. I had to keep control of myself, and I did, in general. But I'll say this: the anger and the hatred was like a banked fire that could flare up an' come to life anytime, and when it did, there'd be hell to pay for anyone between me an' my woman.

I was letting Jake suck some water and take a breather when a pair of shots boomed along the river to me, flattened and softened by the distance but unmistakable. As far as I know, there's nothing that sounds exactly like gunfire.

It was beyond mid-afternoon and I hadn't yet come on a crossing point that didn't look like suicide. I tightened Jake's cinch and covered ground in the opposite direction at a lope, in spite of the heat. I'd been getting a little nervous about the time Ton and I were wasting tryin' to cross the river, and I was pleased that Ton had found a safe place.

I came on Ton and Matthew upstream a few miles. Ton was standing at the shore with Matthew's reins in his hand. I rode in next to them and stepped down from my saddle. The Rio Grande was wide at the place Ton had chosen, and the surface water looked placid, with no rocks or boulders to give us grief. "Wadda ya think?" Ton asked.

"Kind of a long haul to the other side. It'd be good if we knew how deep the water might be."

"Be good if our horses grew wings an' we could fly over to the other side," Ton said. "This is the best I've seen all day. I say we take a run at her right here."

"OK. I think what we ought to do is take a loop around our waists and then tie down to our saddle horns. That way, if we somehow got dumped, we'd still have a chance." I could see Ton didn't much like hearing that, but he agreed with me. Actually, I think we were both scared.

We used our throwin' ropes to attach ourselves to our horses and mounted up. We sat there for some time, looking across the water. Finally, Ton said, "She ain't gonna change no matter how long we look at her, so let's do it an' get it over with."

The far shore was about fifty yards away, but just then it looked like fifty miles. We urged our horses into the river. Matthew acted up a bit, but it was because all this was new to him. Jake, on the other hand, went right on in when I nudged him with my boot heels. I'd crossed water with him a few times before, although not at the kind of distance we now faced.

I couldn't see the bottom because the water was so muddy, but it felt like Jake had decent footing. If it'd been rocky, he'd be picking his steps real carefully, but he walked on out like he was on a Sunday stroll. Matthew wanted to stay behind Jake an' Ton let him do so.

We'd covered about a quarter of the distance before the water began getting deeper. Until then, it'd been not high enough to tickle the horses' bellies. The current was stiff, just like we knew it would be. I could feel Jake shift his weight to kind of lean into the moving water. When we reached the midpoint, there must have been a ledge or dropoff or some damned thing, because in a second, Jake was swimming and a moment later, so was Matthew.

Horses swim much like a dog does, except maybe a horse is a tad more frantic about it. Their legs flail, putting water into the air like a paddle wheeler, and they work too hard at it. The problem for the rider is that even if he knows how to swim, he needs to get way the hell away from the horse if he gets unseated, because those steel-shod hooves can bust a man's head wide open like a rotting melon.

I used the stand of cottonwoods on the other side as a reference point. The moment the horses had to start swimming it looked like the trees were moving right quick to their right — the current had gotten us. At that same moment I saw a wavering line of smoke rising above the tops of the trees.

I looked back at Ton. His face was grim and deathly pale and he was clutching his saddle horn with both hands, like a novice rider on a runaway mustang. I could see Matthew's shoes clearing water and splashing back down with enough force to pound a railroad spike into a boulder. Jake, too, was reaching way out, snorting, on the edge of panic. There was nothing me an' Ton could do but hang on. The horses wanted dry land under their feet as much as we did, and they'd get us across if they could. Trying to direct a swimming horse is not unlike telling rain to stop — nothing happens.

The current was deceiving — the brownish surface looked flat an' steady, but that water was moving, and moving hard. We were being carried downstream at a good clip and those cottonwoods were getting farther away. I was crouched forward in my saddle and I was underwater from my waist down. I knew I was making the swim harder for Jake with my unbalanced weight rocking on his back everytime he surged ahead. I figured I need to push off an' then hang onto that rope like it was a line to life — which it was. I chanced a look back at Ton and saw he was having the same problem I was, 'cept he was half off his saddle on the right side.

"Ton," I yelled to him, "Push off! It's our only chance!"

I took my own advice and eased off my saddle. I hung there for a split second and then the slack was gone from the rope and I felt like I'd been kicked in the stomach when the loop tightened. Jake dragged me along strongly enough, but everything but my head was underwater. I made the mistake of trying to take a gulp of air with my mouth open and must have swallowed half the goddamn Rio Grande. That set me to coughing, and I could taste the dirt in the water and feel it scrape the inside of my nose.

I looked back when I stopped coughing and at first all I saw was Matthew, eyes huge, punching the water with those big hooves of his. Then I saw Ton off to the side, his Stetson down as low as he could tug it, moving along with his horse, his hands in a death grip on his rope.

We were still being swept downstream and it seemed like every foot we moved ahead we moved sideways two feet. I was worried about Jake wearing out. Swimming is even harder on a horse than a full gallop is because his legs are constantly churning against a force a lot harder than the air is when he's running. There's the panic, too, which makes him fight all the harder, burning energy like mad.

The whole swimming thing stopped just as quick as it'd started: Jake's hooves had found some river bottom and he scrambled ahead, snorting, wanting to get to shore. In half a minute I, too, could feel the bottom under my boots an' I don't recall anything ever feeling that good to me. I heard Ton whoop behind me and I knew he'd found the bottom, too.

There was still maybe fifteen or so yards to cross, but the shallower water made it much easier going for our mounts. I was dead tired. Hanging on to a rope doesn't seem like real hard duty, but I guess I was so tight with fear that my whole body was clenched up an' straining.

There must have been a slope or a hill down below that river and we were going up it, because with every couple of steps the water was lower on my body. My legs were shaky, but I could walk and I wanted to get to shore at least as much as Jake did.

When I was about knee-deep a couple of bees buzzed by my face, and I raised my hand to swat them away, wondering what the hell was going to happen next. I'd just almost drowned and I can't see that I really need a few bee stings.

My thought changed in a big hurry when I heard the gunshots. Those bees I heard were the metal kind — bullets. There was some slack in the rope now and I used it like a long rein to slap Jake on the ass with to get him moving as fast as he could. There were more gunshots from the shore but I couldn't see any shooters yet. Behind me,

Ton cursed and yelled to me, "We gotta get outta this water — we're like ducks on a pond out here!"

I couldn't argue with that. A slug cut a gouge in the leather wrapped around my saddle horn and another slapped into the water a foot or so from me. The water was barely at knee height and Jake was only pastern deep. I slapped him again with the rope and then started a clumsy run. The last few yards to the shore were only a few inches deep and my fatigue was forgotten — Jake an' me were haulin' ass, an' so were Ton an' Matthew.

The thing is, both my Colt and my Sharps had been underwater for some time and it was unlikely that they'd fire before I cleaned them out, which I'd planned to do as soon as we crossed. I carried a bit of clean rag wrapped in oilcloth in my saddlebag, but that was to protect it from rain, not being fully underwater. I'd find out soon enough how it'd worked for me — if I made it to shore. I was stuck being a target an' no way to protect myself nor my partner and the shots from shore were coming faster an' closer now, spurting little geysers of water next to and in front of me.

CHAPTER SIX

My boots sank deeper into silt and mud the closer I got to shore, and each step felt like those in a crazy dream where my feet were godawful heavy an' I was tryin' to run from something bad that was breathin' down my neck. Ton was sloggin' just behind me and I heard him cursin' the river, the shooters, and several other things, so I knew he was all right. Then the dream ended an' I was atop that rank bronc in Busted Thumb all over again.

We splashed out of the Rio Grande and hustled for the scanty cover of a small stand of cottonwoods, bullets still hissing past us. I dropped Jake's reins the second we were in the trees and pawed through the soaked contents of my saddlebags for my cleanin' rod and that bit of oilcloth-wrapped rag. I sat on the dirt, breathing hard from the crossing, unwrapping the little sack and feeling of my cleaning cloth. It was more dry than wet. I wrapped the cloth around my cleaning rod and slid the rod and cloth from the muzzle back to the action gently, carefully, not wanting to screw up the delicate rifling inside the barrel. I withdrew the rod just as carefully, put a few drops of gun oil on the cloth, and repeated the process. My ammunition had gotten wet, too, but I quickly dried and lightly oiled a half-dozen rounds. My Sharps was ready to do its job, and it was a piece of work I was lookin' forward to.

"You gonna be much longer?" Ton called from the edge of the copse. "A bunch of those boys are comin' down the shore an' my rifle won't fire."

"Keep your drawers on," I answered. I worked the bolt action on my rifle and jacked a cartridge into the chamber. The action worked as smooth as sweet cream, making that same well-oiled click it always had.

Ton, prone and peeking around a tree, was working the lever action of his .30-.30, squeezing the trigger, hoping that one of the cartridges would fire. When they didn't, he cranked the lever again, ejecting the wet, unused bullet and bringing another into the chamber. I pushed up next to him. There were about fifteen men, all armed with rifles, fifty yards away from us, and coming on fast. "Night Hunters," Ton said.

"Musta been after our horses," I said. "Figured we was easy prey."

"They figured wrong," Ton said. "See that fat one with the sombrero? I remember him watchin' those poor whores when they was all nekkid the other night."

I aimed and fired and asked, "That one?" as the sombrero and a good half of the outlaw's head spun off into the mud behind him.

The thunderous report of the Sharps sent the Hunters scurrying for cover, into the scrub and trees parallel with the river. One unlucky desperado flung himself down behind a good-sized tree that'd been ripped up and carried along by the floodwaters. He made the mistake of looking over the rough bark of the tree to draw a bead on us.

"Nice shot," Ton commented, as the fellow's rifle arced up a few feet and dropped into the water. "Right 'tween the eyes."

The battle had drawn a lot more Hunters from what must have been their camp. The odds weren't looking good: Ton and I had but one functioning weapon. "We gotta pull out," I said between shots. "Let's get a move on."

The horses were tired from the battle with

the Rio Grande, but they set out willingly enough when Ton and I mounted up. Truth to tell, all four us were bedraggled from the crossing and the gunfight that followed it. We rode away from the river and on into Mexico wet, weary, and glad to have the water behind us. When we'd gone a mile or more the terrain began to change from its earlier lushness. Everything had changed from good buffalo grass an' fertile soil to scrub and arid, powdery dirt that looked like it'd never been wet by anything 'cept prairie dog piss.

I turned in my saddle every few minutes, expecting to find the pointing finger of rising dust that'd tell us the Night Hunters were mounted and after us. It never did show up. We rode through the heat of the day and our clothes quickly dried.

A couple of buildings appeared a long stretch ahead of us. It was hard to see because the heat shimmered up from the sand, a mirage that looked like the reversal of rain goin' up 'stead of down a window-pane. "Could might be a ranch," Ton said, as he eyed the buildings.

"Doesn't seem like a hundred acres out here would keep a steer alive, and it's a sure bet that nothin' will grow 'cept weeds an' cactus," I said. "But they're buildings, all right. Scroungin' a meal wouldn't be a half-bad idea, would it? If the Mexicans are like the Texans, they won't let a stranger ride off hungry."

"Least we don't need no baths to be presentable," Ton grinned. "I don't know when I've been this clean before."

We came to large pieces of land that were fenced with posts an' heavy wire, but we didn't see any stock in what looked like big holding pens. The fences were tight and straight; whoever lived here knew what he was doin' stringin' wire. I'd done some in the past and found it damned near impossible to run a straight line with it because it always wanted to snake itself back to the coil. It took a lot of cussin' to fence an acre, an' lots of time, too.

Ton looked down from Matthew's back, inspecting the tracks in the dirt of the empty pen. "This fellow's raisin' mules, is what he's doin — quite a few of them from the tracks. Different ages, too."

"Looks like horse tracks to me — but then I don't know a whole lot 'bout mules."

"There ain't that much to know," Ton said. "A mule ain't but a cross 'tween a stud donkey an' a horse mare. Thing is, a mule has a narrower, kinda more boxy hoof'n a horse does. It wears better an' is stronger

187

an' harder than a horse's. Hardy sons-abitches, them mules."

The buildings, which we could now see were a small home and a decent-sized barn, sat atop a gradual rise. We rode in at a walk, giving whoever lived there time to get his hands full of gun if he thought he needed to. When we were a piece from the front of the house, a man stepped out and walked toward us, a shotgun at port arms across his chest. His skin was brown — much like Anna's — and his hair black but speckled with some gray. It was easy to see he worked for a living. His arms were prominently sinewed, muscular, and his bare chest ridged with power. His gut was as flat as a fryin' pan.

We stopped and dismounted maybe ten feet from the man with the shotgun. He looked us over for a long moment, his gaze lingering on Ton's size, and then his face broke into a wide smile that showed the startling whiteness of his teeth. "Ju are no with the keelers," he said in passable English. "Come — we will put up your horses an' see to them an' then we weel drink an' eat, no?"

His name, he told us on the way to the barn, was Pedro Santa-Dominica. His wife, who hadn't yet appeared from inside the house, was named Blanca. Four men worked for him. At the moment, they were switching ninety head of mules from one pen to another some distance to the rear of the house. "Eeese like a clock," Pedro said. "We move them from number to number in a beeg circle all 'round us. Mules, they don' eat like horses. They do good on scrub an' could be some hay when dry times come an' even the scrub don' grow."

The barn was as neat and orderly as a well-run mercantile. The dirt floor must have been swept very recently; the broom marks still were clear and straight. There was an anvil and a small forge to one side, and that caught Ton's attention immediately. The farrier and blacksmithing tools were arranged on a work table within easy reach of the anvil and forge. The stalls — eight on a side with a wide alleyway between them — were smaller than the usual 10' by 12' or so of horse stalls. Each had a grain feeder, and empty water buckets stood just inside the gates. The hardware was good quality; most horse owners used a small loop of rope over a post to secure a stall.

Ton and I each led our horses into a pair of adjacent stalls, stripped off their tack, and rubbed them down with empty feed sacks supplied by Pedro. The man himself kept up a long, and at times hard to follow, conversation about how he sold mules to the U.S. Army and how well he was paid for his stock. The war, he said, had made him a comfortable man.

Ton checked the set of all four shoes on each of the horses before we left the relative darkness of the barn and walked out into the sunlight toward the house. It was a single story made of something like adobe, and it spread around a central entrance, looking like rooms had been added to the original structure without too much interest in design. It was much cooler inside the house and the air smelled delightfully of spices and meat cooking. Pedro sat at the head of a large table and waved to the chairs on either side of him. Ton and I sat, Ton's chair squeaking a complaint under him as it accepted his weight. Pedro called to his wife, waited a moment, and then called again.

After what seemed like a long time a woman — more of a girl, I suppose — stepped into the room from one of the many doorways leading to it. She was maybe sixteen, at the outside. She was beautiful in an innocent, dewy way. Her eyes, the deepest chocolate, were big enough to drown in, and her skin was almost alabaster in its purity. She stood quietly, hands clutched at her sides, her eyes on only her husband. She was hugely pregnant. I don't know much about things like that, but if she'd been a mare I'd have had her cross-tied in a birthing stall and I'd be standin' by to help if I was needed. I heard Ton gulp as if he was about to choke.

"Theese is my life," Pedro said proudly. At first I thought he'd mistaken the words "wife" an' "life," but quickly realized I was wrong when I saw the pride and the love shining from the man's weathered face. "Soon a son weel be my life, too."

I pushed my chair back an' stood like my ma had taught me to do when a lady comes in a room. Ton looked at me for a few seconds and then stood, too, although the confusion on his face indicated he didn't know why he had.

Pedro motioned us down and then introduced us to Blanca, an' she nodded, never really resting her eyes on either of us. Pedro rattled off a string of Spanish in a soft voice and Blanca turned and reentered the room she'd just left. Moments later she reappeared with a full bottle of clear liquid, three shot glasses, an' three salt cellars on a tray.

I never had much use for tequila since a

few years back when I went swimming in it an' woke up in a jail cell in a pissant town called Lee, Texas. I had no idea how I'd gotten there an' my head felt like a damned buffalo stampede was going on inside it. That day I puked up everything I'd ever eaten in my life, and swore 'fore God an' the world I'd never take another drink again — of any booze or beer, not jus' tequila.

The way Pedro took his was somethin' I'd seen other Mexicans do. He poured himself a shot, made a fist with his left hand, poured some salt on the creases his thumb and first finger made, brought that to his mouth, and followed the salt with the tequila. He was good at it, smooth, as if he'd practiced a lot. He handed the bottle to me. I lifted it to shoulder level to see the fat little worm on the bottom, grinned at my host, said "what the hell" to myself, and poured me a shot before passing the bottle to Ton. I wasn't about to bother with salt. Ton tried it with the salt an' seemed to catch on right quick. Fact is, he did another shot in the Mexican way 'fore he passed the bottle on to Pedro.

After the level of the tequila had dropped considerable, I asked Pedro how he knew we weren't Night Hunters. "I know them, no?" he said. "They are small men an' cowards an' they have no one like my new fren' Ton." He drank another shot. "I've saw them in Santa Lucia," he said. "They are like the wolves, with but one leader, an' they are cowards without him. If you an' Ton were Hunters you would have shot me in the back, not come ridin' up to me like real men."

"The leader is Danny Montclaire, right?"

Pedro laughed derisively. "Who but a li'l boy has a name Danny? But yes, he is the one."

"Do you know anything about him?" I asked.

"Si — yes. That he is a pistolero an' a snake."

"A pistolero?"

"Is true. I watched him face a caballero in Santa Lucia. The boy had the reputation, ju know? He faced Danny Montclaire an' he had three slugs in his ches' before his own peestol left his holster."

I had another taste of tequila while I thought that over. So did Pedro an' Ton. After a bit, I asked, "Why is your ranch still here, Pedro? Why haven't the Hunters burned you out, killed you?"

Pedro smiled that broad smile. "The army, my fren', the army. They count on me for mules an' if that supply is burned out they'd be highly angry — enough to chase those sonsabeeches down. Montclaire, he knows this well an' he leave us alone. Ju see, he ees crazy but no stupid. He know the army need my mules, war or not."

As we'd been swilling tequila and talking, the heady scent of Mex sauce and baking bread had grown stronger and stronger, until my mouth was watering every time I took a breath. "Are you hungry?" Pedro asked.

"You'd best answer him in a big hurry 'fore I eat this here table," Ton said. "We're almos' outta tequila, too." He glanced over at Pedro as he said the last part. Pedro called out to his wife in Spanish and she appeared a minute later with a fresh bottle.

I knew that the second bottle was a big mistake as well as I know my own name. It'd make no sense at all for any of us to take on more of that cactus whiskey. We were already like a trio of steers after getting the sledge at a slaughterhouse. More drinking would be jus' damn idiotic.

Pedro pulled the cork with his teeth, spit it out, an' lifted the neck of the bottle into his mouth, leaning his head back as if he was checkin' the sky for stars. A large bubble rose from the neck to the bottom of the bottle as he drank. He wiped his mouth with the back of his hand an' passed the booze to me, an' I did just what he did, sucking down an inch or so of liquid fire. Then, I passed the bottle to Ton. By the next time around I was dead asleep with my head on the table, mumbling something about Anna, according to what Ton told me the next day.

Ton, Pedro, an' Blanca had one fine meal, Ton told me. Frijoles, refried beans with molasses, a stew all choked full of big chunks of goat meat, an' golden biscuits that were light enough to float away. They passed dishes over my head, not lettin' a drunk an' snorin' bronc man louse up their feast, even if I was Ton's pard.

What purely aggravated me the next morning was that Ton an' Pedro were gabbin' away while stuffing down eggs an' fat meat an' biscuits while I was hangin' over a damn bush behind the barn, upchuckin' everythin' but my boot heels.

They were still eatin' when I first came back in, an' the smell of food sent me right on outdoors an' behind the barn again. After that I drank some water an' felt a little better, but not a whole hell of a lot.

Pedro gave us good directions to Santa Lucia and agreed that was probably where the Night Hunters were headed to sell the whores. It was about eighty miles or so, he said, which ain't that bad of ride, unless the heat was awful bad. He added that around here, the heat was always awful bad. He drew us a map to show us where we'd find drinkin' water on the way. He had one of his vaqueros fill our saddlebags with goat jerky, which tasted like beef jerky, except more so.

I didn't have much to say as we rode out that morning. I thanked Pedro and Blanca an' wished Pedro well with his business, an' Ton did the same. The sun was a cruel, white hot disk that hung in the otherwise vacant blue sky, doing its best to melt me into a foul puddle of pain and tequila residue. The horses were having trouble with the heat, too. Jake had begun to weave slightly, and he was no longer sweating, which was a bad sign. Matthew plodded along like a tired ol' plow horse, dragging the toes of his shoes with every stride.

"This ain't good," Ton said. "We gotta give these boys some rest."

He was right, of course. But, what good would a rest do if we spent it in the hottest part of the day with no shade to hide from the sun in? I said as much to Ton.

"That's true," he said. He took Pedro's map from his pocket and looked at it for a minute. "Looks like we ain't too far from some water an' maybe some trees," he said, handing the map to me.

I looked it over and shook my head in disgust. "Shit. We can't be no more'n six or eight miles from Pedro's ranch. If we stop now, we waste most of a whole day."

"We don't stop," Ton said, "an' we'll kill our horses. I can't see that we got any choice."

We changed direction a bit, taking us kinda east of a direct ride to Santa Lucia. I was dizzy in my saddle an' my gut was rumbin' something awful. If I looked out straight ahead, in a little bit of time I'd start to see little red spots floating in front of my eyes and hear that buzz sound I heard before Ton came on me in Busted Thumb. I let my reins slacken and Jake followed Matthew on his own. I clutched at my saddle horn with trembling hands, renewing my promise to myself that I'd never use alcohol again.

The horses, just as they usually did, caught the scent of water when we were still a good ways from it. Their gaits picked up a tad an' they'd snort every so often, shakin' their heads.

When we saw a few scraggly trees up ahead, we knew we were comin' to our stop.

We had to rein in our horses to keep them from runnin' the rest of the distance. They sure wanted that water.

It wasn't much, but it looked good to us. The water was clear an' wasn't much more'n a big puddle maybe a foot or so deep. There was good, green buffalo grass around it and the trees offered some speckled bits of shade. We stripped Jake an' Matthew and led them into the water. After they'd sucked hard for a time, we dragged them out an' walked them around a little. Then we took them back for another drink. After a while we staked them in the grass an' me an' Ton sat in the shade. Ton rolled a smoke, but I couldn't face one yet.

"You're lookin' a mite wore out," Ton said. "I'm thinkin' some hair from the dog what bit you might pick you up."

"Shit. The thought of it makes me want to puke. Anyway, where'd we get whiskey even if I wanted some?"

Ton stood and walked over to where our saddles an' gear rested next to a tree. He took a bottle of Pedro's tequila out of his saddlebag an' held it up like he was offerin' the key to heaven or somethin'.

"You might give 'er a try, Cal," he said. "Can't make you feel no worse than you do, right?"

That made some sense. "What the hell," I said.

Ton half-filled our tin coffee cups an' brought one to me. I raised it to my mouth but that ugly, oily smell of the tequila made me lower it down. Ton sipped at his cup. I held my breath and swallowed a mouthful, gagging as I did so. I let that set for a couple of minutes an' then finished off the cup. I stretched out on my back, my hands behind my head, an' my hat over my face.

The next thing I knew it was comin' dark an' the air was a tad cooler. I had me some pain behind my eyes but I didn't feel bad at all, considerin'. I sat up and rubbed my eyes. Ton was sound asleep and snorin' to beat hell. There was enough moonlight for me to see that the tequila bottle stood guard next to him and that it was about three-quarters empty. I walked over to where we'd staked the horses an' moved them some so they'd have fresh grass. Then I went back to where I'd been sleeping and laid back down again.

During the night I had vivid, violent dreams. Hunters were close around me an' shootin', but I could barely hear their guns fire. Anna was in a line of shackled, naked whores, silent bullets diggin' up the ground at her feet. I had my Colt in my hand but the trigger was stuck an' no matter how hard I pulled on it, it wouldn't budge. I half woke up a couple of times but then went back to the same bad dream.

The faint smell of smoke woke me. I sat up, saw the pale line of dawn, an' sniffed the air. I lost the scent for a time an' then picked it up again. We hadn't made a fire the night before, an' the Hunters were too far off for even our horses to catch the scent of smoke. I had my fixins in my pocket and I rolled a cigarette. I scratched the head of a lucifer with my thumbnail and lit up, suckin' the smoke deeply. It tasted good, 'specially after not burnin' a single cigarette the day before. Somethin' about a cigarette that makes a man want another one pretty bad after havin' one only a short time ago. But hell, I figured. Tobacco was harmless an' cheap, an' in my mind, that's a fine combination.

Even after I ground out the nub of my cigarette I still smelled smoke. Like I said, it wasn't strong, but it was there. Ton was stirring an' grunting. The line of dawn was brighter now, a kind of purple-yellow color that looked like the flame of a wood fire . . .

"Goddamn!" I yelled. I scrambled to my feet and shook Ton's shoulder roughly. He snorted but came awake. "Whaaa . . ." he began.

"Pedro's place, Ton — those dirty sons of bitches musta burned it! Saddle up, dammit!"

We rode fast and hard back to Pedro's ranch, covering the eight or ten miles right quick. I figured there wasn't nothing we could do about the fire, but maybe Pedro and Blanca had gotten out an' were still alive. The smell of smoke got stronger the closer we got to the ranch. We passed a small herd of a dozen or so mules wandering free. At first they shied off when they heard us coming, but then a few followed along behind us for a ways, as if they were curious to see what the big hurry was all about.

As it turned out, it didn't make a damned bit of difference when we got there. Pedro, Blanca, and a couple of men we didn't know wouldn't have been any more dead or less dead. The barn was still smoldering and twisted little fingers of flame appeared here and there in the charred ruins. The adobe walls of the house still stood, but they were blackened, and smoke drifted from the many open windows.

Pedro lay in the central entrance, his naked chest riddled with so many bullet wounds that it looked like he had the pox. Blanca was off to the side of the house, face-up in the dirt and sand, shot up just as dead as her husband and the two others, who, we figured, were a couple of the hands Pedro had mentioned. The vaqueros were closer to the barn, probably chased out by the flames into a Hunter crossfire that tore their bodies apart. What happened to the other two of the four we never did find out. It could be that they were under the collapsed roof and beams of the barn.

Digging in that soil was like digging through solid rock, an' all we had was a hay fork an' a manure shovel we salvaged out of the wreckage of the barn. It took us the better part of the day, but we got four proper holes dug. We had nothing to wrap the bodies in, but we lowered each of them down as gently as we could, Ton at the head an' me at the feet. Blanca seemed very light when we picked her up, like she was not only empty of life and of her baby, but everything else, as well. Me and Ton avoided looking at the faces of the men as much as we could, 'cause they were terribly shot up. Pedro had taken at least a couple of rounds to his head, and the vaqueros probably more than a couple. Blanca's long dress or smock or whatever it was called had been soaked with blood from her chest all the way to her feet, and the fabric held closely to the mound of her stomach now that the blood had some time to dry out, like blood does.

We couldn't help but look on Blanca's face. The preachers call death a goddamn repose or rest or something, which is pure horseshit. This young girl's face was contorted with fear and pain. Her mouth was open in a silent scream and her eyes — those wonderful deep brown eyes — were open but no longer shone like they had. They'd become pale, without real color. A flat, whitish gray is what they were.

After we'd filled in the graves, Ton said we should say a few words over those people, because that's the way it's done when you bury a good person. I said, "I got nothin' to say."

"Yeah, you do," Ton said. "You got a ton of fancy words about everythin' else, an' there's no reason you can't talk over these folks." His words sounded not far away from a threat. When I looked over at him, tears were runnin' down his face.

"I can say some good things," I told him, "but I gotta follow them with bad things. I can't do it no other way."

"Say what you need to say," Ton said.

I moved a couple of steps 'til I was at the

head of Blanca's grave. I had to think a bit but finally said, "This is a long distance from fair, God. This girl — this wife — was about to have a baby, an' now her an' the baby are dead. Where the hell is the peace an' rest in that?"

I moved a bit to Pedro's grave, next to Blanca's. "This man raised mules, God. You figure lettin' him die like this was proper an' right?"

At the vaqueros' graves, I didn't say much beyond, "These men were good enough to work for Pedro an' care for his mules. They did their jobs, an' that says enough about a man."

Ton started to put his hat on, which he'd been clasping to his chest. I motioned him to wait.

"I got something else to say." I thought for a moment. "God, Ton and me are goin' to put an end to the Night Hunters or they're goin' to put an' end to us. Either way, there's goin' to be blood flowing. If you're of a mind to, give us a hand. If not, that's fine, too — we'll still get it done."

We saddled up an' rode out, even though the day was pretty much over. We wanted to get some miles between us an' Pedro's ranch an' the bodies an' graves, so we kept on moving until after full dark, an' then rode another hour by moonlight.

Pedro's map was a good one. We found water pretty much where it was supposed to be the next day. There were tracks — lots of them, and lots of horse manure around the water hole. The tracks were from shod horses, not from a mustang herd stopping to drink. We camped there that night, eating goat jerky.

"They ain't much more'n a day ahead of us," Ton said. "We ride hard for a day an' part of a night an' we'll be right on them."

"Yeah," I said. "I been thinkin'. If we attack we'll drop some Hunters, but we'll get our own asses shot off in the bargain."

"Maybe."

"Ain't no maybe about it, Ton. But look: I did some buffalo hunting just before the war. The only way to make any money was to find a stand of shaggies, set up on a hill, an' pick them off startin' with the ones farthest away from the cluster, an' movin' in, killing until they finally figured out they were being shot at an' took off. Then we'd follow the rest of them an' do it again an' again until there was hardly none of them left."

"I heard tell a good shot could make a basketful of money on hides."

"Sure. Skinnin' the damned things was tough, though. I had three Indians with me as skinners. They'd peg down the dead shaggie an' tear the hide off him like peeling a glove off a hand."

"We ain't aimin' on skinnin' out no outlaws," Ton said, obviously wondering where I was going with the thought.

"No. We're not. But it seems to me that we can catch an' follow the Hunters until we come to the right spot with a good vantage point. I can commence to go to work there, maybe a quarter-mile or more from the camp."

"An' like you did with buffalo, we keep on after them, shootin' when we get a chance, right?"

"Right."

Ton was silent for a minute or so. "I kinda favor close fightin' with these snakes, Cal. That's what we set out to do."

"We'll get to that, don't you worry. But if we can knock down the odds some, then we go in close. See what I mean?"

Ton nodded. I could see he was after real combat, man-to-man, but he saw the sense in what I'd said.

"Let's give her a try," he said.

It took some long riding, but we had Pedro's map and we were able to find water when we needed it. The Hunters' tracks were no harder to follow than a circus parade. Still they had better'n a day on us. The moon was cooperating. It came full the first night an' we rode through the entire night, only stopping a couple of times to rest the horses. I shot a nice pair of jackrabbits that we cooked up the next morning, and then we pushed on through the day. We were close enough to the Hunters to smell their campfire at the end of that day.

"Now what?" Ton asked.

"We just hang back 'til we come on a good place to shoot from, is all. Then I set up an' go to it."

"These boys ain't complete idjits, Cal. They're gonna figure out we're doggin' them — maybe they know already."

"Look," I said. "Wouldn't we have seen anybody laggin' behind the main bunch of them? Wouldn't we pick up on an outrider?"

"I s'pose so. I'm gettin' awful antsy bein' so close to them an' not doin' nothin' about it, is all."

"Me too," I said. "Me too."

That night I thought about Anna more'n I like to let myself do. I could picture us puttin' together a little spread with me workin' horses an' beef, an' her cooking up somethin' or other in her kitchen. It made my heart hurt to bring to mind where she was an' the things that coulda been happenin' to her — with me not at all far away an' doin' nothin' about it. I knew a full-scale attack would be a damnfool move, but that didn't make things any easier.

I sat up. It was a sure thing I wasn't going to get any sleep. Ton was snoring away, his saddle blanket a pillow. I eased to my feet and walked out toward where the Hunters were camped, maybe a mile or so away. I hadn't thought much about my foot. It was workin' good, an' I expected it would continue to do so.

They didn't make a secret of their camp. There was a good-sized fire still burning, and I could make out figures on the ground near it, sleeping, I guess. If there was a guard posted, I didn't see him. There was a small, separate cluster of figures that I suspected were the women. They were on the ground, too, but farther away from the fire. It didn't look like a good place to camp to me — there was very little natural cover. A small bunch of desert pines showed there was water there or they wouldn't be growin' and there were a couple of boulders. The fire was out in the open, like I said.

If I had my Sharps, I figured I could take out maybe three or four of them. I guess what stopped me was that shooting a man as he slept just plain went against the way I've lived my life. Hunters or not, I wanted to fight them, not slaughter them without them even knowin' who killed them. I wrestled with that thought and tried to override it with what could be happening to Anna, but I couldn't do it. That angered me some, but I still couldn't do it. I walked back to where Ton slept and waited on the sun to start to come up. There was enough moonlight for me to clean an' oil my Sharps, which I could do blindfolded. I hadn't fired it since the river crossing, but I went ahead and cleaned it for somethin' to do with my hands.

Ton woke up with first light. It was easy enough to see that he was feisty that day: his mouth was hard set and his face like it was carved from granite. He moved quickly but not smoothly and he threw rather than placed his saddle on ol' Matthew so hard, the horse flinched and took a couple of nervous steps away. That set Ton to cussin'.

After he'd pulled his cinches he turned to me.

"This ain't workin' worth a damn, Cal. I can't do it no more. We're pussyfootin' 'round like a couple of egg suckin' dogs, not havin' the grit to kill us some outlaws."

I started to say something but Ton stopped me with an upraised hand. "No — you listen 'stead of talkin' this time. Them hunters killed my wife an' burned everything I owned. I won't never let that go by. I give my oath right at Priscilla's grave that I wouldn't let the ones who killed her live. I — we — ain't doin' that. We're actin' like a couple of Indian scouts, is what we're doin'." He stopped, swallowed hard, and went on. "If I gotta bust up our partnership, then that's what I'll do, an' I'll do 'er right now. I don't want to, but I damn well will."

Ton wasn't a man to flap his gums or make threats he wouldn't back up. He stood next to Matthew, glaring at me, the muscles at his jaw kind of flexin', eyes like he was lookin' at somethin' he hated. I cinched up before answering. I met his glare an' grinned at him. "What say we kill us some Hunters today, pard?"

The whores were cookin' breakfast by the looks of the camp. I spied Anna for a second or so, her ebony hair pulling my eyes to her. Then she went behind the larger of the pair of boulders. A Hunter with a rifle walked three women out from the camp an' stood there as they squatted, doin' their mornin' business. Me an' Ton looked away.

I set up my tripod about a half-mile from the outlaw camp. That's a good distance, but the Sharps will eat that up an' more, puttin' that thumb-sized slug right where I want it to go. I'd have preferred a little rise to shoot from, but I didn't have one an' there was no sense in worryin' about it.

I scratched up a handful of grit an' dropped it out in front of me, watchin' it go down. It fell straight, not being moved by wind nor breeze. I dug the legs of the tripod in good so it couldn't wobble an' stretched out behind, resting my Sharps where it belonged. When I cocked the rifle the metallic snick of the action got to me like it always does, making me proud to be shootin' such a quality gun.

It looked like the same outlaw who'd taken three of the women out from the camp was takin' three more. He walked behind them an' musta said somethin' because the women stopped. The Hunter motioned downward with the barrel of his rifle, and the women faced away from him an' began to lower themselves.

"Him," Ton said.

My sight was already on his chest. I took a breath and started an easy, steady pressure on the trigger. The report was like a mortar in a church — it echoed and reverberated an' seemed to go on for a long time after the Hunter's rifle flipped into the air above him an' he was thrown back like a gigantic punch had hit him in the chest. The women got to their feet in a hurry but another outlaw came chargin' out an' herded them back to the stand of desert pines. I took him down with a shot that was a little sloppy, I guess. I didn't hit the big part of him — chest an' gut — I was aimin' for, but must have hit him in his shoulder, spinning him around like a top before he fell. It looked to me like I'd blown his arm clean off, but I'm not certain about that.

The outlaws were rammin' around down there like crazy men. Some — maybe most — of them were smart enough to use the rocks for cover, but four weren't. One stood jackin' a shell into his rifle, as big an' clean a target as I ever seen. He was easy.

Ton was crouched next to me, feeding me cartridges as I needed them. "Lemme try out that buffalo gun," he said.

I rolled out of the way an' Ton took my position. The Sharps looked a lot smaller when he was holdin' it. He aimed a mite too long, I think, but he squeezed rather than yanked on the trigger. His shot tore a jagged piece off the larger boulder an' went whinin' off to wherever ricocheting bullets

212

go. Ton's second shot dropped an outlaw who was tryin' to make his way to where the horses were, in a rope corral. I was proud of Ton — the Hunter was steppin' right out an' he was veering an' swerving as he ran. I couldn't figure out what the damned fool wanted with a horse just then, but it didn't really matter. The only ride he was takin' was straight to hell.

The Hunters figured out pretty fast that they needed to take cover real quick or we'd pick them off one by one. I nudged Ton and he handed me the Sharps and rolled out of the way so I could get back to my tripod. I got a couple more rounds off but didn't hit anything. I didn't want to fire into the stand of desert pines an' cottonwoods because I thought that's where the women were, but a short, blocky fellow peeked out from behind a tree a couple of times, then drew his head back in. I focused on the spot and held my aim. It was getting hot already; sweat was dripping down my forehead and into my eyes. In order to wipe it away I knew I'd have to let go of my rifle with one hand and my aim on the tree would be shot to hell, so I just let the sweat drip and blinked it away as well as I could.

The man held out his hat on a stick for a second, then pulled it in. After a bit he did the same thing again. I'll admit I thought of blowin' the hat away just for the fun of it, but I didn't do so. The outlaw's confidence must have built up each time he pulled his hat trick. I started light pressure on my trigger. Just sure as Honest Abe is president, the desperado stepped from behind his cover, hat on, a rifle in his right hand.

For a long moment I thought I'd missed. The fellow stood there, rifle still in his hand, face under the shadow of his hat. Then, he sort of melted. By that I mean that he kinda sank into himself and eased down to the ground without making another move of any kind. I figure I'd put one of those thumb-sized bullets clean through his heart, and that the slug kept right on going.

There was somethin' goin' on in those trees, some motion, people moving around, one man shouting, although we couldn't hear the words. "What're they up to?" Ton asked.

"I dunno," I said. "They must know that there ain't but the two of us, an' they're plannin' to attack. They gotta know they'd lose a passel of men if they came ridin' at us."

Nothing much happened for a bit except the sun got hotter. Hell, the prairie dogs were wearing sunbonnets. In answer to

Ton's question, I said, "Beats me." I was about to say more when a Night Hunter stepped out from behind a tree with a stick in his hand. Tied to the stick was a long piece of white cloth and the man started walking toward us, waving the cloth from side to side.

"Gotta be some kinda trick," Ton said.

I had my sights on the guy's chest. "I guess we'll find out."

It took him a good amount of time to walk the distance between us and the Hunters. When he got in near enough, Ton and me got to look him over. He was tall and gaunt, lookin' like one of them poor boys at Andersonville. His face was hard edges and angles. He wore a ratty Confederate butternut-colored shirt and had bandoliers of ammunition crossed over his chest. The holster at his right side was tied to his leg with a piece of latigo, gunfighter style. He took long strides and the heat didn't seem to bother him, or if it did he ignored it.

He stopped ten yards or so out from our little ridge. "I come to talk," he said. His voice was raspy and low, and when he opened his mouth we could see that he didn't have any teeth — or at least in the front, anyway.

"I don't see that we got a whole lot to talk

about," I said.

"Why're you doggin' us?"

"Because you're cowards and murderers and you abducted some women an' me an' Ton here, we decided we were gonna do what the army and the law hasn't — step on the Night Hunters like a boot on a worm."

The man grinned showing more of his pinkly yellow, diseased-looking gums. "I doubt Mr. Danny Montclaire'll agree with you on that."

Ton's voice trembled with the anger behind it. "You scum killed my wife. You'll die for it — an' so will Montclaire."

"Lotta talk for two men against better'n thirty," the tall man said.

"I notice you been losin' some of your boys lately," I said.

"Maybe. Thing is, Danny sent me out here to deal to get you off our backs. What is it you want? Revenge? Shit. What do you think the odds are that you two can wipe out the Night Hunters?" He walked a few steps closer. "Tell me what you want an' I'll take it to Danny. If it's a whore or two, we might consider it."

I knew that if I revealed I had any special interest in any one of the women, she'd have hell to pay. "We don't want whores," I said.

"You can take this message back to Mont-claire: we're gonna . . ."

Ton's big body slammed to the ground next to me and the tall man brought a rifle around from his back where he must have had it in a rig we couldn't see. I dropped him in a big hurry with a head shot — the lyin' sonfofabitch, comin' to us under a peace flag — and then I felt warm liquid on my neck and looked to Ton. There was a geyser of blood squirting out of his leg. Another shot came at us from the far left, digging in the sand a foot away from me.

Ton's face had gone to a sickly white in a little part of a second. He clamped one of his huge hands over the wound, but the blood still pulsed strongly out from between his fingers.

CHAPTER SEVEN

The gunfire from the left of us was coming in steady, probably as fast as the outlaw could crank a fresh round into his rifle. He wasn't much of a shot, but his misses were getting closer. The problem was that I couldn't see where he was shooting from.

Ton was pumping blood. A man of his size and strength must have a whole lot of blood, and right then it looked like it all was trying to leave his body through the hole in his leg.

I was in a sitting position, aiming my rifle in the general direction of where the shots were fired at us. The problem with that was the outlaw was behind a king of wind-formed lip of sand and scrub that ran maybe twenty or thirty feet kind of parallel to us. So, he could fire from one position and slide on down to another for his next shot.

Like I said, he didn't shoot worth a damn,

but he was getting closer to us. We had no cover and with Ton down, I'd have no one at my back. The best bet we had was to get to our horses and make tracks. I tore a sleeve from Ton's shirt and wrapped it just above his wound in his right calf. I cut away his denim pants and saw the entry hole, but there was no exit mark — the bullet was still in him. The tourniquet stopped the heavy spurting of blood immediately, but the wound was still weeping. I threw some lead to where the shooter might have been, but saw we had another problem: the Hunters in the camp were chasin' down an' saddlin' up their horses.

"Lookit, Ton," I said. "I know you're hurtin', but we gotta get to our horses an' haul ass or we're gonna chewed up here. You lean on me an' use the butt of your rifle as a crutch an' let's go!"

Some color had returned to his face, but I could see he was in pain. He gritted his teeth and shoved himself to a standing position, rifle, butt down, in his right hand, grasping it by the barrel. I moved to his left side an' he put his arm over my shoulders an' we got moving.

It didn't seem like we'd left Matthew an' Jake that far behind us, but supportin' a man who weighed almost as much as a buffalo made the distance longer. The rifleman was still plinking at us an' in a matter of a couple of minutes the mounted Hunters would be on us.

"Lemme out from under your arm," Ton grunted. "I can manage from here, Cal. You gotta put some lead in the air or that boy's goin' to take us — even though he doesn't shoot worth a damn."

That made some sense, although it'd be hard on Ton. But, I didn't see that we had any options, and at times, a man's gotta do what he needs to do. I sat down as Ton shuffled on toward the horses. I never much cared to shoot from a sitting position, but at times there ain't nothin' else that'll work. Standing, I'd make a good target, and prone, I wouldn't have the line of sight I needed.

That rifleman was getting cocky. He'd stand an' fire an' then drop down an' roll one way or another an' then shoot again. Sitting there I had a chance to figure out what he was doing. I thought like this: there ain't but two directions he can roll in — one side or the other. I made wrong choices twice and my slugs did nothing but dig up soil. The third time I heard a scream that turned into a grunt an' then ended. I waited a bit to see was he toyin' with me, but he wasn't.

The Hunters were still off a bit but they were comin' on hard. Ton was already in his saddle, holding Jake's reins for me. Ton's face was that pasty white again. I climbed into my saddle, took my reins, an' we set out at a full gallop. The horses were rested an' ready — they covered some ground in a big hurry, even with the heat enough to boil a man's brains.

I turned in my saddle pretty often to see if them sonsabitches were breathin' down our necks. Maybe they'd have had a chance if they'd fed and cared for the good horses they stole, but their mounts would give out earlier than ours. The haze of grit the Hunters put into the air showed me where they were. 'Course the sand kicked up by Jake an' Matthew showed the Hunters where we were, as well.

I was maybe half a horse ahead of Ton, tryin' to get Matthew to follow Jake. Matthew can be ornery at times, and he reached over to take a bite out of Jake's flank. I don't know that anyone readin' this has ever been bit by a horse who was mad. I'll tell you what, though: I saw a bronc take such a mouthful of a kid's leg when I was ridin' in a festival outside Wichita that it'd make you

221

gag. The horse got ahold of some skin and then commenced to grind his teeth together 'til he could pull the flesh away.

I leaned way back in my saddle an' punched Matthew in the nose. That calmed him down some an' he quite tryin' to tear skin offa Jake. It's strange: Jake's a stud and I'd never seen him back down from a horse before. He wasn't necessarily backin' down from Matthew, but he showed no small amount of respect to that big horse — the kind of respect men show to a man Ton's size.

I didn't think the Hunters were going to be interested in chasing us for any great distance, and I was right. I expect they wanted to get within rifle range and when they couldn't do that, they said the hell with it and gave up to go back to their camp.

Ton and I were lettin' our horses blow. I climbed down from Jake and loosened his cinches, but Ton didn't dismount. "I'm scared if I get down I won't be able to get up again," he said. He looked pretty bad — shaky, his eyes flitting about, not really focusing, the hand holding the reins dancing in front of him, next to the saddle horn. "I'm awful dizzy," he said.

He was still losing blood. The wound had seeped and was continuing to seep in spite of the shirtsleeve tourniquet, and I didn't want to draw it any tighter, 'cause a sawbones once told me that pullin' one of them too tight is worse than havin' none at all, an' if all the blood is stopped, gangrene can set into an arm or leg. That same doc told me that both the Union and the Confederacy lost more boys to what he called infections than they did from bullets or canister shot. That's why I didn't know what to do for my pard, and was right worried about him.

The patch of dust over the Hunters was headin' back in the direction they'd come from. They may or may not have left a man or two back to stay after us, but I didn't see any sign of that. What me an' Ton needed was a place where we could make camp — a place with some water an' maybe some shade. I didn't know where the hell we were and Ton didn't know anything at all: he was slumped forward in his saddle, mumbling about Priscilla.

Here's how the road thing happened: that same day, Ton was leaning more an' more over Matthew's neck. I figured it wouldn't be too long before Ton ended up with his face on the ground. I moved Jake up next to Matthew and took the reins from Ton's hand. Matthew got a tad cute an' I whacked him one on the neck an' he calmed right down. Jake walked on just as he was supposed to, an' this way I could keep a closer eye on Ton. The truth is I was gettin' a crick in my neck from turnin' around so often.

We needed water bad, both men and horses. We were way off of Pedro's map. The sun was hotter'n a two-dollar pistol an' I was startin' to see little bits of red float about in my vision, which was not at all a good sign.

When Jake stopped and swung his head back to me I found that I'd been more or less sleepin' in my saddle and my horse kept right on walking, although the reins were hanging slack. Matthew snorted next to me an' that brought me further awake. Ton was still aboard, but he looked real bad.

Why the horses stopped an' became confused was that there was a barely discernable road they'd stepped onto. There was a pile of fresh horse manure, too, so the road or trail or whatever it was probably led someplace. Most of the tracks led to the east, and I figured maybe there was a town or something in that direction. There wasn't anything else to go on but the tracks, so it was kind of a crapshoot. It could be that we were ridin' away from a town, too, which I didn't like to think about. Ton was slumped in his saddle, his face that sickly pale color, 'cept now it was coated with a patina of sweat. He was still mumbling some.

I kept on thinkin' that we might well be ridin' in the wrong direction. If that was the case, Ton wouldn't have to worry about takin' revenge on the Night Hunters, 'cause he'd be as dead as the Hunters we already killed.

It seemed like there was nothin' between us and the sun — no sky, no air — nothin' but mind-numbing heat. It was the sort of constant, sweaty, frustrating heat that makes men who'd been tight friends for years come to blows against one another, and turned good dogs mean, an' gave cattle the blind staggers. I scanned the sky all around us and the brightness made me squint, even when I was lookin' away from the sun. There was no smoke an' no dust rising anywhere; there wasn't even a single damned cloud. I reined in and Matthew stopped beside me. I felt Ton's forehead, although I knew he had some fever because of the oily sweat fever brings. His head was as hot as any flesh I'd ever felt. His eyes were almost closed — they were slits, really, and sweat beaded on and fell from his eyebrows. He wasn't making any sound at all now, although his lips would move slightly every so often, as if he was tryin' to form a word.

I sat there for a good bit, baking along with my partner and our horses. It could be that what we were on wasn't really a road at all, but a trail cowhands used to go back an' forth between their herds when they were movin' beef. If we were lucky, there might be water an' shelter a couple miles down the way we was goin'.

I decided to keep on an' not to worry if we were headed nowhere. Hell, there were only two choices to make — go east or go west. Those aren't bad odds. If what I was following wasn't really a road that went somewheres, well, then, we were screwed.

I couldn't keep thoughts of Anna from forming in my mind. Seems like every time I closed my eyes I saw her an' heard her voice. I guess it was the sun poundin' on me, but all of a sudden she was there, right next to Jake, walkin' along as happy as you could want. She was wearin' one of those kinda shapeless Indian dresses with beads woven into it, an' her hair was clean an' shone in the sun.

"You're going the right way, Cal. Just you wait and see. It's not far now. There's a root woman there who can help Ton."

"Root woman?"

"What my people would call a shaman, except a woman rather than a man. She's very old and her magic is powerful."

"How much farther, Anna?"

"Not far. Jake and Matthew can get you there."

I'd been dozing in the saddle an' dreaming, I guess, an' I woke myself up callin' to Anna, telling her to come back. The horses had kept walking for however long I was asleep. When I looked down I saw that there were some wagon wheel ruts, probably made the previous spring, when all this area was mud an' muck. That was a good sign. If someone was haulin' something in a wagon, there must be someone else around to get whatever's bein' carried.

It was well past midday but I couldn't even think about making camp. First, there was no shelter at all from the sun, an' second, the buffalo grass was dry an' dusty an' our horses wouldn't graze it, an' third, Ton would croak.

We came upon the village abruptly, almost as if it had popped out of the earth. I'd been half awake again when Jake snorted and whinnied an' Matthew did the same, bringin' me back to consciousness. There was a church maybe a half-mile ahead an' beyond that there were a couple more single-story buildings that looked like the church 'cept smaller an' without the big cross atop them. Beyond those were some smaller structures that looked like homes. As I got closer I saw that there was a well an' that a few women were cranking away at it, filling buckets, an' talking an' laughing with one another. One of them saw us an' pointed an' then she an' her friends ran off. Within a couple of minutes three men on horseback galloped out from behind the church, the sun glinting off the barrels of the rifles they carried. I could see that they weren't vaqueros. What they wore was some sort of military uniform with brass buttons that captured the sun and fired it back at us. I shaded my eyes with my hand an' watched them ride in.

The first thing I noticed even before I got a good look at the men was that they was ridin' fine stock. Two of the horses were tightly muscled, tall paints, and the third had some thoroughbred blood in him. He was a blood bay an' he stood an' honest sixteen hands.

Some folks say you can tell how a man lives by how he takes care of his horse. If that was true here, these three fellows woulda been declared saints. The white on the paints was that of a fresh-washed an' bleached sheet my ma used to take in to wash from the rich people, an' the bay's coat purely shone.

At first I thought they were young bucks, but when they drew closer I saw that they'd been around for a while — there was some silver in the blackness of their hair, an' the almost chestnut hue of their hands, faces, and necks showed they'd spent a ton of long days in the sun. I'd have bet my boots that their chests, arms, an' legs were as colorless as mine, an' when they stripped down for a bath, they'd look like they was whitewashed.

The three spread out as they came up to us, keeping ten or a dozen feet between themselves in a line, with the center man slightly ahead. They wore the short jackets and tight pants of soldiers, but they definitely weren't regular Mex army — their clothing wasn't nearly fancy enough for that. The man in the lead, the one on the blood bay — spoke. "You are here why?" he asked in passable English. "Why is your friend barely hanging on to his saddle?"

I explained as well as I could that Ton'd been shot by Night Hunters and that the two of us were forging a running battle with the desperados. "Is there a doctor here? Anyone who can help my friend? Far's I

229

know the slug's still in him."

The Mexican nodded. "There is a woman here. The Night Hunters are known to poison their bullets so even a minor wound will kill. This woman has potions and salves and ointments to counter the poison." He turned his horse back toward the buildings. "Come," he said. He rode at a fast walk — almost a canter. If I'd followed suit, Ton would have ended up on the ground. I eased Jake forward. The two men left behind rode on either side of Ton an' me, a couple of feet back.

I pointed at the well. "We ain't had water in some time," I said. "If we could . . ." My voice cracked so I couldn't finish my sentence.

"Si — agua," one of them said. I figured that was his invitation to go to his well and drink and to draw water for our horses, an' that's what I did. But first I rode to the adobe building where the English-speaker stood. He and an old women, maybe half-Indian and half-Mexican from her face and skin color, helped Ton down from his saddle. Ton is no lightweight, but the woman carried the most weight, with the fellow holding up Ton's legs.

"I am Armando," he said as he and the woman entered the building. "Go now and

230

look to your horses and drink for yourself. We will take care of your friend."

When I'd pumped water into a small trough by the well for Jake and Matthew, I drank long and deep for myself. The water was icy cold and sweeter'n molasses candy. Armando came up to me leading his horse as I was cupping water in my hands and tossing it into my face. "You see down there is a corral," he said, pointing beyond the church. "The trees offer shade from the sun and there's good hay. Turn your animals out and join me here."

I did what he told me, unsaddling both horses and turning them into the corral with a dozen or so others. Matthew and Jake stayed together, watching to see if they'd be challenged. The already corralled horses barely noticed the two newcomers. I hung our saddles and blankets from the top rail of the fence and walked back to where Armando stood.

I saw now that Ton had been taken into what amounted to a good-sized adobe hut with small, narrow windows that looked like rifle ports. Armando held the door open and we both entered.

It was noticeably cooler inside the hut, and the air had the taste and smell of a cool forest. A pair of coal-oil lamps shed good light. Ton was stretched out on a mat on the dirt floor with the pant leg on his injured side cut up beyond his knee. The wound was an ugly thing, a dark hole the size of five-cent piece. Its edges were ragged, as if the skin had been torn away, and inflammation was spreading around the opening. The woman was cleaning the wound, using a square of white cloth and some sort of liquid from a shallow dish she held. I got a good look at her as she tended to Ton. She was somewhere between sixty and a thousand years old, and her face was lined and creased by her years. She was rather short and hefty looking, although it was difficult to see the shape of her body because of the loose, robe-type garment she wore. Her hair, mostly gray, tumbled around her face and neck all the way to her waist. I don't know what color her eyes were 'cause she never looked up from Ton during the time I was in the hut. She exchanged some rapid-fire Spanish with Armando. He said to me, "It is as I thought. The bullet has been poisoned and it remains in your friend's leg. Tia will remove it and then bind the wound. He will not die, she says. She says his great size and strength are what saved his life."

Ton seemed to be sleeping peacefully,

hands and arms at his sides, his face un-stressed, his huge chest rising and falling gently as he breathed, even though the woman Armando called Tia was now prob-ing inside the wound with an instrument carved from bone and sharpened at one end. Armando touched my arm and mo-tioned toward the door. "Come," he said. "We will talk." I followed him out.

Armando's home was a simple boxlike adobe building, the two rooms separated by a central wall with an arch. A wooden table with a bottle of clear liquid and two glasses setting on it and its four chairs was the only furniture in the first room. The second room was shut off from the first by a curtain or drape or some such thing made of strung colored beads.

Armando sat at the table an' I sat across from him. He lifted the bottle, pulled the cork, and poured a couple of inches of what looked like oily water into them. "Pulque," he said. "Gringos call it cactus whiskey." I'd heard of pulque but never tasted it before. After my recent go-round with tequila I wasn't ready to drink Mex booze again. But Armando had taken us in and Tia was look-ing after Ton, so I figured I owed the man the basic respect and courtesy of drinking with him. I tipped my glass and took a drink. It wasn't bad — kind of sharp and a tad bitter, but not awful unpleasant.

"Tell me why you and your friend seek the Night Hunters," Armando said.

I told him the entire tale — about Anna and Ton's Priscilla an' how the Hunters burned Busted Thumb. Something had been bothering me, kind of stirring things up in the back of my mind. I drank more pulque and asked, "Why are you an' the others here safe? The Hunters must know about you — an' they've leveled bigger places than this. Why don't they attack you, carry off your women?"

"This they tried not two years ago. Our village looks small, but our people are spread out nearby. The bell in the church is used only for emergencies, to call our people to arms. Our scouts are always out, watching for trouble."

"No disrespect," I said, "but how would a bunch of farmers or cattlemen give the Night Hunters a battle?"

Armando smiled. "We are farmers and some of us raise cattle and horses, it is true. This village has stood for many years. When it was started, there was much danger from Indians. It was decided that each man and woman would be taught to fight against attacks. To this day, when a boy becomes a man or a girl a woman, they're taught to use the rifle and pistol effectively and well. This is mandatory — there are no exceptions."

"But . . ." I began.

Armando cut me off. "As I said, they came two years ago. Our scouts gave us plenty of time to prepare. They rode in and we opened fire. It was as simple as that. We buried their dead in a common pit. We lost only two people. Since then, they have never bothered us again." He poured pulque into our glasses and sat back in his chair. "Thus, we have prospered and we remain peaceful."

It was difficult to find anything wrong with the logic of Armando's statement, so I didn't attempt to do so. "What's your village called?" I asked. "A friend of ours knows the area pretty well and he didn't mention it to us."

"I suspect your friend is a Mexican."

"Yeah, he is. But . . ."

"Many of our people know of this village," Armando said over my words, "and protect it from the gringos and from any troublemakers. It's a matter of honor among us." He paused, and then added. "We call the village Tranquila, which in your language means peaceful."

I was getting dizzy from the cactus whiskey. I put my hand over my empty glass when Armando attempted to pour once again. "I'd kinda like to go over an' see how Ton is doin'," I said. "And thanks again for takin' us in. You're good people." I stood, but Armando remained seated, his glass in his hand. He smiled ruefully. "It is not good to judge my people from my hospitality. It may be that you find some of us do not care for gringos — Americanos."

His eyes fell away from mine and he stared at the bottle in front of him. I went out into the sun and for a moment it made me yet dizzier than I already was from the pulque. I shook it off and started to Tia's hut. There were three young kids chasin' one another around and laughing as kids do — until they saw me. Their game stopped immediately and they scurried around Armando's adobe home as if the hounds of hell was chasin' them. I guessed they didn't see a whole lot of white people.

I knocked at Tia's door and it opened almost before my knuckles had a chance to touch the polished wood of it. Like I said, I hadn't seen Tia's eyes before. I saw them this time. They were a deep chestnut, as I'd expected, but there was somethin' else there. I took half a step back 'cause of the power of her gaze. Her eyes were like those of a sidewinder, wild, evil, an' ready to kill. Wordlessly, she motioned with a gnarled old hand toward Ton, still prone and asleep on the mat. I stepped closer an' crouched down next to him.

Ton's face conveyed nothing but peace. His natural color had returned and his breathing was regular. He snored a bit through his nose when he exhaled. There was a low, small table next to him with several bone instruments on it — curved ones, straight ones, even a tool that looked like a wire cutter, 'cept considerably smaller. There was also a fancy straight razor with pure white ivory grips on the table an' its blade caught the light from the lamps on its honed edge. Next to Tia's instruments was a misshapen lump of gray lead about the size of a man's thumbnail, except without even edges to it. It must have been the slug Tia took out of Ton's leg. That leg was now wrapped carefully and the tourniquet a crumpled, blood-soaked cloth tossed aside, to be disposed of later. I looked back at Tia. That same glare of hate seemed to envelop me, pulling me into it, making me feel small an' weak, like a child. I wrenched my eyes away, stood, an' went to the door. I had nothing to say to Tia and I don't know that

I could have trusted my voice not to tremble, anyway.

I pulled the door closed behind me and stood there in the sun, this time not feeling its strength. Instead, I shivered the least bit and welcomed the heat — at least for a few moments. Actually, the sun was not far from the western horizon, but it was nowhere near shiverin' weather in Tranquila. There were no real streets in the way we think of them. The huts an' larger buildings seemed to have tossed from a giant hand to land where they might. The only thing that actually made them feel like a group is that the windows of each of them faced the church.

I didn't know how long Ton'd be recuperatin' — probably a few days, maybe as much as a week. I wasn't too worried where I'd sleep. I figured down near the corral I could find me a little piece of ground to stretch out on. I started walkin' up that way when I saw that there was a handwritten sign above an open doorway readin', CANTINA. I was glad to see it. I needed some grub an' every Mex cantina I'd been in served food as well as booze. Before I walked in the scent of spices an' cracklin' meat reached me an' my mouth was waterin' when I walked through the door.

The cantina wasn't set up like an American saloon. There was no long bar. Instead, there was a sturdy table against one wall covered with an array of open bottles — whiskey, tequila, pulque, but no beer that I could see. There were a half-dozen or so tables, each with four chairs, spread around the floor. Only three were occupied just then, one with four fellows, one with two, an' one with a loner with a bottle in front of him.

All conversation stopped when I walked in. Again I felt the coldness of the stares, just as I had from Tia. I went to the booze table and said to the barkeep, "English?" He shook his head negatively.

I know some boys who can talk Spanish just as well as they can English. I never gave it much thought, but now I wish I had. The few words I knew weren't going to get me anywhere. I lifted my hands up to my mouth and worked my jaws like I was eatin' and chewin'. Again, the 'tender shook his head. It was just then that a heavy woman came through a doorway that must have led to a kitchen with a large plate of beans an' chicken an' rice in each hand. The food smelled wonderful. I pointed at it and then at myself. The woman took the plates to the table with the two men settin' at it an' put them down, ignoring me like I wasn't there.

I started after her but was stopped by a voice sayin', "There's no food here."

It was the loner with the bottle who spoke. I was getting a tad touchy right about then. Here my partner was shot up an' I couldn't get any grub in a fly-infested cantina. "You speak English?" I asked.

"Mas o menos," he said. He pushed back from the table an' I saw he had an Army Colt in a holster tied to his leg. "What I say to you was there's no food for *you* here." He stressed the "you" so it was much louder than his other words.

The loner wasn't a kid — he was maybe thirty or so. His hair — long, matted, and oily — hung limply beyond his shoulders. His eyes were killer's eyes — flat an' uncaring an' looking like they'd seen everything an' didn't like any of it. I noticed that his right hand, although still flat on the table, was edging toward the edge, just above his Colt. I saw that the bottle in front of him was not even a third gone, so he probably wasn't drunk.

"You don't wanna move your hand any closer to your pistol," I said. "I'm getting right tired of this shit. Maybe you better order up some grub for me 'cause no one else seems to hear me."

He held my gaze for a long time, the flatness of his eyes neither diminishing nor increasing. "You are a gringo pistolero, no? Come to cause trouble in Tranquila, es verdad — is true?"

"I ain't lookin' for trouble with nobody but Night Hunters," I said.

"Maybe I give you some trouble right here, an' right now," he said. "Then you don' need no Night Hunters."

I took a step back and squared myself, my right boot a few inches ahead of my left. My right hand had that spark running through it and out the tips of my fingers that it always had when I've been in a fast draw situation.

The two vaqueros eating an' the four sittin' there drinkin' got the hell out of my field of fire in a hurry, knocking their chairs to the floor as they rushed to hug the walls.

Everything goes silent for me at a time like this. It's much as if me an' the man I'm facin' are the only two people left in the world, an' it ain't big enough for both of us, so one or the other has to die. It's that simple.

"I stand now," the loner said. He kept his hands on the table until he was erect and then moved them to his body, an almost mirror image of my stance. Of a sudden he shifted his eyes to his left. It was a test — a

241

schoolboy effort to see if I'd follow his eyes an' give him a chance to blow me outta my boots.

There was no doubt in my mind that I could take this man. I didn't need a reason an' I didn't have to justify the gunfight to myself. It was what it was, an' no amount of talkin' was goin' to change anything.

He smirked, showing a line of yellowed teeth. "See? I know you were the pistolero when your eyes don't follow mine. Are you fast, gringo? Are you . . ."

I flicked my eyes from his down to his right hand. The talkin' was another stupid ploy to buy him a second when I wouldn't think he'd draw. "Maybe we ought to get this goin' if you're done with your little tricks," I snarled.

The fingers of his right hand curled a bit inward an' with a nice smooth move he reached for the grips of his Colt.

"No! No!" Armando bellowed from the doorway. "This cannot happen — José, you go about your business — now. You hear me?"

Both the loner and I had been in too many life an' death gunfights not to realize that regardless of what or who the disturbance was, it could readily buy a bullet as the price for looking away. Our eyes held, but neither of us drew. Armando barged between us, back to me, and grabbed my opponent's shoulders as one would grab and shake a cantankerous child. "This will not happen," Armando shouted into the loner's face. "You will leave now, José."

José stepped back from Armando, gently freeing himself. His posture was more relaxed now. "I will do as you say, Armando," he said, his voice calm and level. Then he looked at me. "This is no finished," he said in that same calm voice.

I nodded. "You bet your ass it's not finished," I said. I wished my voice was as level as José's had been.

"I saw you go in the cantina and I thought there might be trouble. José, he is crazy-mad at gringos, and the others have no love for Americanos, either. I should have warned you."

"Wasn't your fault, Armando," I said. "You had my pard doctored up an' you've been kind to both of us. Maybe I got too hot at that José, an' then again, maybe not. What's his problem with gringos?"

"All his cattle, they were taken by a gang of gringos two years ago. The animals were all he had. A few good horses were taken, too. And it is rumored that the Night

Hunters killed his father in a town called Agua Verde."

"Well, hell, Armando — I didn't steal his damn livestock or kill his pa. What's he mad at me for?"

Armando pondered that as we walked to his house. After a bit, he said, "Is because you were there and a gringo. José needs no other reasons."

"Damned fool," I muttered.

"Sí," Armando said.

"Seems like there's a lot of that goin' around Tranquila," I said.

"True." Armando stopped walking for a moment, staring off into the distance. "You know," he said, "you and José are not so different . . ." He let his words taper off into silence.

"What do you mean?"

"I . . . nothing. Just a thought."

We moved Ton to Armando's house from Tia's the next morning. I'd slept on a too-small cot at Armando's and was stiff from it. The hefty woman, whom Armando introduced as his hermana — his sister — fed me grandly the night before and again in the morning. Armando confided in me that Juanita, his sister, was past the marriageable age, and that her size and general surly demeanor had cost her a husband and

244

children. She was, he said, ". . . always built like a — how do you say? — a hayf-ferr." Heifer or not, Juanita cooked a hell of a fine meal.

Ton was barely conscious as we moved him. When we got him to Armando's home and settled him down on a blanket, I got a good look at his wound. The lividity of it — that shiny red skin around the bullet hole — was completely gone. The opening itself had a straight cut about an inch long descending from it, which Tia must have made to get the slug out of Ton's leg. The cut appeared to be already healing. There was the smell of pine around the wound, an' a musky but not unpleasant scent that I couldn't quite identify.

"How did Tia come to be here?" I asked Armando.

"I'm not certain she came to Tranquila — it may be that we came to her. I can't give you an answer to that. Maybe she's always been here."

Look: stuff like this always has scared hell outta me — magic an' so forth. I saw a man in Houston who waved a little black ball on a chain in front of folk's eyes an' talked to them real quietly, an' after a bit, he had them pickin' corn from stalks that weren't there, an' dancin' an' carryin' on to fiddle-playin' that nobody else heard. I don't give a good goddamn about religion an' so forth, but the ol' devil, he might be a different story. It ain't that I believe in perdition. But, still, well, shit . . .

My dream, if that's what it was, stayed on my mind. Like I said, I got no time for haunts an' spirits. But, Anna was as clear an' real as everything I'd ever seen, an' wasn't she right 'bout the root woman?

I had to ask myself whether or not some part of Anna came to me as I slept. Maybe the pulque helped. I dunno. But, I'd swear in a court of law that I saw my woman, an' heard her speak, an' what she said came true.

All that ponderin' about Anna naturally led to the fact that the Night Hunters had her an' I wasn't doing a damned thing about that. It's fair to say that Ton an' me dropped a few of them, but the thing is, Anna was still their captive.

Ton's a hell of a fine partner an' I'd take a bullet for the man. I mean that. But, he doesn't have the skills with weapons he needs to have if we're going to destroy this bunch of maggots. He's got all the heart in the world, but the man has worked with horses all his life, not in something that required him to learn how to fight heavily armed men, how to sneak in on the enemy, how to find some pleasure in cutting the throat of a sleeping man. He'd do it. I'm sure of that. But battling Night Hunters — killers and crazies, every goddamned one of them — isn't something that comes natural to him.

I tried to shove all that out of my mind, but didn't do good at it. I kept on reliving the taste of Anna's mouth, the texture of her body, her quiet moans, her way of using her hands. I'd been sitting next to Ton doing all this thinking, and when he began to stir I concentrated on him an' not on Anna an' fighting.

Ton's eyes popped open. It wasn't at all a slow, fluttery thing: one second they were closed an' the next they were wide open and I watched the fog dissipate from them as he looked around the room and then settled his gaze on me.

"What the hell . . ." he said.

"You're in Armando's home," I said. "The Hunters nailed you with a bullet carrying rattler venom. It almost croaked you, but it didn't. It sure did drop you like a rock down a well, though. A root woman or shaman or whatever got you fixed up, took the slug out, an' bound up the hole real nice. Hell, if it hadn't been for the poison, I could've cut the bullet out — get you passin' out drunk, an' then go ahead an' poke around 'til I found the sumbitch."

"How long we been here, Cal?" Ton asked.

"Not far from a couple of days. That don't matter. Armando can send us on to Santa Lucia. You gotta rest up a bit."

"Shit. I can ride today — right now. Let's . . ."

Ton shoved himself to a sitting position an' then, quick as a flea bites, got all pale again.

"You ain't gonna ride nothin' but the floor for a bit, Ton," I said.

He had a hand on either side of him, supporting his upper body. I could see the muscles in his arms begin to quiver an' I pushed gently on his beer-barrel chest. "C'mon, Ton," I said. "You settle back an' catch you some sleep."

I was kinda surprised when Ton laid himself back down without a big argument. "We're still gonna get them, Cal," he said. "I'll be fit to ride in a little bit."

"Right," I told him. "You get some rest an' then we'll head out."

That seemed to satisfy him an' his eyes closed. In a few moments he was breathing an' snoring just as he did when we slept out on the prairie.

The thing is, I had no idea how long the Night Hunters would stay in Santa Lucia. Would they sell the women an' move on? Would they settle in for a day or a week? If they holed up in that town, maybe I could kill one now an' again, an' that'd be fine in other circumstances. But they'd sell Anna as a whore. I couldn't let that happen.

I thought lots of times about Anna peddling her womanhood to any cowhand or buffalo hunter or prairie drifter. That hurt. But I came to know that Anna had nothing to do with it. She'd been passed around like a chip in a long poker game, from the time she was a little girl right up to now. I was sitting on the floor near Ton, listening to him breathe when Armando came in from outside, wiping sweat from his forehead with the back of his hand. He dragged one of the chairs from the table and sat on it, looking at me.

"Three men are stronger than two," he said.

There was no way to argue the point, so I kept quiet. The fact that I didn't know what he was talking about helped to keep my trap shut. After a few moments he went on. "You and Ton have this mission against the Night Hunters, but there are many more of them than there are of you." I nodded.

249

"So," Armando said, "you need another man, another gun."

"Maybe so."

"Look — I, too, have been hurt by the Night Hunters. They killed two of my cousins in a raid a year ago in the village where my cousins lived. They were simple farmers — campesinos — and each was married and had children." He sighed. "We have made Tranquila safe from the Hunters, but I have not taken the lives that are due to me for the loss of my relatives. The people here are safe and they don't care to risk their lives in a war with desperados, and I cannot blame them for that."

I was wondering if Armando was going to offer to ride with me an' Ton. I figured if he did, I just might take him up on it. I waited for him to go on.

"As I said, you and Ton need more men — or at least one good man who has tasted blood and does not fear killing. I know of such a man, Cal. Will you talk with him?"

" 'Course I will," I said. "You're right about the odds against me an' Ton. Maybe one more man wouldn't make a whole lot of difference, but maybe he would, too. If this fella is good with a gun an' has some fire to him, seems like he'd fit right in with us. Where is he? When can I talk with him?"

Armando suddenly had the expression on his face that a schoolboy would have when the teacher caught him dozing off. "You have met him."

Well, hell. The only man I'd met was the gunslinger I damned near killed. Why Armando thought I could ride with that shootist an' not expect a slug in the back of my head is beyond me. "Not on your life, Armando," I told him, "if you're talking about who I think you are."

"José is too brave, Cal, and it's likely he'll be killed by the Hunters because of that. He has no concern for his own life and yet less for anyone else's. I have heard it said that he isn't really brave, but that he no longer cares — about anything or anyone. In my mind, it amounts to the same thing. He's a fine fighter."

"What's a man like that have against the Hunters? Sounds like he should be ridin' with them, 'stead of against them."

"He will want money — the money from the Hunters that you'll recover if you can kill them all, or send the cowards among them running."

"That's fine. He can have part of the money. What I want outta this is to get my woman back. But — if there is a bunch of money, I won't hesitate to snatch it up. I

251

got a ranch to buy, an' seed cattle stock, an' so forth after I get Anna free. Money isn't the problem, though. Suppose José decides to cut me down? He was ready to draw yesterday."

"That will not happen," Armando said. "Will you at least speak with José?"

I'd seen the day before that José wasn't afraid to die an' that he knew a bit about fightin'. If I could keep him from shootin' me, maybe it could work out. Still, I didn't much like the idea. Nevertheless, I said to Armando, "Sure. What the hell — bring him around."

CHAPTER EIGHT

Maybe I was a bit too leery, but after Armando left to fetch José, I stood up and moved a couple of feet out from the wall. I advanced my right boot a few inches in front of me. I eased my Colt out of my holster and that let it drop back in, settling itself exactly where it needed to be if I had to draw. I knew Armando's word was good, but one man's word doesn't have much affect on what another man does.

Ton groaned in his sleep, turned on his side without waking, and was quiet. For a moment his breath sounded quick an' slightly raspy, but after he switched positions, he breathed smoothly and evenly.

I'm not real good at waiting. If somethin' needs to be done, I want to get to it and finish it up an' go on to the next thing. So, I was gettin' a tad antsy just standin' there like one of them dummies from a mercantile

that sells women's dresses an' unmention-
ables.

I gave no little thought to this José fellow.
The first thing I'd noticed about him were
his flat, killer eyes. I was sure he had some
kinda past behind him — maybe the war. I
couldn't see a man like him wearin' anyone's uniform or takin' sides in a civil
fracas, though. He'd probably live by his
own laws an' all the laws of the land
wouldn't make any more difference to him
than a Bible would to a prairie dog. José, I
was certain, could handle a gun. I hadn't
actually seen him draw or fire, but he knew
the little tricks to put a man off guard, and
there was no nervous tremble at all to the
hand that was moving closer to the grips of
his pistol.

When Armando's sister popped her head
around the corner from the cookin' area,
my hand snaked down to my pistol and I'd
cleared leather before I could stop what I
was doin'. Juanita yelped an' leaped back,
tripping over the long tentlike dress she
wore, and ended up sittin' on the floor with
a scared look on her face. The fear went
away real quick, and was replaced by raw
anger. She cussed me out real fine in Spanish, and I was able to pick up a few words I
knew: *chinga tu madre, pendejo, hijo de puta,*

maricón, estupido, bastardo, an' so forth. I hustled over to her an' put my hand out to help get her back on her feet. She spit at my hand and raised herself much like a buffalo will from a mud wallow: kind of getting her legs under her and shoving up with her arms an' hands while trying to heft that immense ass. I half expected her to shake herself like an ol' shaggie bull when she stood. I was standin' there facin' Juanita, looking dumb, not knowin' how to explain that I wasn't out to gun her, when the door in front swung open an' Armando stepped in with José a step behind him. I spun away from the woman, my eyes tight on José's right hand. It moved downward a couple inches toward his pistol, as did my own. Armand stepped between us.

"For this talk," he said, "I will hold the pistols to avoid unpleasantness." Me an' José glared at one another for a long moment an' then we both drew our weapons an' handed them to Armando. "What about his right boot?" I said.

"What about it?" Armando asked.

"See that little lump on the outside? He's got a holdout there — probably a derringer." José crouched and tugged the two-shot derringer from his boot an' handed it to Armando. "Now," José grinned, "we will see what you carry in your right boot." Fair is fair, I guess. I eased my bowie knife with its ten-inch blade from the sheath sewn inside my boot.

Armando carried the weaponry into the kitchen an' pulled up a pair more chairs. José took his, but turned it so that his back wasn't to the window. I did the same thing, feeling a lot more comfortable when I had a wall behind me.

"You are cautious men," Armando observed.

"Probably why we're still alive," José said. His voice was the cigarette-and-booze voice of most every cowhand and vaquero but like his eyes, there was a peculiar flatness to it.

"We will drink?" Armando said. José nodded and, after a moment, so did I. Armando called out to his sister and less than a minute later she appeared with a tray with a bottle of pulque and three shot glasses. She set it on the table and left the room wordlessly. All three of us stood an' poured a shot. Jose slugged his down an' so did Armando. I held back a bit, sipping, while the other two had another shot apiece, drank those off, poured again, and returned to their chairs.

"It's good pulque," Armando said in a hurt voice. "The very best."

"Maybe it could be gringos can't handle Mexican booze — a man's cactus whiskey," José said.

"Well, shit," I said. "If we're gonna talk here about possibly ridin' together, we need to stop the damned sniping. It won't get us nowhere but in a gunfight that you'd lose, José." He grinned but said nothing. The smirk on his face showed what he felt about what I'd just said.

"No more, no more," Armando urged. "Please — Cal. Tell your story about Busted Thumb an' what you an' Ton have been doing."

That's what I did, telling about my rides at the celebration, the money I'd won, about Anna and our room, and how the Night Hunters struck. I told how Ton had saved me and how his wife had been killed.

"You have raided the Hunters?" José asked.

"Not — not raided, not full attacks. Instead, we've been picking them off one by one, from cover. I have a Brendan Sharps —"

The mention of my rifle brought a smile to Jose's face. "Fine weapon," he said.

I nodded and went on. "There's thirty or more Hunters. There's no other way I know of to make the odds better than to pick off the sumbitches as we can an' then run."

"The Hunters — they know you're after them?"

I told him about the white-flag incident where Ton caught the slug.

José got up, walked to the table, and set his shot glass on its surface. Then he picked up the bottle as if was ice-cold water and he'd been thirsty for two days an' took long pulls at it. He wiped his mouth with the back of his hand and returned to his chair. "I have no story except greed. I lost no wife or no woman to the Hunters. I've heard that they are vile pigs — and that they have much gold and American currency stashed somewhere, perhaps in or near Santa Lucia. I will fight them for that, not for women or revenge."

The room was very quiet for what seemed like an hour. I was rolling José's speech in my mind. I didn't care why he was with us — if we could count on him. That was a big "if."

It was as if Armando had read my mind. "Greed can drive a man as hard as love and revenge can," he said.

"The law after you?" I asked José.

"Yeah. I shot and killed a marshal outside of Dodge City, and I'm suspected of a few other killings. There's paper on me in the states."

"How much?"

"Two thousand — dead or alive."

I whistled out a long note. "Lotsa money on your head. How're you sure me an' Ton won't bring you in to the law hangin' head down over your saddle?"

José's mouth moved into a quick grin that was gone as quickly as it had appeared. "Just like you know I'm not going to smoke you outta your boots because of our run-in yesterday."

"OK," I said. "One other thing about yesterday: you were awful fast to want to draw. Why was that?"

"It is my way. Gringos took my cattle and horses and I have no use for any of them." He thought for a moment. "And this: you look fast. I saw you were a pistolero as soon as I laid eyes on you. You were a challenge and I like challenges. It's as simple as that." He stopped talking as if he'd just told me how the weather was a day ago.

"Gamblin' with your life is what you call a challenge?" I asked.

"Oh, yes. Yes, it is. Because, you see, I got nothing to lose."

I didn't try to figure that out. I'd known men who'd lost money and livestock and had their homes and businesses go up in flames, but I never seen one who'd go around pickin' gunfights 'cause of their troubles.

"One more thing," I said. "Whatsay we pick up some empties from the cantina and walk out a bit an' maybe see how good you are with that Army Colt?"

José stood from his chair. "I want to see your shooting, too. All I hear so far is that you top off a horse real good. Other than that, I don't know a thing."

"It's a deal," I said. Neither one of us offered to shake hands to seal things.

We gathered up a grain sack full of empty whiskey, tequila, and pulque bottles at the cantina. José walked in first, with me an' Armando several strides behind. Soon's I stepped in, men at the tables and standing near the whiskey table ran for the walls or dove to the floor, thinkin' yesterday's fight was goin' to play out an' wantin' to avoid stray lead.

We stopped at the stable and I picked up my rifle an' some ammunition. It was hotter'n a coonhound bitch in heat as we walked out onto the prairie, putting Tranquila behind us. I had my Sharps over my shoulder. "You don't use a rifle?" I said to José.

"I got a .30-.06 that's sighted in real good," he said. "But I'll tell you what: I got a ten-dollar gold piece that says I can shoot that buffalo gun better'n you can — if it's sighted proper."

"It's sighted," I said. "You got yourself a bet."

I stopped walking. "Let's do some pistol work first. I'll set up six for you, an' you set up six for me. Fair enough?"

"Fair enough."

I walked out about twenty-five paces an' set a bottle down. Then I walked five steps back to José and set another. I did that with the other three — staggered them in distance, and was about to place the sixth one when glass began erupting around me just as the sounds of pistol fire stepped on the prairie silence. The bottle I'd been holding shattered loudly, leaving me hold a three-inch-long part of the neck. "Ya damned fool!" I shouted. "What the hell are you tryin' to do? Goddammit, you could have . . ."

"You said you wanted to see how I handled a pistol. Wouldn't you say I just showed you that? Hitting all six bottles?" José had no more expression on his face then he'd have buyin' a nickel's worth of cut plug over a counter. That heated me up even more — that, an' how flat his voice was, like nothin' at all had happened. He flicked open his pistol and let the brass cartridge casings drop in front of him.

"You lookin' to draw on me?" I bellowed. " 'Cause if you are, then load that sumbitch an' let's have at it."

José kept a little grin on his face as he plucked fresh rounds from his gunbelt and calmly — and, I think, slower than he ordinarily would — placed them into the empty spaces of his Colt's chambers.

I'm not generally a man who riles easy. I like to live an' let live, kinda. But when somethin' real bad happens to me that I ain't caused, well, then, I get some sand in my craw. This was one of them times.

I drew and fired five shots from my hip, my pistol not rising any higher than my gunbelt. There were five explosions of dirt and pebbles within a couple inches of his boots, with two going betwixt his legs and finding ground by his heels. With the sixth shot I plucked José's hat off as neat as I'd pull a cork on a whiskey bottle. His eyes were awful big for a bit and they found mine in a hurry. For the first time since I'd seen him in the cantina his eyes showed expression. It didn't last but for a couple of seconds, but it was there, that softening, that glint.

Then José began laughing — and so did I. The idea of the pair of us showing off our skills like schoolboys tryin' to impress a little girl purely tickled hell outta both of us. It was the kind of laughter that seems like it's all gone, an' then of a sudden we'd look at one another an' start in all over again.

Finally, when we'd gasped out our last laughs, José motioned to my Sharps. "You ready to do some *real* shooting?" he asked.

I handed the rifle to him. We both sobered up in a hurry — not that we'd been drinkin' nothin', but that we'd been laughing just like we had. There's somethin' about firin' a rifle that punches out enough power to put a slug through a good-sized shaggy an' drop him dead an' then take out the one standing right in line with him, as well, an' maybe a third, if they were set it up just right. I saw the great H. C. Farnam when he was a young stud do just that on a stand he took eighty-seven buffalo from. The barrel of his rifle was getting so hot he had his skinners pourin' buckets of water over it.

José hefted the Sharps, held it out at arm's length and looked it over closely, an' then fitted it to his shoulder. He closed his left eye and moved the rifle across the far horizon, finger outside the trigger guard. "I'm needing one shot so's I can see what this fine gun can do," he said. I nodded in agreement and tossed the sack of bullets to him. He removed one, put the bag at his feet, and fed the cartridge into the mechanism of the rifle.

"See that saguaro out there a piece? The one with the two arms stretched out?"

I squinted an' finally settled my eyes on the cactus I think he was talkin' about.

"If this rifle is zeroed in, I'll take the part of the body right above the arms. These soft slugs you're using ought to tear the piss out of the cactus so we could see it from here."

José didn't do a lot of screwin' about as many rifle shooters would. Instead, he took his stance, raised the Sharps to his shoulder, and, in a second, fired. Pieces of the top of the saguaro were blown twenty feet into the sky and equally far off to the sides. The cannonlike rumble of the report echoed back to us from the far-off hills.

"Madre de Hesu," José murmured. "This rifle — this buffalo gun — is amazing." He swallowed some air an' then handed me the rifle. "This one breathes with me, makes me point it where it wants its death to go . . ."

"Well, I dunno anything about that, but yeah, it's a fine rifle."

José looked out toward the headless cactus. "Damn," he said, almost reverently. Then he looked at me. "You going to throw anything at that cactus?"

"I might," I said. "I just damn might."

I took a couple steps an' loaded the breech of the Sharps with its full six shots.

The sagauro came apart. Its very top was gone 'cause of José's shooting, but I picked off both of them arms and then whittled the body down a foot or so with each round. When I'd shot my six I turned to José. I gotta admit that I liked the look of admiration on his face.

"What do you want to do here, José?" I asked. "We both shoot tolerably good. We both — all three of us, countin' Ton — have some reason to put bullets into Hunters. The only thing is that we have but one leader who calls the shots, an' that's me."

José stared at the ground in front of him for a bit before he looked up and captured my eyes with his. "You gringos — everything goes by your rules. You want to be the jefe, the leader, of an army of three men? That's fine with me, at least until you do something stupid."

I let that go by. "So — you're in?"

José stepped closer to me and extended his hand. We shook. "Let's go kill us some Night Hunters," he said.

We walked back to Armando's house without talking. It was easy enough to see José wasn't real big on conversation. At the door, José nodded toward the cantina. "You need me, that's where I'll be," he said.

I don't have a lot of trust for a man who sets in a gin mill for hours at a time. I don't know that I've seen José drunk, but if he couldn't let the booze alone, I didn't want him with us. A man with the shakes or the visions of snakes and so forth is useless to me an' Ton. They do dumb things an' for the most part, they can't shoot worth a damn.

"José," I said. "Let's talk for a minute longer. How much do you depend on booze to get you through a day?"

"Anybody ever tell you that you run your goddamn mouth too much?" José asked.

"Maybe. But this . . . well, hell . . . I don't care if you drink your ownself stupid every day — but I don't want me or Ton to die 'cause you were drunk."

"Cal," José said, "you can stick your partnership with me in your ass. If you want to put a dozen steps between us and then draw, let's do it. I don't take what you were saying from . . ."

"I'm faster an' better'n you are, boy. I'd put two in your chest before you cleared

266

leather."

"Horseshit."

"I'll tell you what, José: check the holes in your Stetson. Looks to me like my slug went in an' then out without killing you, no? S'pose I'd shot maybe a couple of inches lower? You'd be dead for sure."

"Exact same applies to you, no?" José answered. "I tilt my pistol a bit and take your hand off. I move it a couple or three inches to the side a little an' I kill you."

"That isn't the point," I said, maybe louder than I should have. "The three of us gotta fight together if we want to do this. If we don't, we'll be planted in some boot hill or left for the coyotes and vultures."

"You came to me — or at least Armando did. You wanted a gun and a man who could use it. That's me. I don't have no dead wife of captured woman — I'm in this for the Hunter money. I never made no bones about that. If you an' Ton want to ride out without me, well, hell — you up an' do so. If not, you keep your yap shut about what I do when I'm not killing Night Hunters."

I thought that over for some moments, my mind kind of racing along, tryin' to find the right thing to do. At the end, I didn't see that I had a choice. I had no proof that Jose was a bar rag. Hell, there were gamblers

267

who spent all day every day in saloons without takin' a drink. Thing is, Jose had that bottle in front of him on the table. But, all I knew is that he spent lots of time in the cantina and that he was handy with short an' long guns.

"OK. Soon's Ton can sit a horse we'll head out to Santa Lucia. That work OK for you?"

Neither of us smiled. "Yeah, it does," José said. He turned from me abruptly and walked into the cantina. I guess I had more to say, but none of my words woulda made any difference. A man like José can't be warned or threatened, 'cause it seemed like he'd draw down on his own mother, should she give him any lip. I turned from the cantina and headed back to Armando's house to check on my pard.

Ton was sittin' up on his mat, drinking from a cup of something that must have tasted real bad. He shook his head, gagged, and then looked over at me. "Stuff tastes like rattler piss that's been out in the sun for some hours," he said. "Tia made it up from some stuff she finds on the prairie."

"How's the leg?" I asked.

"Healin' real good, Cal. Another day, I'll be ready to ride."

"That'll be good, but we got to do this

268

cautiously — if you need an extra day or so, you're goin' to take it. You fallin' off your horse an' bein' a target for the Hunters doesn't make no sense."

"Another day is all I need an' all I'll take, Cal." Ton's voice had become cold, flinty.

I took in a breath. "There'll be three of us ridin' out," I said. "The gunman José has pitched in with us."

Ton hesitated before speaking. "I can't say that I fancy ridin' with a man who tried to gun my partner, Cal."

"Me an' him talked about that. There won't be any trouble. He's in it for the gold the Hunters have gathered up. I've seen him shoot, both with his Colt an' my Sharps. He knows what he's doin' real well — no doubt about that."

"He better'n you?" Ton asked.

I considered that. "No — but he's damned near as good. But me an' José aren't goin' to be slappin' leather against one another. We're saving all that for Night Riders."

Ton settled down on his back, staring up at the adobe ceiling. "It ain't my favorite thing," he said. "But we don't have no choice, do we? If he can shoot, I guess we need him."

"That's the way I saw it," I said.

■ ■ ■ ■

We headed out a day and a half later, pretty much provisioned with things we'd need on the trail, thanks to Armando's courtesy. We had enough ammunition to fight Antietam all over again, plus coffee, two canteens each, a bottle of tequila, papers an' tobacco, goat jerky, an' even a small sack of sugar.

José's mount was a right flashy Appaloosa, which he said he'd traded the Nez Perce for; he'd had to give four head of good, fat cattle, a Winchester .30-.30, and a dozen bottles of red-eye. It was, he said, the best trade he ever made.

José said he didn't believe in giving horses names — it was like naming a chicken or a fence post or some such, according to him. He called the Appy "Hoss," or "Boy" or once in a while "Goddammit."

Matthew and Jake reacted to the new animal just as we expected them to: snorting, and prancing about, arching their tails, snapping their hooves up almost before they'd touched ground — pulling all the horse antics they do to show how hard an' tough they are. The Appaloosa didn't pay much attention, except when Matthew got close to him, teeth bared, probably intent on ripping a patch of hide off the new horse. The Appy reared and struck with his right front an' if that shod hoof had connected it would have crushed Matthew's skull like a rotten grape — or maybe José's skull, too. Jake an' Matthew let him alone after that.

The heat gave us a whole lot more trouble than our mounts did. I was kinda concerned about Ton, but he didn't show any more ill effects than me or José. But the sun seemed to drain our minds and our whole world consisted of the "thunk-thunk" of our horses' steps. I swear a damn circus parade could have come by an we wouldn't have stopped to watch it.

We hit a shallow dip of tepid water an' decided to make camp there. There were some scraggly cottonwoods near the water, and a few desert pines that seemed to have croaked and were just standing there, turning brown.

There's been free-range cattle around the water. We could tell they were free range 'cause there were so few tracks — maybe left by three beeves. "One's a calf at his momma's side," Ton said. "We could take him an' do some fancy eatin'." That didn't sound bad to me. After all, free-range cattle belonged to anyone who wanted them — just like buffalo or rabbits or prairie dogs.

José got up on his hind legs about that, all feisty. "We'd waste three-quarters of the meat, leavin' it out there to rot. We'd get a couple steaks apiece an' that's about all. That ain't worth killin' the calf for."

That surprised me. "They're free range, José," I said. "Hell, they belong to us as much as they do anyone else."

"What about the momma he's suckin' on?"

"It's jus' a damned calf . . ."

José swung down from his saddle, his face suffused with the choleric red of anger. "I'll go out an' fetch in a few jacks an' we'll eat good. But we ain't killin' no calf."

Ton and I looked at one another. We both shrugged as if the whole thing made no never-mind to either of us. "Rabbit's always good," Ton commented.

Now, I like rabbit as much as the next man, specially when it's fresh killed and cleaned real good. Some say if there's white spots on the jack's liver, you'd best toss it because the white spots are poison. None of the three José killed had liver spots.

Ton had gotten a nice little fire going by the time we'd cleaned the rabbits and found sticks to skewer them on. The meat was good — sweet, almost, with the tang of mesquite to it. We made up some coffee and

José poured a couple of belts of tequila into our cups. I was still a tad leery of cactus whiskey, but I knew a couple of inches wouldn't hurt me.

The setting sun had cooled things down some, and a vagrant breeze picked up and felt good on our faces. For some time, nobody said anything. We sipped our coffee and gawked into the embers of the fire, as men tend to do.

When Ton talked it startled me — I guess I was off somewhere's with Anna. "Lemme ask this," Ton said, looking directly at José, "what's the difference between a jack and a calf?"

"Shit," José snickered, "it's the same difference 'tween a mouse and a good mustang. I could kill mice all day an' not give a thought, but was I to put a slug in a mustang, I'd sure feel it."

"Feel it?" Ton asked. "How do you mean?"

There was a long silence from Jose. "Let it go, OK? I was talking silliness." He tossed the dregs from the bottom of his cut into the fire and moved off a few feet, beyond the wavering circle of light the embers spread.

The following morning we were mounted and moving before the first light was enough to see by. "No water for maybe fifteen, twenty miles," Ton said, "but when we hit it, it ain't but a day's ride from there into Santa Lucia, if Armando's map is any good."

"It's good," I said. "An' if we can't trust Armando, I don't know who we *can* trust."

Ton nodded at my words. José said, in a very even tone, as if he were asking what time it was, "I'll tell you boys who I trust: nobody. Not you two, not anyone in the world. That's why I've stayed alive all these years."

"You don't have to trust us, but you need to depend on us. There's a difference 'tween the two. Trust means someone gives a good goddamn about someone else. Depending on someone is like expecting a good cattle dog or sheepdog to do what he's supposed to do. 'Cause I'll tell you right now, José, the minute we're finished up with the Hunters, I never want to look on you again — never even want to think about you again. An' if that bothers you, call me out right now or call me out after we bury the Hunters. That's up to you."

"Fine with me . . ." José began.

Ton's bellow is substantial at any ol' time, but this one damned near blew me an' José outta our saddles.

"We ain't got time for this shit!" he

roared. "You two goin' at each other like a couple of fightin' roosters isn't nothin' but plain stupid. Do what you need to do when we're all finished up, but until then, keep your yaps offa each other."

❖ That kinda put a damper on conversation for the rest of the day. I brought Anna to mind. She was there most of the time, but just ridin' slow like we were, with nothin' at all to do, brought her to the forefront. I remembered she wasn't one to do much laughing, but when she did the sound was so pure and so joyous that a corpse would set up and laugh with her. I asked her about that — why she didn't give in to laughter much.

There has been very little to laugh about in my life. If I started to laugh I'm afraid I'd cry. No man can ever know how a woman feels when she's passed around or sold or sent to be with stinking, drunken buffalo hunters except maybe a fieldhand slave. She looked into my eyes for a few moments. *With you it's different, Cal. These short days, they make a difference in how I feel. You make me laugh at times. That is good.*

Long about dusk the horses began getting fractious, which meant they'd cut the scent of water. We let them go into a slow lope rather than wrestle with them, and before

275

long we came upon some trees surrounding a little pool of clear water. The tracks around it showed us that critters drank from it an' didn't die — at least not immediately — so we went ahead and dove in, after shucking our sidearms, 'course. I wasn't surprised to see that José had a Derringer two-shot — one of them over-n-under little guns that have saved many a riverboat gambler's life — hideout in one boot an' a sizable pigsticker in the other.

I led Jake in right off and let him suck while I splashed around like a kid in a swimmin' hole. The water wasn't more than maybe three feet deep, but it was spring-fed, an' colder'n the devil's heart.

We didn't build much of a fire — just enough flame to heat coffee — and we ate jerky and drank java an' that was all any of us needed. José offered his bottle around. I said no but Ton took a belt or two.

"So, jefe, what's the plan? Tomorrow we will hit Santa Lucia."

I ignored the "jefe" José used sarcastically. The word means chief or general in Spanish. "I doubt me or Ton could ride into town. They seen us fairly clear the other day."

"I don't know that they did, Cal," Ton said. "You blew the head clean off the guy with the white flag and the ones shootin' from the sides didn't seem like they was real close."

José shook his head. "A man your size ain't a common sight, Ton," he said. "Even if the Hunters didn't see you close up, they sure saw that you're bigger'n a grizzly."

I said, "I might could slide in after dark, when they're takin' on snootfuls of whiskey. I could get into a card game or just stand at the bar. We gotta see what's goin' on and what their plans are, or we're gonna be runnin' our asses off after them for the rest of our natural lives."

José rolled himself a smoke. I took his lead and built one for myself. "I oughtta go in first," he said, exhaling smoke. "I don't know nothin' about Santa Lucia 'cept the Night Hunters all but own it. It won't be hard to see which cantina has the most horses tied up in front. I'll listen, maybe play a few hands of poker or whatever. Then you come in, Cal — maybe an hour or more after I do. I'm hopin' by then that I'll be palaverin' with a drunk Hunter. We'll see what we can get out of him and his pals."

That made sense to me. "Sounds good," I said.

"An' if any of them recognize you, they kill you on the spot an' tack your hide to the wall. I'd rather we . . ."

"What?" I interrupted. "Attack? Three men against twenty-five or better? That doesn't make sense, Ton."

"Well, hellfire, Cal. What do I do while you boys're are in town?"

"Clean your rifle real good, make some coffee, get some shut-eye."

Ton didn't like it, but he accepted it.

The next morning we rode 'til we started seeing tracks that meant traffic and reined over to one side a couple of miles. There was a seep hole there Armando showed on his map. The water was sulfury and warm but it was better'n none at all. Made the coffee taste strange, though.

An hour or so after full darkness, José saddled up an' rode to Santa Lucia. There was a bright half-moon, so ridin' was easy.

I clean and oiled my Sharps but didn't put it back on my saddle. I did the same cleanin' job on my Colt, even though it didn't need it.

Ton tossed the balance of his coffee into the campfire and grimaced. "Tastes like it ran outta John Brown's boots," he said. After a moment, he said, "You cutting crosses in your slugs?"

"I hadn't planned on it."

"Oh. I seen José doin' it, cuttin' nice deep

crosses into the lead — both the load in his pistol and the cartridges in his gunbelt."

"Some folks say it makes a .45 open up and come apart in a man's body, an' those smaller pieces wreck a fella's guts an' stuff," I said. "I dunno. I never did it 'cause it seemed to me that it might screw up my accuracy, make the bullet not travel quite true."

"I'm thinkin' I'll do her, Cal. If it works like you said, tearin' up a man's guts worse'n a regular bullet, I'm all for it. It'd work for a .30-.06, wouldn't it?"

"I don't see why not. Hell, a slug's a slug."

Maybe an hour after José had left I saddled Jake. I told Ton I'd whistle as I came in so's he didn't shoot me off my horse, an' that I'd tell José to do the same thing, in case we didn't ride back together.

It was a good night for ridin'. Like I said, there was a lot of moonlight. The temperature had dropped some an' that felt good. In a couple of places I let Jake lope a bit, but never let him go into a full gallop.

I heard Santa Lucia quite I bit before I saw it. A piano carries good on flatland, and so do gunshots. When I was about a half-mile outside the town I stopped an' looked things over. Jake swung his head back, eyeing me, wonderin' what the hell I was do-ing.

Santa Lucia was bigger'n I thought it'd be. There was a dome of pale light over it an' I could make out buildings and the cantina where I figured the piano music was comin' from. I rode past the church — seems like every little pissant settlement in Mexico has itself a big church — and down the main street of the town. I went on past the cantina where José had tied his horse — that Appaloosa stood out like a otter in a mess of prairie dogs — and continued down to the stable at the end of the street. There was a breaking pen there, with a bunch of mangy-looking mustang crosses that snorted an' carried on when they got Jake's scent. I swung back, not wantin' to rile the stock too much, an' not wantin' Jake to get all studlike.

A drunken vaquero swung onto a decent-lookin' bay horse an' rode off, swayin' in his saddle. I tied Jake in the spot the cow-hand had left open. I noticed that the others tied there showed scars an' fresh rips on their flanks from spurs. Any damn fool that has to hook a horse like that shouldn't be in a saddle. The cantina didn't have a name far's I could see, but it had a pair of batwings that sure didn't lead into a mercantile or a doc's office. There was no pedestrian traffic on the street, although it wasn't awful late — maybe nine or ten o'clock.

There was a cloud of smoke driftin' past the batwings, along with a ton of laughter, curses, that piano I talked about, and an occasional gunshot. I doubted that the shot was directed anywhere but the ceiling of the cantina, since there was no return fire an' because right after the report came more laughter an' shouting.

It was murky in the saloon. There were three lanterns spread down both sides of the building, but they didn't offer much illumination. The fog of tobacco smoke hindered the lanterns, too. The smell was that of each an' every one of these places: sour beer, spilled rotgut whiskey, vomit, an' the sweat of maybe fifty men who weren't in the least bit fond of bathin' every few months or so. I stood just inside my cantina an' let my eyes adjust as much as they could.

There was a real bar — not a plank or a table — an' there were two 'tenders working it, drawin' schooners of beer and pourin' shots of pulque, tequila, an' homemade whiskey in bottles with American labels on them. I knew how the Mexicans made booze, using wood alcohol and a bit of molasses for color, an' tossing maybe a goat's head or a few dead rats into the cauldron where it was boilin' to cover the taste of the raw alcohol.

I saw José at a table with three men who didn't appear to be Mexican. The tabletop was littered with empty schooners an' a couple of clear bottles — tequila or pulque.

José was slumped in his chair an' appeared drunk, but no drunker than the men with him. He saw me and waved me over. When I got to the table his eyes told me that he wasn't nearly as deep into the booze as the other three men he was with.

"This is the boy I been tellin' you about," he said. "I swear on my mother that he can ride the piss right outta any horse ever born. I seen him do it more'n once, an' I never seen him throwed. An' if that ain't true, well, my name ain't Augusto Milliane."

One of the men tried to focus his eyes on me but didn't do it real well. His grin made him look a idjit. "Ain't a horse that can't be rode an' there ain't a rider that can't be rode — nah, shit — that ain't the way it goes. There ain't a horse . . ."

One of the others held up a hand to quiet his friend. "Here's how it's supposed to be said. Any damn fool knows that. It's 'There ain't some horse what can't be rode an' there ain't no rider who can't be throwed.' "

"Bullshit," José said. "My good friend Cal here can't be throwed an' I'll put money on it right here an' now." Jose turned to me. "These boys say they's got some right good horses in a corral somewhere nearby. They tell me they belong to a bunch of fellas, some who're here in Santa Lucia an' some are at the camp. Their leader, Mountain or some damn thing . . ."

"Montclaire," one of the men interrupted.

Jose flipped his hand as if the wrong pronunciation was no more important than shaking away a pesky fly, and said, "Right, Mount-whatever. But he's supposed to know horses real good."

I pulled a chair over from another table and sat on it sorta behind Jose an' a bit to his left.

"See, Cal, what I'm thinkin' we could do is go on out to the camp they're talkin' about an' maybe make us some money on you ridin' the roughest cayuse they got," Jose said, more to the three Hunters than to me.

I shook my head. "Dammit — I ain't here to ride. You know as well as I do that if the law wasn't after . . ." I stopped right there an' tried to make it look like I'd said too much.

283

The Hunters picked up on that immediately, regardless of their degree of drunkenness. "Well, now," one said, "why'd the law be after you two? Or do they only want Cal?"

I met the Hunter's gaze. "I don't see how that'd be your business — but I'll tell you anyway. Me an' my friend here got into a little trouble tryin' to kinda undeposit some money in a bank. We had to shoot our way out an' a customer an' a teller caught slugs."

"They die?" a Hunter asked.

"Deader'n a boot nail. There's paper on us across the river. That's how we come to be here. If it wasn't some lawman tryin' to gun us, a damned bounty hunter'd get behind us with a rifle an' drop us from a good distance. We figured maybe we'd hook up with some others who was over here for the same reason we are. There's purely a ton of money just cryin' out to be took in some of them jerkwater town banks."

"Cal," José said, angry-like, "none of that means nothin' to these boys. All we're doin' is to set up a ride, maybe turn a few dollars. You got no call to run your mouth about that bank nor the law. Shit. You never was no good at keepin' your yap shut."

I stood from my chair. "I've heard enough of this horseshit, Augusto. You come in here an' get drunk an' the next thing I know, you're puttin' me on a horse. Nossir. I ain't gonna do it."

A Hunter also stood, facin' me. He wore a Colt in a holster tied low on his leg. He didn't seem quite so drunk now. "I'll tell you what," he said, "if me an' my friends say you're gonna ride, then that's the way it's gonna be. Hear?"

I pulled eyes away from him, doing my best to show some fear. I didn't feel good about doing it. The Hunters are used to killin' woman an' kids an' sodbusters. I wanted to draw against this killer — but I didn't. "I . . . but I don't know where this camp is where you keep the horses. How can . . ." I think my voice sounded fearful, or 'least I hope it did.

"You an' this man," he pointed to José, "will follow us from here. We'll take you."

I tried to make my voice sound just a little stronger. "How do we know you'll pay up when I top your horse? If there's a camp, there must be other men there. Me an' Augusto could end up . . ."

"If a Night Hunter wanted you dead, you'd a been dead afore you opened your mouth tonight. Let's go — we got a distance to cover 'fore we see how good you set a horse."

285

José and I walked out to the hitching rail, following the three outlaws. Our horses were easily the finest ones there. "See them spur scars?" José whispered to me as he pulled his cinch. "They're gonna pay for that."

The Hunters climbed aboard their horses and raked their spurs down the animals' flanks. "Yeah," I said. "They're gonna pay for that."

CHAPTER NINE

The outlaws pushed their horses regardless of the darkness. José and I hung back, not wanting to end up with a good horse with a busted leg. The Hunters were far enough ahead of us so we could talk without fear of being overheard, even though one or the other of them would swing back an' tell us to get a move on. They'd brought a bottle from the cantina and were hitting it hard.

"I don't get it," I said to José. "What's the point of this camp? They've got the whole damned town and I saw a stable with a paddock — why set up out here?"

I saw the glint of moonlight on José's teeth as he grinned before speaking. "Seems like you an' Ton been givin' the Hunters a good helping of grief," he said. "That leader of theirs decided breaking up his men was safer, an' there was a better chance of getting you an' Ton between the two groups of Hunters."

I asked the big question: "Where are the women?"

"At the camp. Here's the deal on that. The Hunters will bring them into Santa Lucia the day after tomorrow. They've let whore-house buyers know they'd be runnin' a sale, like they had a bunch of slaves at an auction."

"Sonsabitches," I muttered.

"Yeah. I guess that happens 'round here fairly often. The Hunters will take in a lot of money from the buyers. I want that an' I want what they must have stashed."

"One thing I'm not sure me an' Ton told you about," I said. "Danny Montclaire is mine — I'm the one to take him out."

José nodded. "Don't make no never-mind to me, 'less he's set to gun me an' in that case all bets are off. Otherwise, he's all yours. Don't matter who kills a rattler; what counts is that it's dead."

We quit talking when we saw that the three outlaws had reined in an' were talking to a man on foot, holding a rifle. A Hunter passed the bottle to the lookout and he took a long pull at it before handing back.

"What's this?" the lookout asked, nodding toward Jose an' me.

"We got us a gen-u-wine bronc man here," one of the mounted Hunters said. "He's

288

gonna put on a show ridin' down that rank bay Captain Danny has."

The lookout laughed. "Right. An' pigs fly like shitbirds, too. That horse already kilt a man. Why Captain Danny keeps the sumbitch around beats me."

"So's we can have shows like our bronc man here is gonna put on, that's why," one of the mounted men said. "Who's guardin' up closer to the camp?"

"Al, he's off to the side a bit an' Harry is standin' at the other side. Luke is the one closest to the camp. You boys ride in slow and whistle 'Buffalo Gals,' or you'll eat lead."

It was pretty obvious that me an' Ton had changed things a bit around a Night Hunters camp. The first times we did some sniping, the damned fools didn't have a single lookout. Now they had three or four.

José and I followed the three riders at a walk. One of them began to whistle "Buffalo Gals." He couldn't whistle worth a damn, but he got us past the riflemen posted around the camp.

I couldn't think of a single reason the Hunters would let us go after I rode their horse. It'd be a whole lot easier to kill us an' avoid any tales we might tell about them or their camp. I coughed to get José's attention an' drew a finger 'cross my throat like it was a knife. José nodded back: he was thinkin' the same thing I was. 'Course, the best time for us to bolt had been on the way in to the camp. We coulda shot holes in the three outlaws an' rode back to where Ton was, an' I guess José an' me both knew that. Neither one of us wanted to do it. It was more important seein' how many men we was up 'gainst an' lookin' over how things was run by Montclaire.

There was a hell of a fire going; its flames were licking a dozen feet into the sky an' we could see it from a half-mile away. There were trees behind the fire a few yards, but we couldn't see much more'n that. As we got closer we saw there were some Army tents up, just kinda scattered around the fire. There were lots of Night Hunters standin' around eating, drinkin' coffee or booze, an' tossing wood into the fire. It was hard to get a good count 'cause they were movin' around here an' there. I'd guess there was twenty-five or thirty of them that we could see, an' maybe more in the tents or watchin' the horses.

The Hunters stopped whatever they were doin' to gawk as we rode in, following the three outlaws. I felt like I was on display, like maybe a two-headed calf or somethin' in one of those travelin' shows. The front flap of the tent we stopped in front of opened and a man stepped out. He was maybe 5' 10" tall, with dark hair that was slicked back with oil or lard or some such thing. He wore a Union Army officer's jacket an' tall black boots that were highly polished an' reflected the flames of the fire. He wore a Colt .45 in a holster low on his right leg. There were medals pinned to his coat: I recognized a couple from the Confederacy an' some more from the Union side. He smiled at us an' I saw he had a gold lower front tooth. It was the sort of smile a fox gives a fat hen.

"Who are these two?" he asked one of the mounted Hunters. "Why are they here?"

"One's a bronc man, Captain Danny. I thought maybe you'd want to see him try to ride that bay horse." The Hunter's tone was almost apologetic, like the voice of a kid askin' his teacher whether his sums or his spellin' was right.

Montclaire's smile broadened. "A fine idea," he said. "But I see that they're armed. Take their guns."

Men moved to us, a couple aiming rifles. I handed over my pistol an' José did the same. One of the gang took the weapons an' tossed them into the tent next to the one Montclaire came out of. Neither me nor José had carried rifles in.

"Which one is the rider?" Montclaire asked.

A Hunter on his horse to my side pointed at me. "This boy here," he said. "His pal tol' us this fella could ride a bolt of lightnin' without no problem."

There was a strange silence in that camp, and there had been since Montclaire stepped out of his tent. It could have been respect of the men toward their leader, or simple fear of him. I'd go with the fear if I had to put a name to it. The only sound was the cracklin' of the fire. Jake shifted under me nervously, not liking to be standing stock-still in a group of men and horses he'd never seen before.

Montclaire lit a long, thin cigar and stood for what seemed like a long time without sayin' anything. There was still a half-smile on his face. The light from the fire made his eyes appear to be aflame as well, shiny, seeing either nothing or everything.

"Bring the mare," he said. He nodded to me an' José. "Get down from your horses." We did and I began to work the cinch of my saddle so's I could put my rig on the mare I was to ride. Montclaire's smile got a bit wider, his gold tooth glinting. "No saddle," he said. "You ride bareback. Give us a good show an' we may let you live. If the mare dumps you, we kill you both. It's a fair contest, no?"

This man cared as much about a fair contest as an ant does about the King of England.

A lot can be told about a horse in the way it presents itself in new situations — flighty or arrogant or scared or whatever. The first thing I saw about this tall bay mare was that she was up on her rear feet and striking out with jagged-edged, untrimmed hooves. There probably wasn't a blacksmith in the world who'd trim or shoe this animal.

She was blindfolded with a strip of gunny-sack and they'd gotten a halter over her muzzle. Her muzzle was tied down with several turns of stout rope — she must have been a biter.

The Hunter holding the lead rope stood well to the side, poking her flank with a long pole with a sharp end to it. The mare was bleeding a bit from the pole, but not a whole lot. As he'd stick her, she'd move a step or so forward to get away from the pain. The Hunters got the hell out of the way as the leadman brought the mare close enough to the fire so that she could be seen real well.

She was tall for a mare, and a tad gaunt.

Her coat was mangy and dirty and her tail a mass of burdocks.

Montclaire directed one of his boys to take the reins to Jake and José's horse. Everyone moved back thirty or forty feet from the leadman, the mare, me an' José. A Hunter with a rifle prodded José with its barrel an' he moved back, too.

"Only way we can do this is you swing up an' I'll hand over the lead, pull the blindfold, and haul ass," the leadman said. As I grabbed a handful of mane, he added, "This hellcat's gonna kill you, boy. Already killed a Mex bronc man not a full week ago."

I pulled myself onto the mare's back and grabbed the lead rope in one motion. The Hunter tugged the blindfold free and bolted away from me an' the horse. The mare stood as still as a statue for a bit. Then she purely came apart.

She swung her head back to gnaw on my leg or whatever other part of me she could reach, but her muzzle was tied well shut an' I booted her in the nose, so she didn't try that again.

Some of the horses I've ridden would squeal in that high-pitched, eerie sounding tone of fear or anger that no other animal duplicates. This one didn't waste her breath on squealing; she put her whole self and

294

strength into snaking up to the sky, leaping high, twisting and slinging her backbone while in the air.

I hadn't done much bareback riding in the past few years, but I'm good 'nough at it. I rode out the first jumps in pretty good fashion. I figured her to be a spinner an' I sure was right about that. It seemed like she traded her head for her ass a dozen times a second. I'd never been on a horse that spun like this one did. Funny thing is, the speed of the movement kind of held me to her back — at least until she changed directions so fast I didn't know what was happening. I was watching her shoulders, expecting a move like that, but this hellfire horse gave no sign that I could see, an' I make my damn livin' by seein' things like that on the stock I ride. I ended up way over on her right side, clumsy as a drunken sailor, my legs clamped vise-tight to her, scrambling to right myself.

We'd raised a hell of a cloud of dirt an' grit into the air an' my eyes were stinging from it. I was breathin' hard as a mine-mule an' suckin' all that soil made me cough. There was nothin' I could do about that, but here I was tryin' to ride this hound from hell with my eyes streamin' tears an' coughin' so violently I could barely catch a breath.

Right about there is where the mare started to win our little go-round. I'd never in my entire life of bustin' my ass ridin' come across one that could go straight up from a hard spin. This horse did and she came down on her forefeet an' snaked her back, an' there I was again, hangin' on her side like a leech, but losing precious inches every second, almost blind, with a pair of legs that weren't grippin' like they should anymore. I thought I heard gunshots but at first they didn't really register in my head. When the mare's poll — the skull betwixt her ears — exploded in a geyser of bone an' brain an' blood, it came clear that I had heard some shots.

The mare went straight down, dead before she hit the ground. I was able to push off an' I stood there rubbin' my eyes, tryin' to see what was goin' on. I couldn't figure out why a Night Hunter would kill the horse; they would have enjoyed seeing me get my head stomped in. José didn't have a weapon, an' even if he did he wouldn't have bothered with the mare — he'd have killed some Hunters.

The Hunters around me an' the dead hell-horse scattered. I saw one go down with a bloody chest an' another took a slug in the leg an' was spurtin' red. I guess I heard ol' Matthew before I really saw him — that huge horse shook the earth at a gallop an' he stormed in like a runaway locomotive

I kept rubbin' at my eyes and began to see a mite better. Ton charged Matthew right on through that fire, scatterin' wood an' flames an' embers in all directions making the fire look like a fountain of burning wood and reddish-orange embers. Ton had a pistol in his hand and another tucked into the waistband of his pants. He was placin' his shots real well.

Ton hauled Matthew around in a turn you'd think a horse that big couldn't possibly do and thundered toward me. Ton stuck out his left arm, an' as he galloped by me I grabbed that arm. I swear it was like latchin' onto a tree trunk — as hard as the hardest wood. I swung up behind Ton and we headed out of the camp.

I was about to yell at Ton about Jake and José an' his horse, when José raced up beside us, leading Jake by the reins. José tossed my Colt to me. It felt good to have it in my hand.

Some return fire crackled behind us, but we were too far out for pistols to touch us by then, an' they had no targets with their rifles 'cause of the darkness.

We had to ride harder than we wanted to in the dark, but we had no choice about that. When we figured we didn't have Night Hunters breathin' down our necks we slowed to an easy lope — and even that may have been a bit fast for night ridin'.

Ton led the way. He'd broken the camp we had an' set up another a few miles away. The water at the new camp was lousy, but it was water, an' it worked just fine to clean out my eyes an' cut my coughin' down. Ton had left a small fire an' that's how we found the new camp. We dismounted and un-tacked our horses.

"You were losing," José said.

I turned to face him without speaking. "You were losing," he repeated.

"I don't recall ever sayin' I can ride 'em all."

He smiled when I said that. "You put a hell of a ride on that mare, though."

It felt good to hear that.

Ton told us that he'd be damned if he'd set around like an ol' widow while me an' José was in town. He moved camp to a spot that had a puddle of water an' a few cotton-woods and then waited for us outside of Santa Lucia an' when he saw we were riding with three Hunters, he hung back to see where they were taking us. He took out the guards one at a time, leavin' them tied an' gagged. One of them, he said, called out to him, "You got whiskey?" Ton said he sure did an' rode up to the lookout an' knocked him silly with the butt of his sixgun.

"When I saw what was goin' on with Cal ridin' that crazy horse, I got some concerned. When things started to look kinda touchy for Cal, I decided the best way to come in would be ridin' fast an' sprayin' lead. I dropped that poor ol' mare first, 'fore she got a chance to dance on my pardner. I don't like killin' a horse, but sometimes it can't be helped. She was useless, anyhow. Crazy-like."

José told us his story: "As soon as I saw Ton chargin' in I punched the Hunter closest to me a good one an' knocked him out. I pulled his pistol an' shot the Hunter holdin' our horses with it. It was an Army Colt an' I had to pull the damned trigger three times to get it to fire. I was about to jump onto my horse when I saw I was right by the tent where our guns had been thrown, so I snatched them up, and lit out." After a couple of seconds he added, "I sure was happy to see Ton come barrelin' in."

"Me, too," I said. "Wouldn't have been more'n a few seconds before I was on the ground an' the mare was makin' mashed potatoes outta my head."

We put a pot of coffee on the remains of the fire. I was thinkin' a good slug of whiskey wouldn't hurt, but we didn't have any. After a bit our talk ran out an' we sat there lookin' into the small fire. I got to thinkin' about what Ton did. What it come down to is he risked his life to get me an' José outta the pickle we were in. It takes a pair of brass eggs for a man to ride into an armed camp to try to free a couple of his friends. The image of Matthew highballin' through that bonfire came back to me an' I turned it over an' around in my mind, enjoyin' every little part of it, every ember arcing into the sky: a very big man on a very big horse shootin' the ass offa some desperados who needed real bad to be shot.

It wasn't too long before some false dawn began to tint the eastern horizon. I suppose it might have made sense for us to talk about what we were gonna do next, but we were all whipped an' soon stretched out an' slept. The talkin' could wait a few hours.

The next morning we made up some coffee and palavered. Seems like we each had a different idea about what we needed to do next. "We gotta keep on hittin' them," Ton said, "pickin' them off one at a time." I wasn't sure that was the right way to tie the calf.

"I don't see many choices," José said. "We sure as hell can't charge them. They're crazy but they ain't stupid. They'll have lookouts posted all around them, an' this time them men won't be nearly as stupid as the ones Ton hammered last night. We got to lower the numbers against us, an' the only way I can think of to do that is like Ton said — hunt down the Hunters and use the sons-abitches for target practice."

I'd been doin' some thinkin' about our problem. "How long have the Hunters controlled Santa Lucia?" I asked José.

"I dunno. A few years, anyway. I heard tell that some of the Hunters are Rebel deserters an' others rode with Quantrill. But it ain't that they really own the town, 'cept when they're there. When they're not it's just a dusty little nowhere town. An' they don't show up on no schedule of any kind. They'll ride in, drink the cantina dry, sell some whores, shoot some people, an' ride back out 'til the next time."

"The people of Santa Lucia let this happen?" I asked.

"What're they gonna do? They're a bunch of sodbusters an' clerks an' women."

That didn't sit right with me. "Even a farmer can fire a rifle or a pistol."

"Sure they can. One year a couple tried to fight against the Hunters. You remember seein' the big tree near the well in Santa Lucia? They hanged two men there an' left their bodies to rot for a week. That kinda took the spunk outta the rest of the men."

"I suppose that'd do it," I admitted. "We sure could use more guns, though."

"I wonder if talkin' to them would do any good," Ton said.

"I doubt it," José said. "An' if they'd listen, it sure wouldn't be to us. To them, you two are gringo pistoleros, not much better than the Hunters. They've got me pegged as a hired gun."

"Maybe Armando could get to them," I said. The three of us were silent for a bit. Then Ton asked, "Is that what you was, José? A hired gun?"

José stood and dashed the dregs of his coffee into the fire. "Lemme ask this: You boys havin' any problems with my fightin' since we been ridin' together?"

"I didn't mean . . ." Ton started.

"I don't give a damn what you meant. The three of us agree that Night Hunters need killin', an' that's what we're doin'. I'm not lookin' for a friend nor a partner." When he turned from the fire to face us, his face had gone hard. "I'm a Mexican. I got no great love for gringos. Let's make sure we're right clear on that."

"Well, even with all that said, we still haven't decided what we're gonna do. I want to at least talk with Armando before we do anything else."

"So go an' talk with him," José said. "But go at night an' make sure nobody sees you, 'cause if they do you'd be signin' Armando's death warrant."

"Nobody's gonna see me."

"You gonna gamble Armando's life on that?"

My first reaction was to tell José to go to hell, but I didn't, because what he'd just said was true: I'd be rollin' the dice for another man's life. The more I thought about it, the surer I became that Armando would want me to roll those dice, that he was a strong man and one of integrity — a man who'd leap at a chance to rid his people of the Night Hunters forever. I'd been studyin' on how best to defend ourselves against real bad odds in Santa Lucia, an' my mind kept on comin' back to the church. There was a second floor — a loft type of thing — with windows. The structure itself was mostly adobe, so it wouldn't burn.

An' that adobe would stop bullets real nice. I planned to talk with Armando about it.

Things were quiet around the camp for the rest of the day. Our horses needed rest an' so did we. But what we had wasn't the comfortable type of quiet — it was more like there was somethin' buzzin' in the air around us, makin' us nervous an' jumpy. We watched the sky carefully, looking for the cloud of dust that'd follow even a single horseman ridin' toward us. José saddled his horse an' rode out about dusk, not sayin' anything about where he was goin'.

"Feisty today, ain't he?" Ton said.

"Seems so. But what he said was true," I said.

"But you're still gonna go to see Armando tonight, right?" Ton asked.

"Yeah."

"That's what I figured. See if you can't bring back a bottle."

"Of what? Tequila? Pulque? Whiskey?" I asked.

"We ain't choosy. Whatever you can snatch up'll be fine."

José hadn't been out for more'n maybe fifteen minutes when we heard three pistol shots. It's strange how flat a handgun sounds on the open prairie — it's more like a loud snap than a report. But fire a Colt

.45 in a closed room an' it'll blow out your eardrums. Ton was building up the fire when José rode back in with four rabbits tied together with a strip of latigo and hung from his saddle horn. "I didn't hear but three shots," I said.

For the first time that day, José's face lost its flintiness and his mouth formed a half-smile. "I got two singles," he said. "The other two musta just been married an' was on their honeymoon, 'cause they only took one bullet to drop 'em both."

The sky to the north an' east had started to darken up, an' the grayish-dark clouds were rolling about like water at a hard boil. The breeze picked up, too. After a bit, we could smell the fresh scent of rain. "We might best clean and cook those rabbits," I said, " 'cause our fire isn't gonna last long when the rain hits."

We did just that, skinning and cleaning out the hares an' skewering them on sticks over the fire. It was dark by then an' the lightning lit up the whole sky to the north with that white light one sees when a daguerreotypist or photographer sets off his flash powder. Ton said he seen ball lightning once, leaping from horn to horn on a big herd of half-wild Texas beef. It started a hell of a stampede, Ton said, and it fried a few cows right where they stood. I can't say that I'm partial to lightning, an' never have been since I was a kid.

My Pa tol' me when I was a wee one that lightnin' was God hurling burnin' spears at little boys who touched their privates an' pleasured themselves. I proved that wasn't true 'cause I never got struck, but the idea still scared me a little.

Ton and José rigged up a little shelter of branches that may or may not have been better'n nothin', dependin' on how strong the wind got. I pulled on my slicker, saddled Jake — who wasn't fond of lightning and thunder and was a bit jumpy — and rode out toward Santa Lucia. The wind had more teeth to it and I felt a few stinging drops of rain. Jake danced a bit, shakin' his head an' snorting, but I was able to hold him in OK.

The temperature had dropped like a whore's drawers. Back a couple of days I woulda guaranteed that I'd never be cold again. I was wrong. I was shiverin' within a half-hour since I left our camp.

I held Jake to a fast walk, which was easier to say than it was to do. Horses have a natural fear of lightning. It takes a good number of them every year, both mustangs an' owned stock. Out on a prairie a horse might well be the tallest thing around, an' lightning chooses the tallest thing to lay into. Even if Jake hadn't been actin' up, I wouldn't have let him move faster. The prairie grass got slicker'n snot on a doorknob when wet, an' it was as dark as the inside of a buried coffin.

I got to thinkin' about Anna. Fact is, I wasn't sure whether she was dead or alive. I'd seen her a few days back, but that didn't mean nothin'. I wondered what kinda treatment she'd been getting. It didn't make sense for the Hunters to mark her up, since the Mexicans don't have the fear of Indians whites do, an' she could bring a good price from the whoremasters. That didn't mean that the whole gang hadn't been usin' her. That kinda thing didn't leave marks that'd show.

That picture in my mind tightened me up, set my teeth to grindin', an' made me forget about bein' shiverin' cold. The thought of my woman with those murderous pigs made my thoughts all fast an' red, trippin' over each other, each image worse'n the one before it. It wasn't just raw anger, either. I admitted to myself right then an' there that I loved Anna. A man is supposed to protect his woman, an' I was doin' a piss-poor job of that. Hell, if it hadn't been for Ton, I'd be dead. An' ever since we'd been trackin' those sonsabitches, we hadn't killed but a handful of them, an' they still had Anna.

I felt like I let her down, an' maybe I had. A mad rush — an attack at night, maybe — might could have gotten me into the Hunters' camp an' maybe I could have swept her onto Jake behind me . . . .Shit. It couldn't happen, 'specially since Ton had gotten me an' José out. A surprise like that don't work but once, an' we already used up our once. What bothered me is that I hadn't tried it earlier, hadn't charged in an' come outta the camp with my woman on my horse behind me.

Anna moved to the window an' looked out at the street. She was naked an' unashamed an' a right fine sight. A dog — a big an' young fella — trip-tropped down the middle of the street like he owned the town. Anna laughed an' I went to the window an' watched the dog with her. His tongue was hangin' out the side of his mouth.

Anna moved closer to me. "I like dogs," she said. "I always did. My people ate dog, but even as a child I would not. One day I'll have two — no, three or four dogs — and I'll treat them right."

The rain hit with full force right then an' I was jerked outta that hotel room an' brought back to where I was — in the middle of a damned ragin' storm, freezin' my ass off, an' almost bein' blowed outta my saddle by a howling wind.

Jake didn't like it anymore than I did, and his instincts told him to run. For the most parts, instincts are right — but in this one, it was way wrong. If I'd given him his head he'd run hard an' either bust a leg or go down 'cause of the slippery grass an' mud, maybe on top of me if I didn't push off fast enough. I never use a high-port bit — the ones that give the rider almost enough leverage to crush the horse's jaw. I favor a low-port piece that lets Jake know what I want from him without hittin' over the head with a fence post. We argued some, but Jake gave in.

I'd seen one of them shows in Dodge in a whorehouse where for a penny you crank a handle an' a bunch of cards flip, makin' it look like the people were movin' an' throwin' balls, an' so forth. It was worth the penny; in truth I did it maybe five or six times. My point here is that the lightning was so frequent an' close that it made everything like that card show — a tumbleweed would blow by but it didn't roll smooth — I'd see it once an' then in the next second again, but it'd moved along its way.

Holdin' Jake in was no easy task, but I managed it. I'd planned to leave him staked a good distance from Tranquila and go on in on foot, but the storm changed my plans. For one thing, I doubt there was ever made a stake stout enough to hold Jake back if he was to panic. He groundties good, but not in these conditions.

I got to the livery. I had to do that or give up the trip, 'cause there was no place safe for Jake but in a stall or with me on his back. The ol' geezer who ran the place was settin' just inside the open front end of his barn, smokin' his pipe.

"I gotta leave my horse with you for a bit. You got any problems with that?"

"Can you pay, Bronc Man?"

"Yep."

"I got no problems, then. Slide him into an open stall in the back."

I led Jake to a back stall, the fresh, earthy scent of the good hay baled on the open loft drifting down to me, the smell of leather and horses and muscle liniment surrounding me. I loosened my cinches but didn't pull the saddle. I tossed a flake of hay into the box stall with Jake and went up to the front of the barn again. I could hear the out-of-tune jangling of the piano in the cantina as I approached the old man. "Look," I said, "it might be better for everyone if you forgot I was ever here."

"Es verdad. When you ride with the Night Hunters you ride with the devil, no? An' if you did come back, you don' care for anyone to know, es correct?" He drew on his pipe and it made a wet, gurgling sound. "I should smoke horseshit 'stead of the tobacco the puta at the store sells to me."

"Might smell better," I said. "You know why I'm here?"

"Si. Your friend, he is dead?"

"No. We escaped clean."

"Bueno. Es good."

There was a long silence. We watched the lightning burning holes in the sky. Finally, I asked, "Can you handle a rifle?"

"Like a mama handles a bambino. But I can does no mean I will."

"Suppose I got enough men together from here and from Santa Lucia to bring down the Hunters when they bring in their women to Santa Lucia?"

He didn't answer for a moment. "I will only say this, get enough men and guns and will do a battle with the Night Hunters — but only then."

"Fair enough," I said.

The rain was driving down, sweeping the length of the street like an impenetrable curtain. The cantina was the only place showing light, and even that was obscured by the downpour. There were five or six horses tied to the hitching rail in the front of the cantina, dripping water, dancing an' snorting when the thunder crashed. I wondered why they didn't bolt an' then saw that each mount was hobbled. That's no way to treat a horse.

I went back through the livery barn an' out the door. It was like stepping into a flood — the rain hit me so hard it was like a punch in the face, and the wind whipped at my duster, flapping it around me. A shimmering bolt of lightning showed me that the way to Armando's house was clear, an' I was just about ready to make a run to it, when I saw the figure of a man standing hunched in the rain maybe ten feet off to the side of the house. I waited for another bolt an' when it came, I saw the figure was holding a rifle.

I made a big loop from the back of the livery barn, squishing through the mud, battered by the rain an' wind, an' came up behind the lookout. I waited for another burst of thunder and then shot him down. I don't much care to fight like that, but there wasn't no way around it that I could see. It wasn't like I was fighting against men who had a cause they believed in, but shooting down blood-thirsty animals who thought nothin' of killing anyone in their path. If that was wrong, then I was wrong, too, but that didn't make a speck of difference to me.

I didn't have time to stand outside an' knock on Armando's door, so I shoved it open and stepped right in. I found myself facing a pair of gaping maws of a double-barreled shotgun aimed about chest high at me. If Armando had fired either or both barrels at me, he'd have blown me all over his door. He didn't.

There was a small candle in a glass globe flickering on the table in front of Armando, an' a bottle of tequila an' a glass. Tia, I saw, was huddled down where Ton had lain while recovering from the poisoned slug. She glared at me an' made the sign of the cross.

Armando brought both hammers of the twelve-gauge back to rest and put the shotgun down on the table, still pointed at me and at the door. I pulled the door shut and got the hell out of the way.

"Montclaire trusts no one," Armando said. "He has posted a lookout outside to watch me and my amigos. He may have seen you."

I shook my head. "He didn't, an' he's

never goin' to see anything again."

Armando nodded. "Sit," he said. I moved to the table an' took a chair to Armando's left side — I wasn't about to sit across from him with that shotgun pointing at me. That sort of thing makes me a tad nervous, be the weapon cocked or uncocked.

Armando pushed the glass and the bottle over to me. I didn't really care for a drink jus' then, but I took one anyway. Fact is, I needed this man an' I didn't want to do anything that might show a lack of courtesy or disrespect to him. His eyes, almost black in the poor light, pinned me. He didn't look real happy to see me.

"You endanger both Tranquila and Santa Lucia, Cal," he said. "Killing the lookout was stupid. You've declared war on the Night Hunters — although I guess you'd already made that clear to them."

"I think it's real clear to Montclaire and his boys," I said. "I dunno how me an' Ton an' José could make it any more apparent." Armando's gaze didn't soften an' it didn't move away from me. I poured myself a couple of inches of tequila and slugged it down, as much to have something to do with my hands and as a way to break our eye contact as anything else.

"The reason I came tonight is that . . ."

"I know why you're here," Armando interrupted. "Do you take me for a fool? You want me to use my position in Tranquila to put together an army to battle the Night Hunters." He shook his head slowly from side to side. "They are killers, murderers, rapists, pillagers. My people are simple farmers and laborers. They know nothing of war, of fighting. What kind of ragtag group could I assemble? Yet you come here to me and in doing so you kill a Hunter, and for that they will kill two of us — two of my people."

There was a lot of anger in Armando's voice. I didn't answer him right away. "How many of your people will be killed whether or not they fight?" I asked. "Anybody who gets in the way, correct? Armando — you yourself have told me that this happens year after year. You don't know when they're coming in an' when they do there's hell to pay. And the women — what about the women who are sold off here like cattle to the highest bidder?"

Armando stood and moved behind his chair, his hands gripping the top of it, his posture military-straight. "If you fight the Night Hunters and somehow win, you ride off with your woman, Ton and José get their revenge, and your battle is over. But us —

we bear the brunt of the Hunters' wrath long after you're gone."

"Not if there isn't enough of them to be a force, Armando. That's my point. These aren't brave men. They're backshooters and deserters and cowards. If we can drop enough of them in Santa Lucia, the rest will fade away like smoke from a dying fire. And you'd best believe that the other killer bands out there will hear of what happened here, and they won't come."

"These things are easy to say. No matter what happens, you will be out of it. You'll either be dead or be with your woman. You don't know the Hunters. You don't know the other bands of killers. Talk is cheap, Cal. Blood is not."

I poured myself another inch of tequila and felt it burn its way down my throat and into my gut. "Everything is set for the day after tomorrow. I'll be there an' so will José an' Ton. We'll give the Hunters the best fight we can, but . . ." I let the sentence die. There wasn't much to add to the words left hanging in the air.

Armando sighed quietly. "This I can do: talk with some of my people — my amigos. I make no promises. Is understood?" I nodded. "Bueno."

"Fair enough," I said. "I have one more

favor to ask. Can you get .45 an' .30-.30 ammunition to the second story of the church in Santa Lucia sometime tomorrow? As much of it as your general store has?"

"Our mercantile is small, without large amounts of stock. I will do the best I can. But why will you fight from the church?"

"A couple of reasons. From the higher vantage point, I'll be able to use my Sharps to bring down some of the Hunters as they ride in. Plus, there are windows on all four sides of the loft — we can move about quickly, firing where we need to. This is good, too — there's a single stairway that leads to the second story, the loft. That'll be easy enough to protect."

"And the fact that the church is the house of God means nothing to you?"

I met Armando's stare. "Not a damned thing, my friend. Not a damned thing."

I left Armando's house and pushed out into the still-raging storm. I remembered approximately where I'd shot the lookout an' I stood still, lettin' the lightning light things up for me. Sure enough — there was his body. I grabbed him by his boots an' dragged him after me back to the livery. He skidded along right nice; the mud was slick an' watery an' just right for pullin' a dead body along. I put the outlaw outside the back door of the barn an' then fought the wind to the front. The ol' man was still settin' there suckin' on his pipe. I got in outta the rain.

"What do I owe you for puttin' up my horse?" I asked.

He ignored my question. "Armando goin' to help you boys out, come day afta tomorrow?"

"I don't know. Hard to say right now."

His wrinkled old face took on a slight flush of anger that stood out in the light of his lantern. "Git your horse an' skedaddle, son. You ain't never been here."

I nodded. I had one more question, and I didn't really want to ask it, but I did. "You don't happen to have a bottle of red-eye around, do you? Me an' Ton an' José could use a taste on a night like this."

He stood. His back was curved forward with a growth like a buffalo hump betwixt his shoulders. When he walked away I saw how bow-legged the old jasper was. He went into what must have been a tack room, cursed the darkness some, an' walked back out with a clear quart bottle with no label on it. He tossed it to me. I started to thank him but he waved me away. "Git your horse," he said.

I tightened my cinches an' led Jake out

the back door into the rain an' the wind an' lightning and thunder. That didn't make him real happy.

I wrapped my slicker around me as well as I could an' kinda hunched in the saddle, Stetson pulled way down in front of my face. It was gonna be a long damned ride, an' a wet an' cold one, to boot, even with the bottle I had to take a toot out of every so often.

My mind wandered free. For some reason I got to wonderin' if Anna was warm enough on such a foul night. I knew that was probably the tiniest of her worries, but the thought stayed with me, makin' me madder an' madder.

I thought a good bit about Ton an' José an' me in that church tryin' to hold off between twenty-five and thirty or so gunmen, an' I had to shake my head. It was a stupid damned plan, but it was all we had.

After what seemed like a few months in the saddle, Jake whinnied to Matthew an' José's horse, an' I was able to ride in guided by the little fire they had goin'. They'd spread their slickers over the top of the lean-to they'd built an' I saw they'd reinforced the half-assed little shelter with some larger cottonwood branches. It wasn't much, but it beat hell outta sittin' out in the rain.

Both of them were lookin' glum, cold, an' miserable. I tossed the bottle to Ton an' both their faces lit up considerable.

I led Jake into the scanty cover the trees provided from the rain an' pulled his saddle, carryin' it to the lean-to with me. I made a promise to myself that I owed Jake a double ration of good feed with a few dollops of molasses mixed into it for his work this night.

I sat as close to the fire as I could get without burnin' myself an' told the boys about everything that happened an' everything that'd been said.

The bottle got empty pretty fast an' we did our best to get some sleep.

CHAPTER TEN

The next morning the sun shone as if there'd never been a storm. Dry wood was hard to come by, but we found some branches and kindling that weren't too damp and made up a fire to brew coffee.

We decided to spend the day where we were and, at dark, head for Santa Lucia. We knew there'd be guards out, so we planned to go in one at a time, stash our horses at the livery, and then hightail it to the church. We'd gone all over that, an' it became obvious to the three of us that the church was our best point of attack when the Hunters rode in with the women and the best place to defend until the battle went one way or another.

The three of us realized but didn't speak of the fact that there was an awful good chance we'd be killed by the outlaws — that the odds against us couldn't be much worse.

The day heated up in a hurry. We lazed

about in the copse, cleaning and oiling our weapons, drinkin' coffee, not sayin' a whole lot. I went out on foot midday an' fetched back a pair of fat rabbits. Ton cooked 'em nice an' they made a good meal.

After we ate we built cigarettes. José was kinda starin' off into the distance an' at first, he didn't say much. But, when he got rollin' it was like a dam busted open — the words chased after one another, as if he couldn't talk fast enough to say what he wanted to say. He didn't look directly at us. I guess watching the embers of the fire burn out an' lose their white an' orange color was more comfortable for him.

"I have killed uno short of a dozen hombres in gunfights," he began.

That kind of jolted me because it came from nowhere. We weren't talking about killing or gunfights — in fact, we weren't talking at all just then. Anyway, José got our attention in one big hurry.

"My first," José went on, "was when I was a niño — maybe fourteen years of age. My people — mi familia — dropped me with a tia an' tio when I was but a bambino. My tio — my uncle — was a cruel son of a beech who used the hickory stick too often. My work was like that of the black slaves in Los Estados. As I grew older he began us-

322

ing his fists and boots on me when he thought I sassed him or was slackin' off in my work. My tia, he hit her with his fists, too."

José rolled a smoke and I noticed that he was shaky, spreading good tobacco on the ground. He got the cigarette made, though, and picked a twig out of the fire to light it.

"One day, my uncle, he beat me for not cooling down his draft horse. We kept an ol' muzzle-loader in the barn for snakes. I killed him with it, no? Just as I had snakes. Now he rots in hell." José took a deep drag of his cigarette and exhaled the smoke.

"I liked pulling the trigger." He pronounced the word 'treeger.' "I took his best horse an' his Colt an' I — how do you say? — practiced all the time. You see, no? I found I liked the kill, the taking lives."

He paused again before going on. "I never had no amigos — an' I never wanted none. Maybe I be killed by the Night Hunters, but I cut many of those gordos — those peegs — down, no?"

"Sounds like maybe you done the right thing, José," I said. "It ain't for me or Ton to say that your uncle didn't have it coming to him."

José ignored my comment. "I like pullin' the treeger on an hombre. La morte — the death of otra hombres, it keeps me alive."

The three of us were silent for a long moment. Then José continued. "I kill one of Quantrill's pistoleros in a fair fight, but Quantrill, he don' like his men bein' killed, 'less he does it. Quantrill, he's been after me like the pero after a bone."

I wondered where José was going with all this. "I tell you boys this: I keel the Night Hunters for you an' then I ride on. Don' theenk we are amigos. I am a machina de morte — a machine of death."

"Fair enough," I said. Ton nodded. "OK with me," he said.

José went over to where the horses were staked an' swung up on his mount bareback an' jogged off.

"Crazy as a goddamn bedbug," Ton said.

I saw no reason to disagree with him.

"I never met a man who would say he enjoys killin', Cal. I knew a couple, three fellas who come back from the war an' said they had no problem with takin' down blue-bellies, but José is different." Ton's forehead wrinkled a bit as he looked at me, an' something or other was rollin' about in his head. He looked away from me an' said quietly, "Can you take him, Cal? Are you faster an' better? 'Cause it seems to me if we get into the Hunters' script an' gold,

José ain't gonna want to share with us."

I pondered that for a moment, but not a very long moment. "I'll say this, Ton," I said. "There ain't a gunman who can't be beat. I can be beat — but not by José. I suspect he handles a rifle good an' a pistol even better, but I don't see in him what I seen in men I knew could take me. Earp — Wyatt, that is, not them brothers of his — coulda dropped me, an' maybeso that crazy Doc he ran 'round with. Cassidy might have matched me. But all of them, they were crazy in a different way than José is."

"I don't know what you mean," Ton said.

"Well, Earp an' Doc an' Cassidy wanted to stay alive, is my take on it. They was fighters, but they wanted to hold onto their lives. José, I think, is lookin' to die. You ever look close into his eyes, Ton? There's nobody in there — nobody who gives a good damn about anything or anyone. That's where I think my advantage is. I wanta live, an' run a spread with Anna, an' raise some horses, an' sleep every night with my hand on Anna's ass, 'stead of on my pistol under my pillow."

" 'Cause you want somethin' don't mean you're going to get it, Cal," Ton said.

"Maybe not. But wantin' somethin' as bad as I want Anna might just give me that speck of time I could need to drop José. But, it doesn't make sense talkin' like that. Me an' José got nothin' to tangle about."

"Well, that's true enough," Ton said. "An' right at this time we got a man to fight with us against Night Hunters, right?"

"Sure."

"Then let's let it set the way it is."

"Fine," I said. "Let's do that."

Our plan was a simple one. Like I said, that night we'd slide into Santa Lucia separately an' leave our horses at the livery. Then we'd go to the church an' make the loft as secure as we could. After that, we'd wait 'til the Hunters came into town with the women an' set to takin' as many of them down as we could. We'd either kill most of them or they'd kill us. That's the way it is sometimes: there's not much that's complicated about men shootin' guns at one another.

It was maybe a half hour when Jose came back from his ride. Apparently he'd been thinking about the coming battle.

"That church ain't bad — with the thick walls an' all. The Hunters, they cannot burn us out. Maybe the pews on the first floor will burn, but nothing else." He grinned, but it was like the grin of an executioner. "We say 'Gracias, Dios Mio' with each

Hunter we kill, no?"

José settled himself on his haunches and rolled a cigarette. "You see the cross that's cut in the front wall of the loft, no?" he said.

Tom and I nodded.

"The padre who served there had it cut as a symbolica. But it's better than a window for us, 'cause we can shoot up, down, an' to either side an' still be covered good. You see? Jesus is good to us, no?"

"I didn't think of that," I said. "Good point."

"It's a good place to make a stand," Ton said.

"The only big problem is the stairs leading to the loft an' that door. It's the only real way the Hunters have at getting right to us, an' we'll need to have one of us watchin' it all the time," I said.

"The door any good?" Ton asked.

"No. It's a flimsy thing a strong man could spit through."

"Them pews could be good cover at the head of the stairs," José said. "All we gotta do is haul some up the stairs an' pile them in front of the door."

Ton stood and stretched. "How 'bout one of you goin' out an' bring back some dinner? I'm a mite tired of rabbit, but it beats hell outta starvin'."

"I'll do that," I said, getting to my feet. I wasn't awful hungry, but sittin' around talkin' was makin' me antsy. I didn't see much sense in debating a battle we really couldn't control. How the Hunters came at us — in a mass, or from behind cover — was somethin' we couldn't predict, an' chewin' on it too long didn't accomplish anything.

It was still very hot an' the ground seemed to be radiating the heat it absorbed back upward. I lifted my Colt a couple of inches above my holster an' then released it, letting it settle itself.

The sun had begun its downward arc, but I was walkin' to the east so the glare didn't bother me. I'd never been much of a walker, figurin' that pretty much everything that needed doin' could be done from the back of a good horse. Still, I was enjoyin' the quiet an' the fact that I was alone with my thoughts — which, of course, were about Anna.

I'd never before given much thought to dyin'. Whether a man bleeds out on a battlefield or croaks in his home in his own bed didn't make much difference: He was equally dead either way. But now there was somethin' added to that thought. I was no longer responsible for only my own self — I had Anna to look after an' care for an' I couldn't do that if I was dead. Ever since Ton found me crawlin' around in Busted Thumb after the Hunter raid, I'd devoted my life to getting Anna free an' livin' out my life with her. That felt good to think about, an' I turned the thought over an' around in my mind, savorin' it like a kid with a peppermint stick.

What stepped on those mind-pictures was the treatment Anna was no doubt getting at the hands of the Hunters. If it hadn't been for me an' Ton an' José, she'd be sold like a horse or a milk cow the next day an' put into a whorehouse 'til she got too old to bring in customers.

My hands began to sweat a bit as I tried to push that thought away. A rabbit popped out from behind a rock an' my draw was smooth an' fast in spite of my damp palm. I put the hare down with a single head shot. He was good sized, but I'd need at least one more to feed the three of us. I took the second one maybe ten minutes later. When I picked that second rabbit up, his fur was warm in my hand an' the coppery smell of blood hung about him. I stood there with a dead rabbit in my hands an' another at my feet in the dirt until the warmth of life seeped out of the second hare.

"Well, hell," I said aloud to no one, "might just as well get to it."

Like Ton had said, we were weary of rabbit meat, but that didn't stop us from eatin' the two I brought back. We sat back smokin' an' drinkin' coffee without sayin' much, watchin' the little fire go to embers an' then begin to die. It seemed like the sun was kinda stuck in position, an' was goin' down awful slow. Eventually darkness came, but it was a long time comin'.

I'd told Ton an' José that I'd go into town first an' they didn't question that or have a problem with it. There was a half-moon, an' it gave some light. I saddled Jake an' climbed aboard an' was off to Santa Lucia. I hadn't mentioned to the others that I wanted to do a bit of shoppin' before I holed up in the church, 'cause Ton sure as hell would have wanted to come along.

About a mile out of town I was able to see a riderless horse cropping grass at the side of the road. I slumped in my saddle an' began singin' loud an' off-key, which isn't hard at all for me. The lookout was standin' about ten or so yards down the road from his horse.

"Shut the hell up, you son . . ."

I straightened, drew, an' put a round into his throat. The sound of a gunshot — if it

330

even carried to town — wouldn't raise any interest there.

I heard the out-of-tune piano before I saw any of the few lights in Santa Lucia. I let Jake pick his own way on the rutted road at a walk. I wasn't in a hurry.

When I walked down the central aisle of the livery barn the livery owner didn't seem surprised to see me. I handed him a twenty-dollar gold piece. "I've got two others comin' to leave their horses here," I said.

He took the gold piece from me. "I'm headin' to the cantina," he said. "Them Hunters can't hold me responsible for what happens in my barn when I ain't here, right? An' I'll be there with the drunks an' gunmen from now 'til early mornin'. I imagine I'll get drunk an' pass out by the cantina, is what'll happen. The Hunters'll see me there."

I watched him scurry off. I figured there'd be a lookout close by to Armando's house, just as there had been the last time. So I went out the back of the barn and circled back to the rear of the buildings on the main street. I heard the sound of retching several buildings beyond where I stood. I figured it was a Hunter who'd taken on too much of a load of pulque or whatever and was getting rid of it. After another eruption he went back into the cantina.

The mercantile — and the other buildings — had loading doors in the rear. The mercantile's was secured with a cheap hasp lock and the plate it was attached to was rotted wood — I could see that much even in the pale moonlight. I got my hand tight on the lock and pulled the whole assembly away. The door swung open, as if welcoming me.

I found myself in a dark storage room, which is precisely where I wanted to be. I tugged the door shut and then struck a lucifer. The ammunition was piled in wooden boxes against one wall, along with some farming equipment. I picked up a box of .30-.06s and two boxes of .45s. There was another, smaller box by the farm supplies and I picked that up, too. I looked for loads for my Sharps but didn't find any and didn't really expect to. There weren't enough of the rifles around for a store owner to purchase ammunition for them. There was some weight to the load I was carrying, and I was beginning to feel like a pack animal by the time I reached the church. I thought the front door was probably not locked, or at least I gambled that it wasn't and sprinted up to it, balancing my boxes. The door swung open easily with a nudge from my shoulder.

The dark church smelled like candle wax and incense, just as all the churches I'd ever been in did. I hustled to the stairs and onto the loft and put my boxes in the middle of the room. Every sound — my boots hitting the floor, the creaking of the stairs — seemed as loud as thunder inside the church. I sat away from a window, built a cigarette, and smoked it down to a nub before immediately lighting another one.

Ton was the next one into the church. He didn't make any more damned noise than a bull buffalo would have, but there was no one but me to hear it. Ton started across the floor toward me and almost tripped over the supply of ammunition. He looked closely at the boxes an' grinned. "You done good, Cal," he said. "I was kinda thinkin' of bustin' into the store, myself. I'm hopin' we can fire every last round into a Hunter." He paused for a moment. "You didn't happen to pick up some booze now, did you?"

"I already had too much to carry, Ton."

"A bottle don't weigh much."

"Dammit, Ton — it ain't the weight. Where the hell was I going to put a bottle with all I had to carry?"

"I'll tell you right where you can put it," Ton said. After a second we both started laughing. It felt good.

José showed up maybe an hour later. "Killed a lookout on my way in," he said. "Too much cerveza and pulque — he could hardly stand up."

We sat there for a century or so. It became real apparent that the piano player didn't know but three songs: "Buffalo Skinners," "O Susanna," and "Texas Boys." Even then, knowin' those songs, he couldn't play them worth a damn. While it was still light, we saw men who didn't look like they belonged in Santa Lucia, some of them dressed fancy like bankers, riding good stock, with saddles carryin' a lot of silver decorations. Some were gringos and some were Mex. A couple of two-horse covered wagons had pulled in, too. "Whore buyers," José said.

I dozed some, an' so did Ton. Fact is, his snorin' woke me up. I hadn't gotten to any kind of good sleep, anyway. I was tense an' nervous an' . . . what? Scared? If I was scared, it wasn't 'cause I might get my ass shot off in a few hours, but fear that if I were killed, Anna's life would be pretty much over, as well.

I remembered talkin' with a friend after he'd come home from the war, minus a foot that'd been cut clean off by canister shot. He told me that on the night of the second day at Gettysburg, there probably wasn't a Rebel who got a minute's sleep. Rumors were scampering around that Bobby Lee was going to try a head-on charge at the stone wall the Yanks were behind. My friend said they all knew it was a damn fool move, an' most suspected Pickett knew that, too. For one thing, it was a big, open field goin' up a grade with not a bit of cover once the boys were on that field. He said the air was jus' buzzin' with the men's nerves, feelin' like the sensation just before lightning strikes close by — that edgy, jagged, scary feeling.

José was settin' next to me rollin' a cigarette with hands as steady as could be, an' like I said, Ton was sleepin'. I figured it was my own nerves actin' up an' that Ton an' José knew a fight was coming but couldn't do anything about that 'cept fight when the time was right. That doesn't mean they didn't think about it, but that they knew what was gonna happen was gonna happen, so why waste time studyin' on it?

I kinda faded out for a time, but the raucous, pre-dawn racket from a rooster nearby woke me. I never saw any sense to havin' one of those damn things around, but maybe that's jus' me. So, I went to the window and watched that damned fool bird standin' atop a backyard chicken coop, raisin' hell with that screechy, ear-splitting racket.

He'd have been a fair to middlin' pistol shot, but there was no wind to make a slug wander, an' I was sure I could do it. I didn't, though. Instead, I stood at the window watchin' Santa Lucia come awake. There wasn't much to see: some women were fetching water at the well, and I heard the clang of a heavy hammer against an anvil from the livery.

I think that's what woke Ton up. It must have been one of the most familiar sounds in the world to him. José woke, too, stood, an' stretched. I backed away from the window and José an' Ton took my place, as if a big parade or circus was comin' by right outside. They didn't see any more than I did. José stayed at the window, but after a bit, Ton went to our supplies an' ate some jerky an' washed it down with water.

Ton was about to say something when José said, "Here they come." He said it calmly, like a man would say, "Looks like rain." I went to take a look, an' so did Ton. José was right: There was a brown cloud of dust risin' a few miles out of town, an' whatever was makin' it was comin' this way.

Even though it was still early, some of the

fancy-dressed men began to gather at the cantina, standin' around out in front, smokin' those long, thin cigars gamblers an' whoremasters tend to favor. Every so often a laugh or a loud voice would carry up to us.

A half-dozen Night Riders came to the cantina on sweated horses an' kinda looked things over. They talked real briefly with some of the buyers an' then rode back out the same way they'd come from. In another twenty minutes or so a good-sized Conestoga wagon rolled into sight, pulled by a pair of stout draft horses. There were four riders in a line maybe fifty feet ahead of the wagon and two on each side of it. Behind, eating dust, were about twenty men, spread out in a ragged line. Each carried a rifle in one hand rather than in the scabbards on their saddles.

The driver of the wagon had bandoliers of ammunition draped both ways 'cross his chest an' a shotgun rested across his lap. Next to him on the driver's seat was Danny Montclaire, his various badges an' ribbons an' brass buttons shining in the early morning sun. I left the window and unrolled my Sharps from its deerhide wrap. It would have been a ridiculously easy shot to put an end to Montclaire right there an' then, an' I sighted in on him from the window but hadn't cocked the rifle. That wasn't the way I wanted to take him down.

The Conestoga pulled up in front of the cantina. Montclaire climbed down an' Hunters moved about, positioning themselves all around the wagon, some aboard their horses, an' some on foot. Montclaire walked through the batwings like he owned the cantina, an' the buyers who'd gathered followed him inside.

"What's goin' on?" Ton asked.

"Dealin'," José said. "The sonsabitches are talkin' price. They do this every time they have whores to sell."

"But," Ton protested, "them buyers ain't even seen the . . ."

"They will," José cut Ton off.

I had to walk away from the window. I'd seen a slave auction in Natchez one time, an' I didn't think a whole lot about it. I figured that's how blacks are bought an' sold. I wondered why the women — an' some of the men, too — were carryin' on an' cryin' about their families being busted up an' sold off. The slavers said that the blacks didn't feel nothing like whites do. Right here in Santa Lucia I knew how those blacks felt about their people bein' sold. Nobody ever called me an abolitionist before. I guess now they'd have to, 'cause that's what I am. I been right where those slave men were. The only difference is that I could do somethin' about what was happenin', an' they couldn't.

It was getting hot in the church loft. Nothing was happening on the street except that the guards around the wagon were passing a bottle around. "We should get some of those pews jammed into the stairway," I said. "How about one of us watchin' the street and the two others carry pews? We can switch off every so often."

The pews were long an' heavy an' made from some sort of wood that had been polished so often that it felt a tad greasy. The stairway wasn't wide an' it wasn't hard to block. Me an' José hauled three of the pews up into the loft, an' then jammed as many others as we could into the stairway. The three we'd brought up to the loft we piled right at the doorway. It wasn't the best blockade in the world but it'd sure slow Hunters down if they tried to attack us from inside the church. We'd just finished that job when Ton called us to the window.

Montclaire had walked out to the Conestoga with a group of buyers taggin' after him. He went to the rear of the wagon, lit himself a cigar, got it goin' good, and then pulled the tarp that was coverin' the rear of the wagon aside. He said somethin' we couldn't hear an' motioned the women inside to come out.

There were thirteen of them. They were roped together at the waist with maybe three feet of rope between each of them. Anna was the third one out. Montclaire directed them to stand in a line an' the buyers approached them like cowhands do a horse auction, lookin' for the best stock.

The women didn't look good at all. They must have spent a good deal of time inside that wagon where it'd be pretty dark 'cause they were rubbin' their eyes an' walkin' unsteadily. They were dirty — we could see that from where we watched — an' their hair was all matted and wet with sweat. They — regardless of their actual skin color — were a pasty white, like a person looks after a battle with a long fever. They were dressed in whatever they were wearin' when they were carried off, an' for some of them, that didn't amount to much at all.

The buyers walked slowly up an' down the line, stopping to look at a face, or to lift a blouse or shirt to inspect a woman's breasts. Some were told to hike up their dresses to their waists so the buyers could get a better look at the commodity they were after.

My hand was sweating against the stock of my Sharps, an' I could feel a sort of trembling all through my body. A buyer stopped in front of Anna an' reached down to lift her dress.

"You boys ready?" I asked.

"I been ready for a long time," Ton said.

"Si. I am ready," José said.

My first shot took the buyer who'd been lookin' over Anna in the chest an' tossed him maybe four or five feet, into the middle of the street. The roar of the Sharps in that loft was godawful loud — so loud, in fact, that I could see José next to me firin' his rifle but couldn't hear the reports over the ringin' in my ears.

The Hunters an' the buyers scurried for cover either on the other side of the wagon or in the cantina. The women were left where they stood, cowerin', hands to their faces.

José was doin' a nice job pickin' off those who were tryin' to make it to the cantina, dropping a pair directly in front of the batwings so that others would have to jump or climb over the bodies.

Hunters put lead into the air real quick, slugs pounding the adobe walls around the window. A round hissed past my ear and buried itself into the wall across the room from me. I stepped back to load my Sharps an' Ton took my place, keepin' his head as low as he could an' still draw a bead on a target.

I went to one of them crosses I told about before — the one over the entrance to the front of the church. The vantage point wasn't as good, but I was able to place some shots.

The Night Hunters were as crazy a bunch of killers as could be found anywhere. They were bloodthirsty, sadistic, and had no regard for human life whatsoever. But, they knew fighting. Their return fire was withering, spraying the church, blowing fist-sized chunks of adobe from the outside walls, an' lots of their rounds were making it through our window. I crossed the loft as I reloaded, heading for the window on the opposite side. It's a good thing that I did: two Hunters were runnin' hell for leather to the church, hopin' to take us from the inside. I put a bullet through one Hunter's head an' took the other one with a chest shot. My slug must've caught one of the shotgun shells in the bandolier across his upper body, 'cause there was a flash like that of a gun's muzzle an' of a sudden, the Hunter's legs from the knees down were red pulp.

I hustled back to the window Ton and José were firing through. It was hotter'n hell up there an' the gunsmoke was so thick it was hard to see across the loft. The right side of my face was smartin' some an' in a couple of places was torn right open. The blow-back from a Sharps will do that, particularly when the rifle has been firing rapidly.

When José ducked back to reload his .30-.06 I took his place. Several Hunters had run out of the cantina and dashed to the wagon, diving through the canvas and into it. I thought it was a damned fool move. My rifle could shoot through a whole lot more than wooden side panels, an' I didn't doubt that our smaller rifles an' maybe even our .45s could reach through that wood an' find itself an outlaw.

I sighted in on a fellow who'd just made it into the Conestoga an' squeezed off a round where I was pretty sure he'd be. Nothing happened — or at least nothing I expected. I fired again and again splinters of wood sprayed out from where the slug struck, but that was all. I wiped the grit an' tears from my eyes an' peered a bit closer. There was the glint of metal where I'd blown the wood away.

The sonsabitches had reinforced the wagon with steel plates.

The women were down in the dirt of the road, hands an' arms over their heads, not moving. If they were screaming, I couldn't hear it. My ears were buzzing an' ringing so loud I couldn't hear much of anything. More Hunters piled into the wagon, but more important than the number of them was what I saw as I watched: the barrels of rifles poking through the flimsy wood panels from the inside. Montclaire must have had holes bored the length of the steel plates, maybe figuring he'd get into a battle like this one. The gunfire from the wagon became heavier an' more accurate. The Hunters had time to take good aim rather than attempting lucky shots, an' they were taking advantage of that situation. The window we'd been using to fire through got useless in a fairly big hurry — the riflemen of the Hunters weren't even waiting for one of us to pop up an' shoot. They were keeping six or ten or whateverthehell number of bullets comin' through that window all the time. And this was bad: the way the Conestoga was positioned in the street in front of the cantina gave us a good view of one side of it an' the back end, but that was all. When it started to swing out into a long arc to bring it closer to the church, José shouted, "Shoot the horses! We can't let them get too close!"

I was down on the floor loading my rifle an' Ton had just finished putting rounds into the .30-.06 he was using. Our eyes met. Ton's were tearing from the acrid gunsmoke an' so were mine. "I ain't shootin' no horses, Cal," he shouted.

The fusillade through the window continued. Not one of the three of us could hear worth a damn, but we could shout into one another's ears. "I ain't shootin' no horses," Ton bellowed again.

I wasn't real happy about that, either. Plugging horses that were doin' not a damned thing but following orders from their driver went way the hell against my grain. Problem was that the Hunters had a bunch of boys in that impervious wagon, an' the closer they got to us, the more they poured bullets into the window.

José was shooting out the window, keeping his head as low as he could. Standing off to his side, feeding bullets into my Sharps, I saw the lead horse stop, stand stock-still for a moment, an' then drop to the ground. I guess maybe José was right. We had to stop that wagon from comin' in closer — our barricade of pews wouldn't make no difference at all, if there was enough Hunters getting into the church.

I'd been crouched an' loading my rifle, an' I put my hand on José's shoulder to tell him I was ready to move into the window space. Of a sudden, I felt a splash of somethin' warm an' grey on my hand and José fell backward, a not real big hole a bit above an' between his eyebrows. As he went down I saw a sight I never care to see again. The Hunters were shooting soft slugs — the ones that expand when they hit a man. The back part of José's head was blown out an' brain stuff an' pieces of skull splashed against the wall on the other side of the loft.

I stood at the window and saw that the Hunters had already cut the dead horse outta the harness an' reins an' gotten the other horse moving. A mule skinner with a long whip popped up every so often to keep the rig moving. He popped up once too often an' I put his lights out.

Things were happening quick down on the street. When the Conestoga blocked our sight of the women the Hunters must have dragged them to their feet an' herded them into the cantina. I saw the last two going through the batwings.

I had no choice. The horse didn't feel a thing — it was a clean, perfect shot. I hated to do it but I had no choice. The wagon was stopped, one side to us, about fifty feet from the church an' maybe a bit more. That was a long piece of ground for a man to cross when he had no cover an' was bein' shot at by a couple of fellas in good position with good cover.

It seemed like the hottest part of the day lasted a lifetime. There wasn't much shooting from the wagon, an' only an occasional round from the cantina. I was certain Montclaire had told his men in the wagon to sit tight until dark an' then make a run for the church. Once they were inside our pile of pews wouldn't stop them for long, an' both me an' Ton knew that.

We tried to avoid looking at José's body, but finally I dragged him away from where he'd fallen an' put him alongside the opposite wall. A metal locket fell from his vest pocket as I hefted up his hands to get a grip on him. "I ain't figured him out," Ton said, "but I guess he was doin' what he had to do, bein' here with us."

"Yeah," I said. I clicked open the locket with my thumbnail. Inside was a photograph of a woman's face and a couple inches of reddish-blonde hair. It was hard to make out the lady's features, but she seemed comely enough. I tossed the locket to Ton. "Could well be this was the reason," I told Ton. Ton looked at the photograph for a long time without speaking. Then, he clicked it shut, walked over to José, an' gently put the locket back into the dead man's vest pocket.

Each of us had brought a canteen, an' Ton an' I sipped at them for the balance of the afternoon. When ours were empty we drank from José's, but felt strange about doin' it. Still, we needed the water to kinda replace the buckets of sweat that soaked our shirts an' faces. Our only consolation was the fact that the Hunters — we figured maybe twenty men — jammed into that iron-plated wagon were probably hotter'n we were

As the sun began lowering, Montclaire appeared at the batwings for a moment, looked things over, and retreated again to the cantina. Not a minute later three men slammed through the doors, runnin' hard for the wagon. I stopped one with a single shot. Ton fired two rounds an' may have clipped one of the others. It was hard to say 'cause the back of the wagon was out of our line of sight.

Once it started to get beyond dusk, the darkness dropped like a shroud over Santa Lucia. That worried me. I'd figured on havin' the fightin' over by night, one way or another. A Hunter fired from the cantina and the muzzle flash seemed like a stroke of lightning 'cause there wasn't another light anywhere — not in the cantina, homes, or stores. The moon was new and there was so much cloud cover we could barely see the stars.

"They're gonna rush us soon, Ton," I said.

"Can we hold 'em off?"

"Not for long — we've got two guns against maybe twenty-five or thirty an' we're trapped up here like a couple of mice backed into a corner by a hungry cat."

"What do we do, then?"

"I'll show you," I said. I moved over to where our ammunition was stashed and tugged out the third wooden box I'd picked up at the mercantile. I used my boot knife to pry it open. In what little light there was, I could see the sticks of dynamite laid out in a nice, even row of three, resting atop another row of three. I picked up a pair of sticks, wrapped their fuses together to form a single strand, an' joined Ton at the window. I could see his teeth in the gloom when he smiled.

"Ain't you somethin'?" he said.

"I really didn't want to use this stuff," I said. "I didn't want to kill that horse, either. I don't see no way around it, though."

I held the dynamite out toward Ton. "Get back from the window, strike a lucifer an' get the fuse burnin', an' then get the hell outta my way."

I hefted the dynamite in my hand, feeling its weight. There was a waxiness to the wrapping and the sticks had a slightly chemical smell to them. I cocked my arm and said, "Light 'em."

The flare of the lucifer brought a couple of shots from the wagon. I waited until the dual fuses were sputterin' along good an' then leaned back and pitched the sticks. Like a clumsy fool, I ticked the dynamite against the side of the window, cutting the strength of my throw in half. The white burning of the fuse pointed at a place maybe a dozen feet from the wagon, struck the ground there, sputtered for a few seconds, an' then exploded. It was like opening the gates of hell.

A sheet of orange-red flame erupted upward, hurtling dirt and grit with the velocity of bullets. The sound was impossible to describe; it made the report of my Sharps sound like the mewing of a kitten.

Night Hunters piled out of the wagon an' charged toward the church. If my dynamite had gone where I wanted it to, the men rushing us an' shootin' at us would have been dead. There wasn't time to rig another pair of sticks — not even time to light and throw a single one. Me an' Ton shot down at the attackers, but the numbers made it impossible for us to even the odds.

A slug slammed into the barrel of my Sharps, ripping it from my hands and flinging it across the loft to bang off the wall. I grabbed up José's rifle as Ton moved away from the window to reload. "We're screwed," he said. I was about to agree when Santa Lucia seemed to light up with muzzle flashes — from Armando's home, from the well, from the houses. Hunters scrambled but had nowhere to go for cover but back to the wagon, an' they were bein' cut down by the hail of bullets. Several Hunters stampeded out of the cantina, which was a stupid move. Not a one of them took more than three steps before being dropped.

"Hot damn," Ton said, almost reverently.

I ran to the stairway an' began shoving and pulling pews outta my way. I climbed over a couple, heaved one ahead of me and clambered down the stairs, breaking through the last of the barricade. I shoved through the big oak doors an' hit the street runnin' to the cantina. I heard the moans of some of the men bleedin' out into the dirt of the road.

There was a light in the cantina now, but it didn't seem to be bright enough to be a lantern. I busted through the batwings an' saw the light was a candle, placed about halfway down the bar. Montclaire stood just outside the selfish splash of light the candle yielded, but his ridiculous medals reflected some of what little light there was.

The women were off to my right sittin' against the wall, tied again, it looked like. I couldn't give them more than a quick peek — I had a gunman standin' twenty feet from me, wantin' very bad to kill me.

The flame of the candle grew larger for a moment as a breeze touched it. The quick light showed Montclaire's eyes to me: they were glistening almost wetly, an' seemed to spit light back at me. "You're a tenacious son-of-a-bitch, I'll give you that much," he said. His voice was level with not even a tint of fear to it. I didn't trust my own voice not to quiver if I spoke, so I didn't.

"What's with you boys?" Montclaire said. "You want a woman or two? All you had to do was ask, maybe pay a few dollars. Whores are cheap."

I'd shifted my gaze from Montclaire's eyes to his hands. They hung quite naturally at his sides, the fingertips of his right hand just grazing the grips of his Colt. I swallowed a couple of times to generate some moisture in my mouth and said, "You an' your men are animals — disease-carrying animals. You killed my friend's wife. You stole my woman. You've killed and burned an' looted and now this is the end of it."

Montclaire chuckled and it didn't sound at all forced. "The end of it?" he asked. "Only if you're as good as you think you are. Those dead and injured men out there are real easy to replace."

I shifted my left foot back a few inches to steady my balance. I squeezed my right hand into a fist and then relaxed it. What began happening then is what's always happened to me when I faced a gunman: everything slowed way down. The flickering dance of the candle flame became sluggish, and its light seemed to travel more slowly around it. Even my breathing slowed. It was as if I'd been riding a galloping horse that suddenly slid to a stop and began a very slow walk.

Montclaire's right hand began a downward sweep to his pistol, but it seemed I had all kinds of time to match him, to beat him. He made a sound — like a low grunt — as he began his draw.

My Colt cleared leather as if it did so on its own, as if I had no control over what was happening in that cantina, like I was watching a scene on a stage play out. My first shot struck Montclaire just above his belt buckle. I kept cranking my trigger until the hammer snapped sharply on an empty cartridge and everything lurched back to normal speed.

I walked over to Montclaire. I'd hit him with all six rounds, mostly in his upper chest. His pistol hadn't quite left his holster when my first round found him. He was probably dead before he hit the floor.

The smell of gunpowder and the coppery scent of blood suddenly made me gag an' I tasted bile in my throat. I swallowed that away and pulled my boot knife as I walked over to the women. They were all quiet, and motionless as if they were paralyzed. I cut the rope between each of them. They all stood as soon as they could.

Anna's eyes seemed to put out more glittering light than they received from the candle across the room. "I knew you would come," she said, her voice only barely above a whisper. She covered the couple of steps between us quickly and put her arms around me, and I held her close.

Maybe or maybe not we'd find some of the Night Hunters' money. I didn't really give a damn.

I had gotten what I came after.

The employees of Thorndike Press hope you have enjoyed this Large Print book. All our Thorndike and Wheeler Large Print titles are designed for easy reading, and all our books are made to last. Other Thorndike Press Large Print books are available at your library, through selected bookstores, or directly from us.

For information about titles, please call:
(800) 223-1244

or visit our Web site at:
http://gale.cengage.com/thorndike

To share your comments, please write:
Publisher
Thorndike Press
295 Kennedy Memorial Drive
Waterville, ME 04901